PARTING SHOTS

"Listen," said Bernhardt, "I'm going to find Betty Giles. I'm going to try and square this."

Slowly, meaningfully, Dancer shook his head. "No you're not. You're going to forget about it, Alan. You're going to let it die. We're clean now. That's the way I want to keep it. We were hired to do a job, and we did it. Maybe the client lied to me, maybe he didn't. Maybe the whole thing is a coincidence. But whichever way it comes down, we're clean. Which means we aren't going to ask questions." Abruptly, Dancer hitched his chair closer to the desk, dropped his eyes to the scattered piles of paper in front of him. The audience was ended.

Bernhardt remained motionless for a moment, standing rigidly behind the desk. When he spoke, measuring each word, he was conscious of his actor's craft: "I'm going to find her, Herbert. And that's a promise."

For a moment Dancer held Bernhardt's gaze. Then he shook his head. "If you do that, you're through here. You understand that. You'll go broke."

"I've always been broke. I survived. Good-bye, Herbert. Watch the newspapers."

Bernhardt's EDGE

BY
COLLIN WILCOX

A TOM DOHERTY ASSOCIATES BOOK
NEW YORK

BERNHARDT'S EDGE

Copyright © 1988 by Collin Wilcox

A TOR Book

Published by Tom Doherty Associates, Inc.
49 West 24 Street
New York, NY 10010

Cover art by Stephen Peringer

ISBN: 0-812-51148-4

Library of Congress Catalog Card Number: 87-51398

First edition: June 1988
First mass market printing: January 1991

Printed in the United States of America

0 9 8 7 6 5 4 3 2 1

This book is dedicated
to Mickey Friedman,
my old friend

MONDAY
September 10th

1

As the Falcon jet's wing dipped, Justin Powers' grip tightened on the arms of his seat as he unconsciously tried to right the airplane. Then, mind over motor reflex, he deliberately lifted his hands from the arms, flexed his fingers, clenched his right hand into a resolute fist, lifted his left wrist, checked his wristwatch. Four o'clock, exactly. They were about to land, then, probably turning to the final approach course. They would be on the ground by 4:15, at the Oakland airport, where limos were allowed on the tarmac. Forty-five minutes, he'd been assured, would be enough time to get into downtown San Francisco, even in the rush hour. Powers tightened his seat belt, reached for his gold-bound appointment book, placed it on a small coffee table. He looked at the notation he'd made on a perforated half page. Yes: Herbert Dancer, Ltd., 350 California Street, Suite 1705. Time of their appointment, 5 P.M. Probable length of the interview, forty-five minutes to an hour. The limo would wait. By seven o'clock, he'd be back in the Falcon, airborne. A catered meal would be on board: cold cracked crab, green salad, French bread, and Chardonnay, all very San Francisco. By nine o'clock he'd be home—or almost home. Sylvia and their guests would still be at the table. Adroitly, Sylvia would have arranged matters so that he'd join

3

them for dessert—chocolate mousse, she'd promised, one of his favorites.

Now the airplane was rocking gently as the landing gear and flaps came down. Through the windows, Powers saw a line of hills higher than their flight path. He checked the time, 4:08. Good. Even concluding an agreement that he dreaded, initiating a sequence of events that could conceivably ruin him, it was nevertheless essential that everything happen on schedule, predictably. For Justin Powers, there was no other way.

• • •

"I should be finished by six o'clock," Powers said. "To be safe, you'd better plan to be here by five-forty-five."

"Yes, sir." Holding the door, the driver nodded. "Five-forty-five."

Powers turned away, began making his way purposefully through the press of liberated office workers to the revolving doors of 350 California Street. Dressed in a medium-dark, three-piece suit, white shirt, discreetly striped tie, and narrow-brimmed hat, a man of medium height and medium build, Powers' manner and his appearance were a perfect match, projecting the image of the successful, assertive, assured executive. His face completed the image: a tightly compressed mouth, dark, level brows, impersonal eyes. It was the severely sculpted face of a man who seldom allowed himself to smile. He carried his attaché case as a soldier carries his weapon, a part of himself.

An empty elevator awaited him; at five minutes to five, everyone was leaving the building, not entering. He pressed "17," and was gratified to see the doors immediately slide shut. Solitude, Powers felt, suited his status.

4

• • •

As his office door opened and his secretary performed the introductions, Herbert Dancer rose, moving out from behind his desk.

"Mr. Powers—" Smiling, Dancer extended his hand. "Nice to meet you."

"Thank you." Powers perfunctorily shook hands, put his attaché case on Dancer's desk, sat in a tufted black-leather chair, crossed his legs, arranged his trouser creases, checked his cuffs. He decided not to return Herbert Dancer's smile. Instead, pointedly, he consulted a gold Piaget wristwatch. When he raised his eyes again to Dancer's face, he saw the other man's smile fading. Good. Dancer had gotten the message.

"You were recommended to me by Gardner MacCauley, Mr. Dancer." Now, deliberately, Powers smiled. And, yes, the other man couldn't quite decide whether to venture a smile in return. They were making progress, then, defining their roles. Employees smiled by permission only.

"MacCauley has handled several, ah, matters for me in the past," Powers said. "And when I told him that I needed someone with Northern California—San Francisco—coverage, he suggested you."

"Fine." Expectantly, Dancer drew a pad of legal paper close, clicked a ballpoint pen.

"Actually," Powers continued, "it's the same, ah, problem that concerns me in both cases. That is, I called MacCauley when I—" He frowned, interrupted himself. He was digressing, losing momentum, compromising his authority. He allowed himself a moment to organize his thoughts. Then:

"First, I'll give you the background. I'm based in Los Angeles, as I told you when we talked on the phone. I'm in investments. Venture capital, primarily. Powers,

5

Associates . . ." He produced a card, leaned forward, placed the card on the gleaming walnut desk, leaned back, recrossed his legs, rearranged his trouser creases, cleared his throat. "I'm the, ah, principal. It's a corporation, of course. But I'm the C.E.O. I've got three vice presidents, and five or six third echelon people. Below them, there're another four or five secretaries, plus several clerks and typists."

Writing on the yellow pad, Dancer quickly noted 3 VPs, 5–6 assts, 10–15 flunkies. "Yes, I see."

"The problem," Powers said, "developed with one of the third echelon people. Her name is Betty Giles." He leaned forward again, opened the attaché case, withdrew a single sheet of paper, which he slid across the desk. "That's a fact sheet on her." As Dancer dropped his eyes to the sheet of paper, Powers broke off. Quickly, Dancer scanned the page, obviously extracted from a personnel file:

ELIZABETH (BETTY) GILES, born 1953, San Francisco, CA. Parents divorced. Father's current whereabouts unknown. Mother, Norma Heckler/Giles/Farley, currently divorced from her second husband, living at 456 Brady Street, San Francisco. Betty Giles currently resides at 5022 Klump Avenue, apt. #603, Los Angeles.

Education: B.A. art history, U.C. Berkeley, 1975.

Employment record: 1976–1978, Researcher, Appleton Systems, Inc. San Francisco.

1979–1982, Assistant Director, Standard Oil Community Development Program.

1983–present, Researcher, Assistant Supervisor, Powers, Associates.

Evaluation: Excellent.

The evaluation was handwritten, signed, and dated.

"This is her picture—" Powers handed over a colored 3″ × 4″ head-to-waist picture of a young, dark-haired, dark-eyed woman with regular features. Her mouth was upcurled in a hesitant smile. Her eyes didn't pick up the smile. She wore a demurely tailored blue dress, pleated in front. Her face was oval, her torso was slim. Her breasts were indeterminant.

"You'll notice," Powers was saying, "that she was born in San Francisco, and her mother still lives here. Her mother's name is Nora Farley."

"Yes."

"That's why I've come to you."

Dancer nodded, but decided to say nothing. Almost twenty years as a private investigator had taught him the value of strategic silence.

With the air of someone reluctantly getting down to unsavory business, Powers paused heavily. Then: "That report doesn't really tell much about the nature of Betty Giles' work. But the truth is that, during the past year, especially, she was involved in developing some very, ah, sensitive material for us. We have interests worldwide—Europe, Asia, South America. And research—information—is absolutely vital. The more we know about a given situation, the better we can predict the future. And when you're involved in multinational investing, the future is what it's all about. Educated guessing, in other words. Do you follow?"

"Yes."

"Good." Briskly, Powers nodded. His manner was more decisive now, as if the hardest part was behind him. "Well, especially during the last year, as I say, Betty was doing some highly classified work for us. Which meant that she was dealing with material that could be very damaging, in the wrong hands."

"And now she's disappeared," Dancer said. "With some sensitive material."

Powers was satisfied with his reaction. His face, he was sure, revealed nothing. Without allowing the cadence of his speech to change, slightly flattening his voice, he said, "MacCauley called you, then."

Dancer shook his head. "No, I haven't talked to MacCauley in months. You mentioned educated guessing. That's my business, too. Educated guesses."

"Well," Powers answered, "you're right." He glanced again at his watch. Almost five-thirty. Marginally on schedule. "But that's only part of it. The rest of it is that she's demanding money, to return what she took."

"Whether or not she returns it," Dancer said, "she could make copies."

"That's true. But it's also a matter of what she knows."

"So you want to talk to her. You want us to find her, so you can talk to her."

Gravely, Powers nodded. "That's it exactly."

"We can't hold her. We can't restrain her. You know that."

"Yes."

"She's committed a crime. Embezzlement. Do you want us to contact the police, once we find her?"

Quickly—too quickly, Powers realized—he shook his head. His reply, too, probably came too quickly: "No—no. When you find her, I want you to contact me. I want you to keep her under surveillance. Then you—" He frowned, began again: "Then I'll decide how to handle it, when you've found her—when you've contacted me. But the important thing is, you're not to contact anyone but me. I want to stress that." Across the desk, he stared at Dancer, making hard eye contact. Yes, he could see the urgency registering, even though the other man refused to drop his eyes, as a hireling should. Irritated, Powers took his confidential card from his wallet, slid the card across the desk. "Those are my private numbers. Day or night, you can get in touch with me at one of them. They're, ah, classified. Do you understand?"

Deliberately, Dancer allowed a moment to pass as he used an outsize plastic clip to fasten the fact sheet, the photo, and the business card together inside a fresh manila folder he'd taken from a drawer. Then, initiating his own eye contact, seeing the other man's gaze almost imperceptibly falter, he finally nodded. "I understand."

Another silence passed as Powers looked away, frowning. He'd known this would happen, this insubordination, these knowing looks, that subtle sneer. But he was helpless. Totally, abjectly helpless. As surely as a murderer was destined for the gas chamber, he was destined to be here, enduring this indignity inflicted on him by the man across the desk. This was his destiny, sitting abjectly in this chair, shuddering deep inside himself. Impaled.

He'd forgotten what remained yet to be said. Certainly they must sign something, a contract, with a retainer. Once more, he glanced at his watch, 5:32. Every hour, disaster came closer. Yet he was forced into this meaningless charade, this pretense of equanimity, of urbane unconcern.

"Do you have reason to think she's here, in San Francisco?" Dancer was asking.

"Not specifically. But she's close to her mother, keeps running to Mother, apparently, when she's in trouble."

"She's in trouble?" Dancer frowned. "How do you mean?"

"It's a—" He broke off, searching for the word, the phrase: "It's a figure of speech."

"Hmmm . . ."

There it was again: the insolence, the suggestion of a knowing leer.

"Was MacCauley looking for her, in Los Angeles?" Dancer asked.

He'd known the question would come. For this question, he was ready. "Briefly, he was looking for her. But he didn't find her. And it's pretty clear, MacCauley says, that she left town, left Los Angeles. We think she's traveling with a man. His name is Ames. Nick Ames. They lived together, and they both disappeared at the same time, just about a month ago."

Nodding, Dancer noted the name, then slid open his center drawer, withdrawing a single sheet of paper. "This is our standard contract, Mr. Powers. We have a minimum charge of five hundred dollars a day, for three days. Then there's travel outside of San Francisco, of course, and lodging, if that's necessary. I'll report to you, personally, three days from now, whether or not there's any progress. If you'll read the contract, and sign it, then all we need is an advance of five hundred dollars."

Powers put on horn-rimmed glasses, skimmed the contract, signed it, quickly wrote out a personal check, flicked both away from him. The time was nine minutes to six.

"Will you be handling this yourself?"

Dancer shook his head. "Sorry. I can't. I've got twelve full-time people, plus another five people that work part-time, investigating. Then there's another four, in the office. It's all I can do, frankly, to keep everything on track. Actually, I'd like to get out in the field. But it's impossible."

"If it's a question of the fee . . ."

"It's not. Believe me. But I promise you, I'll put one of my very best people on it."

"I'd assumed," Powers answered brusquely, "that that went without saying."

Aware that the tone of the other's voice demanded a counter in kind, Dancer nodded curtly. "Then you assumed correctly." As he said it, he saw Powers' mouth tighten slightly. Yes, he'd scored a point, found a small chink.

Recovering, also countering, Powers sharpened his tone, hardened his gaze. "There's one thing—one restriction." He waited until he'd compelled Dancer's full attention. "You're not to contact any of my people. None of them know anything about this. And that's the way it's got to stay. Is that clear?"

Eyes steady, Dancer nodded. His voice, too, was steady. "Perfectly clear."

"Good." Powers stood up. "I'm counting on you, Mr. Dancer. I don't know whether you've checked on Powers, Associates, but our balance sheet would impress you. We're simply too big to let someone like Betty Giles threaten us. Do you understand?"

Also rising, Dancer shook his head. "I'm not sure I do, Mr. Powers."

"What I'm saying is that she's got to be found. She's got to be—" He hesitated. "She's got to be neutralized. There's simply no other way. And cost, as I'm sure you know, is of no consequence."

"I understand. I'll be in touch. And thank you for contacting us."

Powers nodded, put on his hat, took his attaché case from the desk. "You're welcome." He turned abruptly to the door.

Dancer waited until he judged Powers had left the outer office, then pressed an intercom button, spoke into a speaker phone: "Has everyone gone, Marge?"

11

"Yes, sir."

"Okay, you can go. Any calls? Anything important?"

"Nothing that can't wait until tomorrow, I'd say."

"All right. Good night. Lock the outer door."

"Yes, sir."

Dancer turned to the room's single window, a large one, behind his desk. He'd chosen the building for its views, and now, reflectively loosening his tie, he stood looking out over the rooftops of Chinatown. Beyond the northern edge of the city, the waters of San Francisco Bay were deepening into purple as the sun began sinking slowly toward the great orange arc of the Golden Gate Bridge.

Dancer drew a long, deep breath. Expanding his chest, he arched his back, lifted his chin, rose on his toes, raised his arms high over his head, exhaled, drew another deep breath. He was a compactly built man, impeccably dressed in a three-piece suit that could have been made by Justin Powers' tailor. At forty, Dancer was as slim as he'd been at twenty, and just as wiry. His gray eyes were shrewd, yet curiously empty. His small mouth was slightly pursed: a corrupted cherub's mouth. His chin was small, slightly indented. His nose was curved, a little too large. His forehead was broad; his sandy hair was receding. Except for the eyes, so cold, so empty, the face was mild, even benevolent. But it was the eyes that defined the man—as many had discovered, too late.

Neutralized . . .

Had Powers meant to say it?

Some people used words very precisely. Others didn't. Powers was a precise man, a man who obviously understood words, and could calculate their impact. It must be assumed, then, that "neutralized" had been carefully chosen.

Meaning that, when Betty Giles was found, Powers

12

would call MacCauley. And MacCauley would call the leg-breakers.

Because, behind his suave banker's face, Powers was badly frightened. Terrified, perhaps, of Betty Giles.

A rich client, a terrified client . . .

Potentially, it was a promising combination, one that Dancer had often turned to considerable profit.

Dancer smiled and turned to his desk, and the phone. From memory, he touch-toned a number.

2

The six of them sat in the front row of the Howell Theater, a ninety-nine-seat house located in San Francisco's Eureka Valley district. With the house lights up and the work light on, the theater plainly showed its age: fifty years, at least, originally built as an Odd Fellows' Hall, later used as a neighborhood community house.

One of the six rose to his feet. He was a tall, lean man with dark, thick hair and an angular, deeply etched face. The face was Semitic: olive-hued, with a long, thin nose and an expressive mouth. Unmistakably, it was a Jewish face, a face that reflected both an ancient sadness and a new, gentle hope. The tall man wore corduroy slacks, an Icelandic wool sweater, and an open-neck shirt. Beneath heavy eyebrows, his vivid blue eyes moved restlessly as he spoke to the five still seated:

"I guess I should introduce myself. I'm Alan Bernhardt. I'm forty-two years old, and I'll be directing this play. It's the fifteenth play I've directed at the Howell. I came to San Francisco eight years ago. Before that I

13

spent several years in New York, mostly acting off-Broadway—and sometimes on Broadway, if the part was small enough." He smiled: a slow, rueful, half-shy smile. He waited for the chuckles, then continued. "I directed off-Broadway, too—and had a play of mine produced at Circle in the Square. It didn't have a very long run, I'm afraid—" Now the smile twisted slightly, quietly ironic. "But at least I've got the clipping, and a photostat of the check." He paused, looked at the five aspirants: three men, two women. One of the women, on his far right, interested him. Her name, he'd learned, was Pamela Brett. She was in her middle thirties. Serious. Attentive. Pretty face. Great body. Not on display, the body. But definitely there, beneath the jeans, and the loosely worn fisherman's sweater.

"The reason I'm telling you all this," Bernhardt said, "is that I want to make the point that, as far as I'm concerned, the Howell is the best theater of its kind I've ever worked in. The people who run it are very, very serious about what they're doing—serious about producing damn good plays. That takes dedication, and stubbornness, and vision, and a feeling for what the public wants. And integrity, too. It takes a lot of integrity. And it also probably takes a touch of mild insanity, the kind of insanity that Don Quixote had, I suppose. Quixote, and Dave Falk, the man who's run the Howell for as long as I've been here. If you haven't met Dave, you will. Maybe you've already seen him, and didn't know it. He could've been answering the phone, or selling tickets, or sweeping out the lobby, or—"

A small, shrill shriek interrupted: Bernhardt's pager, clipped to his belt, under his sweater.

"Oh, oh—" He switched off the pager. "I moonlight, like a lot of people in this business. Either you moonlight, or you have an inheritance. And that's my master's voice. I'll just be a minute. Then we'll do some reading, from the beginning." He smiled, this time at Pamela Brett, who quickly returned the smile. Bernhardt pushed himself away from the edge of the stage, and walked up the center aisle. Slightly stooped, he moved purposefully, eyes to the front, as if his attention were focused just ahead. In profile, with his long, slightly hooked nose, his sharp chin, with his thick, roughly cut hair growing low across his forehead and over his collar, Bernhardt could have played the part of the younger Lincoln.

• • •

In the tiny lobby with its worn carpet and its vintage playbills tacked to the walls, a pay phone hung beside the table used to serve coffee and pastries during performances. Drawing a deep, resigned breath, Bernhardt dropped a quarter in the slot, punched out a number.

"Yes?" the familiar voice answered.

"It's Bernhardt."

"Can you come in tomorrow at nine?" Dancer asked. "I've got something for you."

"Is it local, or out of town?"

"I'm not sure. A little of both, maybe."

"How long will it take?"

"Hard to say. Two or three days, at least." As always, talking to an employee, Dancer's voice was take-it-or-leave-it flat. Then, because it was Bernhardt, he added, "It's a skip trace. There's a twenty-five percent bonus, if it works out. But you've got to tell me now. Right now."

"All right. Nine o'clock."

"Good." The phone clicked, went dead.

• • •

Bernhardt flipped the script closed, put it on the edge of the stage, stretched, looked at his watch. "Okay, that's the first act. What I'd like to do, I think, is go through all three acts, reading the way we have

15

tonight." He pointed to his clipboard. "I've been taking notes, the way directors're supposed to do. So far I haven't put down any 'wows,' but then there aren't any 'ughs,' either. The way I like to work is to read through the whole play. Then I get together with each of you separately, and we decide whether we think it's going to work, with the parts you're reading. Okay?"

As he spoke, the five auditioners folded their own scripts and rose from chairs that had been placed in a semicircle on the stage.

"Today is Monday," Bernhardt said. "Can everyone make it Friday at the same time, six o'clock?" He looked at the five faces: three men, one woman—and Pamela Brett, who'd obviously acted before. A month from now, four or five rehearsals into the play, some of them would have given up, forfeiting the money they'd paid, to pursue their fragile dreams.

Thank God he believed it, what he'd said about the Howell. It *was* the best little theater company he'd ever worked with.

"So study your parts," he said, concluding. "Read them over. Make the characters *you*. That's the best advice I can give. Decide what your character has for breakfast, what he does for kicks—how his love life is going, or not going. I always encourage actors to write bios of their characters. Believe me, it helps. And it's fun, too. So—" He put the script on top of the clipboard, put his ballpoint pen away. "So I'll see you Friday night. If I should have a conflict—that moonlighting, I told you about—I'll call you. It'd help if you give me all the phone numbers you can, where I can get you, or leave a message. Okay?"

As they nodded, some of them thanking him, some not, the group dispersed, moving up the aisle, individually. Was it intentional, Bernhardt wondered, that Pamela Brett had lingered, the last one up the aisle?

Hastily, he vaulted up on the stage, switched off the work light, jumped lightly down, took up the clipboard and script, walked up the aisle. Ahead, she was already pushing open the door to the lobby. He couldn't run after her; he could only walk like this, briskly, believably, hoping she'd linger.

And, yes, through the lobby door's small round window he saw her. She stood with her oversize leather purse and script hugged close, staring gravely at a reproduction of a turn-of-the-century playbill, Elwood Carrington's *Hamlet.*

He pushed open the door, went to the fusebox, switched off the lights in the auditorium. At the sound of the switches she turned, smiling when she saw him. *Had* she been waiting for him? He would probably never know.

"You're a ringer," he said, returning the smile.

"A ringer?"

"You've acted before."

"Maybe I shouldn't admit it."

"Why not?"

"Because when I tell you how long, you'll think I should be better."

"That's the wrong attitude. I should've given my positive-thinking spiel." He widened his smile, stepped closer, looked into her eyes. "Anything's possible, you know, as long as you don't give up. And it's true. I've seen it work. Acting—working—marriage. It all comes down to determination."

Still hugging her script and purse to the swell of her breasts, she shook her head, then dropped her eyes. Her voice was pensive as she said, "You think so?"

The three words, spoken so softly, revealed a certain sadness, a hidden vulnerability. Unintentionally, he'd touched a nerve—a very raw nerve.

"Do you feel like coffee, a sandwich? There's a place

17

around the corner. Mike's. They stay open until midnight. And they've got great pastrami sandwiches, the best outside of New York."

Quickly, her head came up, the smile returned. "On rye, of course. Dark rye."

"Of course."

• • •

As he chewed a mouthful of pastrami, he studied her face: a small, oval face with a good, straight nose, dark, lively eyes, expressively arched eyebrows, a mobile mouth, generously shaped. Her hair was deep auburn, shoulder length, simply gathered at the nape of her neck. The modeling of the face was delicate, but the play of her expression was animated, inventive, fleetingly mischievous, sometimes bold. The pensive vulnerability he'd seen as she responded to his "positive thinking" quip hadn't returned, even momentarily.

"What's the name of your play?" Watching him over the rim of her glass, she sipped her apple juice. "The one the Circle produced?"

"It's called *Victims*."

"Is it three acts?"

He nodded.

"I'd like to read it."

"When I know you better, maybe."

"Why do I have to know you better to read it?"

"Because it's part of the past. My past, anyhow. I can do better, now."

"You're working on another play?"

He looked away. "Always."

She bit into her own sandwich, watched him as she chewed. Finally: "You're shy. You didn't seem shy, earlier. But you are, really."

"Most actors are shy. Or at least self-protective."

"Is there a difference?"

18

"Probably not." He drank an inch of beer from one of the mugs that Mike allowed his favorite customers to use. "What about you? Where'd you do your acting?"

"Los Angeles. I grew up there, went to Pomona College. That's where I got hooked on acting, in college." She hesitated, blinked, bit her lip. Her earlier vulnerability had returned, darkening her eyes, saddening her smile. "My husband is—was—a screenwriter. He got me some bit parts in movies."

He let a moment of silence pass, then said, "When you say 'was,' does that mean—" He let it go unfinished.

Which was it? Dead? Or divorced?

With obvious effort, she raised her eyes to meet his. "It means we're divorced. I got married right out of school. And he'd already been married, twice. We kept at it for ten years. Eleven years, really. But—" She shook her head, drew a deep breath, bit once more into her sandwich, almost gone. Her appetite, Bernhardt noted with satisfaction, was good. Finally she said, "That was two years ago, that we got divorced. I decided I wanted a change, wanted to get out of town, at least for a while. So I came here, to San Francisco."

"Do your parents still live in Los Angeles?"

She nodded. "They teach at U.C.L.A. They're both sociology professors."

"Impressive."

Her smile returned, along with the playful lilt in her dark, quick eyes. "What about you? I'm sure—I'll bet—that you're an easterner. Am I right?"

He chuckled. "Right. New York. But you could've guessed, couldn't you? From what I said earlier, to the cast."

"So what's your story, Alan Bernhardt? You know why I'm in San Francisco, hiding out. What about you?"

With his eyes on the circles of wetness that his beer mug left on the tabletop, making designs of the circles, he let the silence lengthen so long that it would have been an embarrassment not to have told her.

"I was married pretty much right out of college, too—a couple of years out, anyhow. She was an actress. We were married until—it's been eight years, now. Eight and a half, really. And she—" He swallowed, realized that he was helplessly blinking. He felt the familiar ache, the palpable suffocation of terror and dread as he remembered answering the door, remembered seeing the badge, seeing the man standing there, in the dimly lit hallway.

He'd known what had happened. Instantly, he'd known.

"She was mugged. They—they knocked her down, and she hit her head on the curb. She—" He swallowed again. "She never regained consciousness. Her name was Jennifer. Jenny."

"Oh, God. I—I'm sorry. I shouldn't have—I always seem to—"

"You didn't know. It's been eight years. That's time enough."

"Are your folks in New York?"

Still with his eyes lowered, speaking very deliberately, he said, "I don't have any folks, not really. None except in-laws. My father was killed in the war. He was a bombardier. And my mother died sixteen years ago, of cancer."

"Jesus, Alan—" She reached across the table, to touch his hand. "I'm not—I'm not trying to—"

"It's okay—" He raised his eyes, smiled, saw her answering smile, slightly misted. "Really, it's okay." He rotated his hand, to clasp hers. "I like you. So it's okay."

Between them the moment held. Until, gently, she withdrew her hand. Saying: "I like you, too."

They sat for a time in their separate silences. Then, venturing a tentative smile, she said, "I almost hate to ask any more questions. But all evening I've been wondering—" She paused, waited for him to smile, to nod encouragement.

"It's the buzzer," she said. "Your pager. What are you, a part-time brain surgeon?"

He laughed: a full, explosive laugh, filled with pure pleasure.

"I'm a free-lance investigator—a private detective. And a pretty good one, if I do say so."

"You're kidding."

He shook his head. "I'm not kidding. Actors make good private investigators. There's a lot of role-playing —pretending you're someone you aren't, making people believe it." Watching her, he realized that she was deciding whether she believed him. "I'm serious. You should try it, sometime."

"I'm not very tough, I'm afraid."

"Neither am I," Bernhardt answered. "I'm a lover, not a fighter."

Gravely returning his smile, she nodded. "Yes, I can see that."

"Good." He nodded, too.

TUESDAY
September 11th

1

Dancer slid the manila folder across the desk. "That should be all you need. Remember, don't contact anyone at Powers, Associates, where she worked. That's important. And I don't think you should talk to her, make contact with her. Just call me, when you find her. I'll contact my principal."

Picking up the folder, Bernhardt smiled. "'Your principal.' How many times have I heard that? They never have names, these principals."

Dancer, too, was smiling: a small, supercilious smile, mocking the man across the desk. With their business concluded, he could afford a few minutes of relaxation, baiting Bernhardt.

"It's called the edge. I sign your checks. That entitles me to an edge."

Leaning back in his chair, crossing his long legs, Bernhardt accepted the gambit. Deciding on a condescending tone, he said, "Your edge is expediency, Herbert. Sometimes called borderline dishonesty. Face it." As he spoke, he put a wry twist on his smile.

"It's a dishonest world, Alan. It's also a very messy world. You're—what—forty-two? And you still haven't figured out how the world really works. Have you ever considered what would happen if everyone suddenly started telling the truth? You've got a fertile imagination. Take a couple of minutes, sometime. Think about it."

"Sure, it's a messy world. But you make it messier. You steal children for a living, Herbert. You're smart enough to rationalize it. But you can't change it."

A pale gleam of pleasure shone in his gray eyes as Dancer smiled. "I steal children for a *good* living. The distinction is important."

"To you. Not to me."

"People get divorced. It's a way of life. They can usually agree on the money, and the houses, and the cars. But the children—they can't afford to agree on the children, on custody. The mother can't afford to admit that, really, she doesn't want the kids, because they'll cramp her style. And the husband feels guilty, for not wanting them."

"So either way, you show a profit."

"Either way." Complacently, Dancer smiled.

"I don't think I've ever known anyone as cynical as you are. I really don't."

"That's not the question. The question is, am I right? And the answer is, you know damn well I'm right. Look around you. A woman doesn't have an orgasm, she calls her psychiatrist, the first time it happens. The second time, she calls her lawyer. And the lawyers call us."

"Not 'us.' You."

Dancer shrugged. "The only real difference between us is that I make more money than you do."

"Wrong. The difference between us is that you're bleeding internally." Pocketing the check, Bernhardt rose, picked up the folder. "This Betty Giles—she's not dangerous, is she?"

"I don't think so. She stole some papers, and her employer wants them back. He wants to talk to her, too."

"Why do I get the feeling there's more to it than that?"

"Because that's the feeling you always get."

"And I'm usually right."

"Yes," Dancer admitted, "you usually are. For whatever good it does you."

"We're back to the edge, then."

"We always come back to the edge. It's your fate, Alan."

Aware that he was probably behind on points, Bernhardt decided against an exit line. Instead he rose, collected himself, delivered a theatrical snort. He left the office, went to an unoccupied desk in the adjoining office. He consulted a pocket address book, touch-toned a number, waited, frowned, broke the connection, tried another number. Finally: "Yes—is Lieutenant Friedman around, do you know? It's Alan Bernhardt calling." As he waited, sitting on one corner of the desk, he flipped open the file folder, looked at the colored picture of Betty Giles. Her face, he decided, looked a little like Pamela's—the same oval shape, the dark hair, dark eyes, generously shaped mouth, the same—

"Yes, all right. Yes, I'll wait. Thanks."

Pamela . . .

Over the remains of their pastrami sandwiches, they'd talked till after midnight. He'd walked her to her car, a Honda Civic, parked two blocks away. She'd opened the driver's door, tossed her shoulder bag and script inside, then turned to face him. They'd smiled at each other, said something meaningless to each other. The moment of truth was upon them—upon them and beyond them. As she'd extended her hand, for a handshake, he'd put his hands on her shoulders, as if he'd meant to give her a comradely clap, or perhaps award her a medal in the French fashion.

Would it ever change, for him? That sophomoric awk-wardness, that eternal comic relief, would it ever—?

"Hello—Al?" It was Peter Friedman's familiar, good-natured rumble, gritty but cordial.

"Where were you? On the pot?"

"I was trying to figure out what buttons to push on our new six-million-dollar Japanese fingerprint computer. It's not easy, believe me. What can I do for you?"

"If I give you a name and an address, can you give me a rundown on a car?"

"If you buy me a ten-dollar lunch I probably can. That's the standard arrangement, you know."

"It's a deal. Can you run it this morning—and have lunch today?"

"No problem. What's the name?"

"It's Betty Giles. G-I-L-E-S. Or maybe Elizabeth." He looked at the fact sheet, read off the address in Los Angeles. Friedman read it back, and they agreed on The Castle Grand, at twelve-thirty.

2

As he always did when he saw Friedman, Bernhardt smiled, quietly amused. Whatever the occasion, Fried-man always managed to look vaguely incongruous, dressed for the wrong place, at the wrong time. Yet, obviously, Friedman couldn't possibly care less. At two hundred forty pounds, graying, with a smooth, swarthy Buddha's face, Friedman projected an air of amiable in-difference to his surroundings. His dark eyes were heavily lidded—seeing everything, revealing nothing.

During the five years they'd known each other, Bernhardt had never seen Friedman surprised, or flustered, or at a loss for words.

Now, lolling at his ease, belly up, Friedman airily waved, beckoning for Bernhardt to join him at the tastefully set French country table. As always, the homicide detective was dressed in a wrinkled, rumpled three-piece suit, a haphazardly knotted tie, and a shirt with its collar mashed by Friedman's sizable double chins. And, yes, Friedman's vest was smudged with cigar ash. As always.

When Bernhardt sat across the table, Friedman handed over a slip of paper.

"Is this Betty Giles a skip?" Friedman asked. "Is that it?"

"That's it."

"Then you may be in luck." He pointed to the paper. "There was a moving violation issued against her car in Santa Rosa, two days ago. That's the citation number, and the license number, and description of the car."

Gratefully, Bernhardt pocketed the paper. "This could help. A lot. Thanks, Pete."

"No problem."

"Are you ready to order? Or do you want a drink first?"

"Let's order."

After they'd made their selections, Friedman leaned back in his chair, eyeing Bernhardt quizzically. Bernhardt knew that mannerism, knew what was coming next. He was about to be interrogated.

"So what's doing?" Friedman asked. "How's life?"

Bernhardt shrugged. "It goes on. What can I say?"

"Have you got a girlfriend yet?"

Slowly, Bernhardt smiled. "You're a real busybody, you know that? You're incorrigible."

Friedman considered. "How about 'persistent'?"

"How about 'persistently incorrigible'?"

"You haven't answered the question. Anything?"

Bernhardt shrugged. "I know a few women, naturally. There's one, especially—we get together once in a while, get our rocks off. We're friends, too, which always makes it nice. But we're never going to get married."

"A nice Jewish boy like you—you were programmed for marriage, don't you understand that? Preprogrammed."

Sipping a chilled glass of white wine, Bernhardt looked at the other man. Should he tell Friedman about Pamela Brett?

No. God, no. Not yet.

And he didn't have to tell Friedman about Jenny, about their marriage, and how she died. They'd gotten past that years ago, he and Friedman. And they'd never talked about it since.

So, instead, he shifted his ground: "I'm not really so sure I *was* programmed for marriage. Maybe I was programmed for exactly what I'm doing. My father died in the war, as you know. And my mother never even considered getting remarried, as far as I know. She did modern dance, and marched for peace, and civil rights, and Israel. That's all she really cared about, I think. Dancing, and marching."

"You think."

Bernhardt shrugged again, thanked the waiter as he served them.

"What about Dancer?" Friedman asked. "What's he up to—the low life?"

"Same as always—making money. He's got the knack, you know. I finally figured it out. He decided, early in the game, that he wanted rich clients. Powerful clients. And he's smart enough, and smooth enough—" Bernhardt swallowed filet of sole, gestured with his

30

fork. "He's smart enough to cater to them, these power structure types. It doesn't take any longer to send out a bill for ten thousand than it does for a thousand, you know. It's the same postage."

"Dancer has the morals of a puff adder," Friedman pronounced.

"No argument."

"Why d'you stay with him? What are you, his conscience? Is that it? Is that why he keeps you around?"

"I stay with him," Bernhardt answered patiently, "because I want to direct plays—and write plays, too. Which means I have to have outside income. Dancer pays me twice what anyone else in town'll pay."

"No one else in town does what he does—divorces, custody work. And child stealing, for God's sake."

"That's not fair. A lot of agencies do divorce work, and you know it. And, anyhow, I don't do those things. We've already been through this, Pete. I don't *do* that work. So why's it get to you, about me and Dancer? Every time I see you, it's the same old song."

"Maybe it's because we're both Jews, who knows? Or maybe it's because I spent a couple of years down in Hollywood, making the rounds with my eight-by-ten glossies in my hand. Did I ever tell you about that— when I was young and slim, hitting the talent agencies?"

"Several times." Bernhardt paused, considered, then decided to ask, "Do you ever wish you'd kept at it, in Hollywood? Any regrets?"

Friedman dropped his eyes to his plate, concentrating on the task of twisting linguini neatly around his fork. Finally, in a lower, softer voice, he said, "If you don't have regrets, my dad told me once, you haven't been trying very hard. And my dad was—" As Friedman's gaze shifted to the door he broke off, nodding. A friend was coming toward them. Turning, Bernhardt saw

Frank Hastings, Friedman's co-lieutenant in Homicide. Waiting for a beleaguered busboy to awkwardly shoulder a trayful of dirty dishes, Hastings was nodding to Bernhardt, quietly smiling. Hastings was Friedman's exact opposite: laconic not verbose, trim not tubby, methodical not intuitive. Bernhardt had known Hastings before he'd known Friedman. Years ago, after her divorce, Ann Haywood had volunteered to paint sets at the Howell. When she began seeing Hastings, she'd introduced them. Half joking, Bernhardt had once told Hastings that he looked like a casting director's stereotype of the photogenic police lieutenant: a big, muscular man who'd once played professional football, six feet tall, with good, regular features, understanding eyes, and a knack for choosing the right clothes and wearing them well. Characteristically, Hastings had turned aside the compliment. But Ann had been delighted.

"Hello, Al." Hastings gestured to their food. "More payola, eh?"

Also gesturing, Bernhardt said, "You're welcome to join us. Two lieutenants in the pocket's better than one."

"I've eaten," Hastings answered. "Besides, we've got work to do." He turned to Friedman. "There're four people dead out in the Sunset, on Forty-fifth Avenue. Murder and suicide, it looks like—the whole family. When you're finished here, why don't you go back to the office and catch for me? I'm going out to have a look, with Canelli and Marsten." He smiled: dark eyes subtly alive, generously shaped mouth slightly quirked as he dropped his eyes to Friedman's bulging belly. "Maybe you should pass up dessert. It couldn't hurt."

"It couldn't help, either." Friedman wound more linguini around his fork. "But I'll give it some thought. Do the troops know where I am?"

"Yes."

"Okay—" Friedman swallowed the linguini, waved his fork. "I hope all the victims voided before they expired." He looked at Bernhardt. "Sorry—an old homicide joke."

"I'll be in touch." Hastings nodded to Bernhardt. "See you soon, Al. Come over for dinner sometime, why don't you? Ann would like to see you."

"Fine. Give me a call." Bernhardt nodded in return, watched Hastings turn, walk away. Hastings moved like an athlete: smoothly, economically, confidently. Bernhardt could imagine Hastings in high school: a star football player, quietly sure of himself, aware of the girls giggling as they passed him in the hallways, secretly adoring.

Friedman finished the linguini, nodded when the waiter offered more coffee. "So what's next?" Friedman asked. "Will Dancer spring for a trip to Santa Rosa?"

"Of course he'll spring. How else can he pad his bills? First, though, I'm going to talk to Nora Farley—Betty Giles' mother. Then I'll go up to Santa Rosa, stay for a couple of days." He signaled for the check. "I'll let you know what happens."

"Santa Rosa is a sizable place. You'll have to get lucky, to find her."

"Maybe her mother will have something for me. Anyhow, I can make the rounds of the hotels and motels."

"Good luck. Incidentally, you can also come over to my house, for dinner. My wife cooks as good as Ann. Better, maybe. Kosher."

"It's a deal. Thanks."

Nodding, Friedman finished his coffee and stood up, at the same time checking his pager. "Ready?"

"Ready."

3

The address for Nora Farley was a small bungalow in the Ingleside District, a marginal neighborhood in slow, grim decline. The street was potholed, the sidewalks were cracked, and most of the streetlights were broken. A vacant lot was littered with refuse. To his right, Bernhardt saw a derelict car, completely stripped, resting on its brake drums. The Ingleside was an "R-3" district, where fast-buck real estate speculators had taken advantage of a lapse in zoning laws to throw up the small, cheaply built "low rise" stucco apartment buildings that were crowding out the few remaining single family dwellings.

Nora Farley was obviously doing her best to hold her own against the decay that surrounded her. The bungalow's small front yard was neatly planted; the frilled curtains at the windows were freshly starched and carefully hung. But the bungalow's stucco walls were cracking, and badly needed paint. The gutters were rusting, and a vent pipe leaned at a precarious angle. Nora Farley apparently had the will, but lacked the money.

Bernhardt pushed open a sagging gate, stepped up to stand on the "welcome" doormat, and pressed the bell button. He was wearing a sports jacket and tie; his hair was carefully combed. When the door opened, he was ready with a reassuring smile and an extended business card.

"Mrs. Farley? Nora Farley?"

She was a short, dumpy woman with a pale, lumpy face, washed-out eyes, and dark brown hair, imperfectly dyed and haphazardly arranged. She wore belly-bulged blue jeans and an incongruous "49ers" sweatshirt that outlined large, pendulous breasts. She was squinting into the afternoon sun, eyes puckered, mouth askew, as a child might squint up at an adult. Except for harshly penciled eyebrows, she wore no makeup. As she searched his face, she nodded. Yes, she was Nora Farley.

"I'm Alan Bernhardt, Mrs. Farley. I've come about Betty."

Sudden apprehension clouded her eyes, twisted her mouth. Stepping away from him, she raised anxious hands, as if to defend herself.

"Wh—what is it? What's happened to her? Is it—was there an accident?"

"Nothing's happened to her, Mrs. Farley. As far as I know, she's fine. I'm a private investigator. My firm has been retained by Betty's employer to try and find her." He paused, watching her face, waiting for her reaction. He'd given no thought to his opening questions. Long ago, he'd learned to improvise, relying on moment-to-moment impressions for his cues. And, yes, he could see fear in her small, dull eyes. He'd reassured her, told her that Betty was all right. But, still, she was worried. Deeply worried.

It was a good starting point. Nora Farley was a simple person, essentially a defensive person. Properly manipulated, her vulnerability should prove a plus.

But first it was necessary to gain her confidence, convince her that they were on the same side. He must therefore smile, make warm, reassuring eye contact. He was an actor again, turning on an actor's charm.

"Have you got a few minutes, Mrs. Farley? Can we talk?"

"Well—" She hesitated, glanced uncertainly over her

shoulder, finally stepped back. "Well, okay. The place is kind of a mess, but—" She turned, walked into a small living room. The room was furnished in department store early American. Everything was ruffled: curtains, lamp shades, chair skirts. A huge TV in an early American cabinet dominated the room. Soap opera characters moved on the screen, soundlessly. The plastic recliner in front of the TV still bore the outline of Nora Farley's buttocks. A calico cat crouched on the back of the recliner, watching Bernhardt with yellow eyes. Another cat crouched on the back of a maple rocker. Ignoring the calico cat, Nora Farley sat in the recliner, used a remote control wand to switch off the TV, and gestured Bernhardt to a maple loveseat. As he sat down, Bernhardt sneezed. For as long as he could remember, he'd been allergic to cat fur.

"Where's Betty, anyhow?" she asked. "Do you know?"

"I don't. That's why I'm here. I'm hoping you can help me."

The brown-penciled eyebrows drew together; the small mouth puckered, as if she were puzzled.

"You say you're with Powers, Associates?"

"I'm not *with* them, not on the staff. They've hired us, my firm." He gestured with the card, placed it on the coffee table. "I'm with Herbert Dancer, Limited. We've been retained to find her. By Powers, Associates, you see. They're—" He hesitated, deciding on the next phrase: "They're concerned about her, at Powers, Associates. She left without telling them, giving notice. So, naturally, they're worried. You are, too, probably."

"You bet I am. I'm worried sick."

"We're on the same side, then. Good." Smiling again, another actor's turn, he produced a spiral-bound pocket notebook and a ballpoint pen. "You, Powers, Associates, my people—we all want the same thing."

"Except that I don't know where she *is*." It was a plaintive, resigned protest, addressed more to the deity than to Bernhardt.

"When's the last time you heard from her, Mrs. Farley?"

"About—let's see—about a week ago, I guess. Maybe ten days. I forget, exactly."

"Ten days—" According to the handwritten note he'd gotten from Dancer, Betty Giles had disappeared four or five weeks ago, in Los Angeles. "Did you actually see her? Or did she phone?"

"She phoned."

"As I understand it, she moved out of her apartment in Los Angeles about a month ago. Is that right?"

She nodded. "About then. And that's what worries me, see. I mean, it's not *like* Betty to do something like that—just pick up and move, leave town, like a—a thief in the night, or something. She wouldn't *do* that." It was another complaint, directed toward heaven.

"How many times have you talked to her since she moved out of her apartment?"

"Well, she called just the night before she left L.A., the way I get it. And she talked real strange, when she called. *Real* strange. She was nervous. I could tell she was nervous, just the way she talked, and everything. She was trying not to let on, but I could tell."

"What'd she say, exactly, when she called? Do you remember?"

"Well, that's the point, see. I mean, she kept interrupting herself, and every once in a while she covered up the phone, and said something to—" She grimaced. "She was talking to that—that Nick. I know she was. He's the cause of all this, sure as hell. I know he's at the bottom of it, whatever's happened."

"Who's Nick?"

"His last name is Ames. He moved in with her about

37

a year ago, I guess it was. I never knew he'd moved in for about three months, which shows you, right there, that she knew it was wrong, to be living with him. And then, maybe three, four months ago, they had a fight, I guess. Anyhow, he walked out on her, for about a week. And she called me, and it all came out, how he started by moving in for a weekend, and then he just never left." Dolefully, she shook her head. "That's always been Betty's problem. Men. Even when she was in high school, she always went out with the—you know—the greasy-haired ones. It never failed. *Never*." She drew a deep, agonized breath. "It happened to her just the way it happened to me, with men. They just—some men—they just walk right over you. The nicer you try to treat them, the worse they act, honest to God."

"Have you ever seen Nick Ames, ever met him?"

"No. And the only time Betty ever talked about him was just that once. That's because she was ashamed of him."

"What does he do? What kind of work?"

She shook her head, sucked sharply at her teeth, waved a peevish hand. "How should I know what he does?"

"When you talked to him the night before she left Los Angeles, what'd she say, exactly? Do you remember?"

"Sure, I remember. She said that her job folded, and that she was going to leave—get out of town, she said. But I could tell, just by the way she was talking, that she wasn't telling the truth. I don't mean she was lying, I don't mean that. Because Betty doesn't lie. It's just that she was keeping something back. I could feel it, that she was keeping something back."

"What'd you think it was, that she wasn't telling you?"

"Well, it's nothing I could put my finger on, like I

said. But mostly—" As if she were laboriously puzzling out the problem, she frowned, shook her head, pressed her lips together. "Mostly I guess it was what she said about her job. I mean, Betty had a *good* job. Like, that time she called me, when Nick walked out on her, and she was crying, and everything, she talked about it, how good her job was, and how much money she made. She was saying it like, you know, like she couldn't understand it, how she did so good in her work, and everything, but she always ended up with these losers, these men. I mean, my God, one of them even had a prison record, if you can believe that."

"That wasn't Nick Ames, though." Asking the question, Bernhardt thought of Friedman, and another favor for another lunch. Invariably, Dancer questioned the chits Bernhardt submitted for his "Friedman lunches."

"No," she answered, "that was years ago, that she was hanging around with that crook, whatever his name was. He stole from her, that guy. Stole from her purse, for God's sake."

"What's Betty do? What kind of work?"

"Well, I've never been sure, not really. I mean, I know she worked for Powers, Associates, and I know she did research for them. But that's all she ever said, about her job."

"What's her field?"

"Well, that's the funny thing, see. Because her field is art history. And I can't see what that'd have to do with investments, which is what Powers, Associates does, the way I understand it. But Betty's smart. She's always been real smart. I mean, let's face it, she never had any of the advantages. I mean, her father—Giles—he walked out on me when Betty was six months old, if you can believe that. And Farley, he walked out, too, when Betty was about five. So, God knows, I could never do much for Betty, at least not financially. But

Betty worked at the dime store, all through high school. And she got into U.C. Berkeley on a scholarship. And she worked when she went to college, too. It took her five years, because she had to work. And then, a few years out of college, she got this real good job, with Standard Oil."

"What kind of a job?"

"It was in their—I think they call it their—" She broke off, shook her head resignedly. "God, my memory, I swear. I can't—" She interrupted herself: "It was their Community Arts Program, something like that. Anyhow, they used—you know—paintings, and statues, and everything, in their offices, and when they put on exhibitions. And Betty and one other person—a man—they did it all. It was—" Unpredictably, she blinked, wiped at her eyes with awkward, stubby fingers, swallowed hard. "It was wonderful, what she did. Just wonderful. I—I was so proud of her. I mean, I just—you know—graduated from high school, and—" She broke off again, swallowed again, wiped at her eyes again. Then, speaking in a low, clogged voice, she said, "I always did everything I could for her, though. Always. I've always worked. I never made real good money. But we always managed, Betty and me. And I—I—" She shook her head, silently staring down at the floor. Almost whispering, she said, "I always loved her. She—she was all I had, you see—all I ever had."

Surprised at the sudden emotion that momentarily blocked a response, Bernhardt cleared his throat—while one corner of his playwright's mind registered the scene, for future use.

He let a moment pass, while she recovered. Then, gently, he asked, "When did she go to Los Angeles, Mrs. Farley?"

Sighing raggedly, she raised her eyes. "It was about three years ago, that she went. She didn't really want to go. I mean, she didn't apply for the job, or anything. They heard about her, came up here, asked her if she'd like to apply for a job, in Los Angeles."

"Did she say what the job involved?"

"Well, as far as I could see—the way she talked—it was going to be the same kind of work she was doing for Standard Oil. And I guess that's what she thought, too. But the thing is, she'd never say anything about what she was doing, down in L.A. She'd never talk about her work, when she used to come up for weekends. But then—" Sadly, she sighed. "But then, I never knew anything about art, or anything like that. I never—" She began picking at the plastic arm of her recliner, watching her fingers. "I never—you know—went to the exhibitions, or the openings, or anything. Betty would always invite me, like she really wanted me to go. But I—I knew better. I'd—sometimes I'd go by, when no one was around. But—" Biting a trembling lower lip, she let it go unfinished.

Looking away, Bernhardt sat in silence for a moment. Then, softly, he asked, "Does Betty know anyone in Santa Rosa, Mrs. Farley?"

"Santa Rosa?" Uncertainly, she looked at him, then slowly shook her head. "No, I don't think so. Why?"

"Just curious. When you talked to her last week, did she tell you where she was, what she intended to do?"

"All she said was that she and Nick were traveling, that they'd probably be traveling for another month or so."

"Did she plan to go back to Los Angeles, after she'd finished traveling?"

She frowned. "I don't know. She never said. I guess I just always thought that—" She shrugged. "I don't know."

"Mrs. Farley—" Bernhardt leaned forward, pointed to the card he'd left on the cluttered coffee table. "I've left my card. It's got both numbers, my home and my office. I wish you'd keep it, and call me when Betty calls again. Maybe, when the conversation is fresh in your mind, you can think of something that'll help us find her. Will you do that?"

"Okay—" Transparently doubtful, she spoke warily.

Rising to his feet, smiling as reassuringly as he could, Bernhardt said, "I'll be going now, Mrs. Farley. But I hope you'll call me. And if I find out anything, I'll call you. Okay?" As she rose heavily to her feet, Bernhardt began moving to the front door. With his hand on the knob he turned back, as if he'd just remembered a wayward thought.

"I meant to ask you," he said, "was Betty in any trouble, when she was younger?"

"Trouble? What kind of trouble?"

"Oh, you know—" Still smiling—fatuously, he knew —he waved a casual hand. "The kind of trouble that kids can get into, in high school. Drugs, things like that. Did she—?"

"I've already *told* you—" Indignantly, she raised her chin, bowed her back, truculently planted her feet before him. "I've already *told* you, Betty is a good girl. A *good* girl."

WEDNESDAY
September 12th

1

It was, Bernhardt knew, a predictable phenomenon of the trade: whatever the target, whether it was a middle-aged, overweight, red-haired woman, or a child with a missing front tooth, or a man with a limp carrying a black-leather attaché case—or a Toyota registered to Betty Giles—the world was suddenly filled with people or vehicles who seemed to fit the description.

And Nissan, and Mitsubishi, and, yes, even Chevrolet, all of them were manufacturing Toyota look-alikes.

He'd already spent six hours in Santa Rosa, driving from motel to motel, hotel to hotel, vainly looking for a 1985 Toyota, color unspecified, license plate PVH 264 J.

He'd give the surveillance until Friday noon, he'd decided. Then he'd call Dancer, tell him he was coming in. He'd scheduled the second act read-through of *The Buried Child* for Friday night. They were counting on that read-through. Pamela and the rest of them, they were counting on it. He could see it in their eyes, hear it in their voices. Vividly, he could remember how it had felt, the ache of memory, echoing and re-echoing out of his own past, evoking the years of tryouts and casting calls. You couldn't admit it, even to yourself, how desperately you wanted the part, *needed* the part, to keep the fragile dream intact. Because, whatever the price, it was always necessary to protect that dream, somehow keep it whole, even when the director smiled sadly, shook his head, said he was sorry.

So he'd give the surveillance until Friday noon, he'd decided—two full days. Then he would—

A white Japanese sedan—a Toyota?—was stopped ahead, in the lane to his left. The Toyota was signaling for a left turn. He slowed, glanced in the mirror, saw there was no chance of easing into the left-turn lane. But, despite the angry horn-bleating from behind, he could slow enough to see the license plate as he passed. A man was driving the Toyota. A man, not a woman. So it was unlikely that—

PVH 264 J—

Why—for God's sake why—did it always happen that his first thought was of Dancer: how pleased Dancer would be that he'd scored? He didn't need Dancer's approval, didn't *want* Dancer's debit-credit approval. But it always happened like this. Always.

Looking straight ahead, he passed the Toyota on the right, moved into the center lane while he watched the Toyota in the mirror. He saw the driver make his left turn, then disappear. Ahead, a pickup truck was stopped, signaling for a left turn at the next intersection. The oncoming traffic was light. But the driver of the pickup was hesitating, dawdling. Bernhardt touched his horn, saw the driver start, look sharply back over his shoulder. And, yes, there was the stiffened middle finger. About to angrily respond, Bernhardt caught himself, suffered through the other driver's insolent moment of motionlessness before he turned left. Following, Bernhardt turned left at the next intersection, then right. He was behind the Toyota, with two cars between them, all four proceeding at a sedate rate along a four-lane highway leading to the southern fringe of Santa Rosa. On the right, a large green sign announced an entrance to the Route 101 freeway, south to San Francisco, north to Red Bluff. But instead of moving right, into the freeway-bound lane, the driver of the Toyota was signaling for another left turn, which he made immediately, clear of oncoming traffic. The two cars between them continued straight ahead, so that Bernhardt's Ford and the Toyota were alone, traveling east on a two-lane feeder road.

If he were a policeman, a detective, Bernhardt would have called for backup by now. He could have fallen back, let another car take up the rolling surveillance. Or, better, he could have passed the Toyota, ostentatiously turned off in another direction while he listened to his radio, heard his fellow officers closing the electronic net.

Electronic networking—forensics—fingerprint technology—firepower—computer printouts—these were the basic tools of law enforcement, all of them beyond the P.I.'s reach. Leaving him doing now what he'd done so often before, vainly trying to make himself invisible while he kept a suspect vehicle in sight.

He let the Ford slow as, ahead, the Toyota turned into a briskly traveled four-lane highway, keeping to the right. Cautiously following, Bernhardt saw the Toyota suddenly turn again, this time driving beneath a large arched sign that proclaimed the Starlight Motel. Beneath the sign, red neon letters spelled out "vacancy."

Smiling to himself, eyes front, Bernhardt drove past the motel entrance. He would circle the block, return, register at the Starlight Motel. Then he'd give Dancer the good news.

• • •

Sitting on the edge of the bed facing the room's single window, phone cradled to his ear, Bernhardt shook his head. "No, I haven't actually seen her, seen her face. And I didn't want to ask the clerk about them, for fear they'd hear about it. But it's almost six, so they'll probably be going out to dinner." He broke off, listened, then nodded. "Right. They're directly across the court. Unit number twelve. I can see their door, so there's no way they can leave without my seeing them. And I've seen a woman inside, moving around." He paused again, listened again. Then: "So what'd you think? Maybe you should send someone up. I mean, I can't stay awake all the time, and they could leave in the middle of the night."

The line went silent as Dancer considered. Finally: "I'll get back to you in an hour or two," Dancer said. "Do you have food?"

"No. But there's a grocery store right across the street. So I'm—" As he spoke, the door to number twelve swung open. A woman was coming out—a brunette, medium build. Unmistakably, Betty Giles.

"What is it?" Dancer was asking.

"It's her," Bernhardt answered, instinctively drawing back from the window as he watched the man lock the door to number twelve and follow Betty Giles along a brick walk toward the motel's coffee shop. "It's her," he repeated. "And they're going to the coffee shop, not even leaving in the car. So everything's cool." As he said it, he was aware of the small, secret rush he'd always felt, on first sighting. It was a primitive pleasure, he realized: an elemental huntsman's thrill, catching his first clear glimpse of an elusive prey.

"Good," Dancer was saying. "*Good.*"

2

Naked except for a pair of mulberry-colored bikini briefs, Willis Dodge lifted his chin, sucked in his stomach, arched his back, clasped his hands together, and tensed his torso, the muscleman's trick, posing for beefcake. Critically eyeing the head-to-toe effect in the bathroom's mirrored wall, his attention centered on the waist. Yes, there was a thickening, especially on each side, just above the hip bones. Holding the pose, he turned a quarter to the left, checking the stomach.

"A quarter turn to the left, guys," the loudspeaker had blared. *"Give us a profile, how about it?"*

In the voice—the sergeant's voice, amplified—he'd heard it all: the boredom, the hate, the total indifference, the cheerful, impersonal cruelty, and, always, the casual contempt. Because at that time, in that place, they were two different kinds of people, the officer and the inmates. Nine to five, the sergeant knew he was going home that night. Whoever waited for him, whatever waited, the sergeant would be going home to something—anything.

But in his cell that same night, Willis Dodge had felt the loneliness close in on him, a vise, clamped across his chest, a fist, squeezing him dry.

He'd cried, that night. He'd been seventeen, as tough as they come, he'd thought. But he'd cried. He'd thought about his mother, and he'd cried. And his father, too—the father he'd never seen—he'd thought about him, too, the man without a face.

He let his muscles relax, took a white terry-cloth robe from an ornate golden hook, slipped into the robe, cinched in the belt at the waist, lifted the collar snug around his neck. The robe smelled laundry-fresh. It was a smell he needed, one more proof that, yes, he'd gotten it all. In eleven years, dating from that same night in his cell, that first time he'd ever been arrested, beginning probably with those hot, desperate tears of loneliness, of utter terror, he'd never looked back. He was twenty-eight now, with money in the bank, clothes in the closet, a BMW in the garage—and a white woman in his bed, whenever he felt like making the call.

Willis Dodge . . .

Black, beautiful Willis Dodge . . .

Black, beautiful, rich Willis Dodge.

Once a month, at least, he visited the old neighborhood, never at night, because of the BMW, always in the daytime, so he could see the car through his mother's front window. He always—

From the living room, he heard the telephone warbling. As he walked down the hallway, he checked the time: a little after eight. In a half hour, Diane would be there.

Leaving the living room in darkness so he could see the city's sparkling skyscape, he lifted the phone from its cradle.

"Is this Mr. Fisher?"

Fisher. Meaning that "Mr. Carter" was calling.

"Yes, this is Mr. Fisher."

"Well, we've—" A small, nervous pause. Good. Nervousness meant more money, more profit. Always.

"We've found him for you," the voice said. "He's in—ah—California. Northern California, a town called Santa Rosa. That's about fifty miles north of San Francisco."

"Good. That's good. I can take care of it right away. How d'you want to arrange it?"

"You want—ah—half now, up front. Is that right? Cash?"

Willis Dodge nodded. "Yes. Just right."

"Well, what about if we—ah—if I send someone up to San Francisco—the San Francisco airport. I'll give him the money, and all the information, in a sealed envelope. You could meet there, at the airport. Then you could rent a car, drive up to Santa Rosa."

"That's fine," Dodge said. "The airport, that's fine. But I want you to come, Mr. Carter. Just you." He spoke softly, distinctly. "I don't deal with flunkies. I already told you that, the last time we talked."

"Oh. Well—" A cough. "Well, yes. I—ah—yes, that'll be—" Another cough. "That'll be fine."

"Are you calling from a pay phone?"

"Yes, I am."

"Okay. I'll make a reservation, and call you back in a few minutes. I think I can get out tonight. It's only six o'clock, your time. If I can get there by midnight, one o'clock, can you have the money?"

"Yes—"

"Okay. I'll see what I can do. Maybe you'd better stay in the phone booth, pretend you're talking. If I can work it out, get a reservation, it won't take long. Then I'll call you. One way or the other, I'll call you."

"Yes—"

"All right. What's the number?" As he spoke, Dodge switched on the antique brass desk lamp, the lamp he'd just bought, for five hundred dollars. He copied down the phone number, repeated it, broke the connection, slid open the center desk drawer, and took out an airline schedule. He spread the schedule on the desk and tapped-out the number for American, his favorite airline. As he waited for the connection, he ran his fingers lightly over the intricately tooled leather top of the antique desk. Price: eight thousand dollars, at auction.

3

Lying full length on the king-size bed, pillows propped behind her head, she watched the TV screen, seeing figures that meant nothing, hearing sounds that didn't register. Through the thin door, she was aware of

Nick's bathroom sounds: his urine splashing in the toilet, his flatulence, finally the sound of the toilet flushing, followed by water running as he washed his hands.

After a big dinner, Nick frequently relieved himself. And in the mornings, too. Always, in the mornings. For Nick, regularity was a major preoccupation.

Now he would be standing before the bathroom mirror, carefully combing his hair, wetting the comb under the tap, critically examining the effect, arranging and rearranging, fitfully frowning. At age thirty-six, Nick was beginning to lose his hair. In the year they'd been together, the hair loss had been obvious. And, yes, the rate of loss was accelerating.

And, yes, it bothered him. A lot.

Because, yes, Nick was a vain man, therefore secretly a vulnerable man. In Porterville, a valley town just north of Bakersfield, he'd been a star high-school athlete. He'd been co-captain of the football team in his junior year—the same year he'd scored his first piece of ass. Of course, according to Nick, the girl had been a cheerleader, a blonde sophomore with the biggest boobs on the squad.

The biggest, the best. Whatever it was, Nick had to have it—have it, or believe he'd had it.

It was, she realized, a braggart's giveaway, a telltale admission of insecurity that would always dog him. When she was a young girl, still in grade school, she'd felt the same need to brag, to make up the stories of classroom triumphs that she would take home to her mother. Even in high school, still searching for an identity, desperately trying to impress others, she had invented petty triumphs. Some of the stories she told to her mother, but most she told to other girls.

God, how she'd envied them, the other girls who seemed so incredibly secure, so supremely self-confident, therefore so blasé. She could still remember the names: Angie Hill, so smart, so vivacious; Helen Patterson, so friendly, so sunny, so popular; Maxine Leamy, so beautiful, so incredibly assured. Once, when she was a junior, Helen Patterson had invited her to a pajama party. She'd been ecstatic, hardly able to believe it would really happen. But then, lying in bed that night, three nights before the party, the terrible truth had struck: If she went to Helen's, and to Maxine's, and Angie's, then she must reciprocate, must invite them to her mother's small, dark, third-floor apartment, must introduce them to her mother, of whom she was ashamed.

At the thought, the shameful memory, she closed her eyes, bit her lip, fought back a sudden sob. Because it was now, only now, at age thirty-three, that she finally realized how much her mother loved her. Only now, during these last terrible days, these deadly dangerous nights, did she realize, fully realize, that in all the world only her mother really cared for her. That fat woman, living alone with her two cats and her enormous TV and her grotesquely ruffled furniture— someone named Nora, who had briefly loved someone named Charlie Giles—that woman named Nora was all she had. And she was all her mother had. They'd started together, and might end together. Because the clocks were ticking: the temporal clocks and the biological clocks.

And, somewhere, a murderer's clock was ticking, too.

Because if the wages of sin were death, then the wages of stupidity were—

The bathroom door opened. Wearing only his Calvin Klein jeans, Nick stood motionless for a moment in the doorway. He was a solidly built man, slightly bandy-legged, with bulging shoulders, a short, muscular neck, and strong, short-fingered hands that he carried away from his body, as if he were ready to defend himself. His face was self-indulgent, heavily handsome, with dark, thick eyebrows, a wide, muscle-bunched jaw. The mouth was thick-lipped, the nose was short and broad. But if the face was heavy, often combative, the eyes were a clear, vivid, celestial blue. And the voice was quiet—tight, often, but seldom harsh, almost never loud.

"What's that?" He gestured to the TV. "I think I saw it." He frowned, looked at the screen. Charlton Heston was driving alone through dark, deserted city streets. A submachine gun lay on the seat beside him. "I *did* see it. What's the name of it?"

She shook her head, shrugged. "I don't know. I haven't been paying attention."

"I know I saw it." Still watching the screen, he stepped to the closet, took a plaid sports shirt from a hanger, took a clean undershirt from a drawer. She watched the play of his muscles as he slipped into the undershirt.

The feel of his muscles straining against her naked body was part of her permanent consciousness, she realized, her secret obsession. Constantly, she—

"*Soylent Green*," he said, snapping his fingers. "It's one of those after-the-atomic-war things. Ten, twelve years old, something like that." As he spoke, he unbuckled his tooled leather belt, unbuttoned his jeans, began tucking in his sports shirt. On the TV screen, Charlton Heston was striding purposefully across piles of rubble, his machine gun cradled in the crook of his arm. She looked away from the screen, away from Nick, who now sat in the room's single easy chair.

"Why don't you turn it off?" she said.

Eyes still on the screen, he let a long, deliberate beat pass before he looked at her. "Where's *TV Guide*?" he asked. "Maybe there's something else on."

"I want to talk, Nick. We've got to talk."

He sighed petulantly, got up, switched off the TV,

returned to the easy chair, which he swiveled to face her. As if the dead TV screen had snapped some essential connection with the make-believe world beyond, she saw his face sag, saw his eyes go suddenly hollow. This, she knew, was the face of fear.

And in her face, certainly, he could see the same sag of fear, the same emptiness behind the eyes.

She sat straighter in the bed, drew up her legs. She was wearing a T-shirt, and she saw his eyes drop appreciatively to her breasts. Sometimes she thought her breasts were all that drew them together. Sometimes it seemed that, since her teenage years, the swell of her breasts was her sole definition. Did her identity depend on the stares she could attract? Did any woman's? Was anything else a self-deceiving illusion? A scholar had once written that, when man began walking upright, the relationship between the sexes began to equalize, because intercourse was then accomplished face-to-face. It was, the scholar had continued, the essential difference between men and the apes. Then he'd gone on to equate the buttocks of apes with the breasts of women, both contrived to invite the male, quicken his sexual appetite, the buttocks inviting intercourse from the rear, the breasts inviting "frontal entry," as the scholar had put it.

"We've got to go back," she said. "This isn't any good. We can't live like this."

His eyes darkened. "You can go back if you want to. I'm not going back. Christ, they tried to *kill* me. Can't you get that through your head?"

"It could've been robbery, Nick. Attempted robbery."

Emphatically, he shook his head. "No. He was going to kill me. That's all he wanted to do. I was lucky, just plain goddam lucky. But I'm not going to give them another chance. It's easy for you to say we should go back. You're not the one they're after."

"I can square it, though, make it right. I know I can make it right, if we go back."

"You're kidding yourself, Betty. For all you know, you could be next. Me, then you. It makes sense. Perfect sense. Think about it."

"I'm willing to take the chance. It's all we can do. It's either that, or keep running."

"You might be willing to take the chance. But I'm not."

"I want to call him. I want to tell him you're sorry— *we're* sorry."

"Sorry." Contemptuously, he shook his head. "Christ, you make it sound like a—a kid's prank, what we did. A game."

"It's what *you* did, Nick. You. Not 'us.'"

"*Christ!*" He jumped to his feet, paced furiously to the door, turned to face her. "Is this what it's going to be like—blaming me, putting everything on me? I thought—Christ, I thought we—" He gritted his teeth, chopped the air with a flattened hand.

"It was a crime, what you did, Nick." Eyes downcast, she spoke quietly, regretfully.

"Wait. *Whoa.*" He stepped forward: one coiled, light, stiff-legged step. "It was a crime what *he* did, don't forget that."

"But it didn't hurt you, what he did."

"And it won't hurt him, either, what I did. I— Christ—you talk like I'm a stickup man, or something. A fucking hoodlum."

Still sitting with her legs drawn up, with her shoulders and back pressed against the bed's headboard, eyes still lowered, she made no reply. In the silence, she heard voices from the driveway outside—young, eager voices, laughing, cavorting. Had she ever laughed like that, ever felt like that?

Still angry, he was speaking again, belaboring her

with words: "I'm thirty-six years old, and I come from a long line of losers. And I decided—really decided—that I'm not going to eat shit for the rest of my life, like everyone else in my family. I decided, by God, I'm going to make people pay attention. Very goddam close attention."

"They'll pay attention, Nick. When you go on trial, they'll pay attention."

"Jesus, that's just what I need, you know that? That's just what I fucking need, right now. Thanks, Betty. Thanks a lot." He turned, went to his suitcase, took the revolver from beneath the clothing. He thrust the revolver in his belt, grabbed a poplin jacket from a chairback, slammed the door on his way out. Moments later, she heard the car's engine come to life, heard the tires squeal as he pulled away.

4

Moving smoothly, Dodge flipped open the large saddle-leather suitcase on the bed. The suitcase was already partially packed with underwear, socks, a sweater, slacks, loafers, a toilet kit. He turned to his wardrobe closet, opened the doors, stood still for a moment, considering. Santa Rosa—Northern California—a medium-size town. Meaning sports clothes, nothing flashy, nothing citified. He stripped shirts from hangers, selected a casual jacket, two pairs of slacks, a pair of sport shoes from the shoe rack. He threw everything on the bed, then carefully folded the clothing, packed them, put the shoes in plastic bags. He straightened, took his practiced traveler's last-minute inventory, then closed the suitcase, locked it with a key from his key ring. He returned to the closet, slipped out a matching leather case from the shelf. He took the second case to the bed, where he unlocked it, opened it. Both halves of the case were filled with scalloped foam. Embedded separately in the foam were a Smith and Wesson .357 magnum with a four-inch barrel, a .22 caliber Colt Woodsman with a six-inch barrel, and a UZI machine pistol, along with a silencer for the Woodsman, three clips for the UZI, and two boxes of cartridges, one for the .357, one for the Woodsman. Two ice picks, both with weighted metal handles, completed the cache. Quickly, he checked the contents of the cartridge boxes, checked the operation of the two handguns and the UZI. Working with the guns, his touch was as deft as a musician's, handling his cherished instruments.

He closed the second suitcase and tested the lock. Now he slipped into a blue blazer, took an envelope from the first suitcase. He opened the envelope and riffled the contents: approximately five thousand dollars in used bills. He put the envelope in an inside pocket of the blazer, checked for his wallet, checked again for his keys, and his pocket change.

Next stop, San Francisco.

5

Powers touched the breast-pocket-bulge of the envelope, recrossed his legs, cleared his throat. Now he lifted the *U.S. News and World Report* so that it screened his face, as if he were nearsighted, and was concentrating on reading the magazine. His instructions had been simple, recognizably ingenious. He was to sit in the observation area, ostensibly reading. On his lap, placed so the logo could clearly be seen, he was to put a copy of *Time*. Both magazines were to be the current issues. Carefully, Fisher had repeated the instructions, then gone on to elaborate: If American flight 324 from Detroit was on time, and if Powers hadn't been contacted by midnight, then he was to phone the Detroit number, and make new arrangements.

Meanwhile, dressed casually in slacks and a golf jacket, he was playing the part of the ordinary, work-a-day traveler, or the suburban husband, waiting to greet his returning family.

Time, 11:40 P.M.

What were the odds of his being recognized? How many people did he know in San Francisco, in Northern California? If it happened, if he was recognized, he'd say he was traveling incognito, suggesting that he'd been sent on a secret mission, business related. It was important, he knew, to have a prepared story, should the unexpected happen. Role-playing, staying one step ahead—in every field of endeavor, it was important. In the boardroom or the back alley, it was important to be prepared, constantly anticipating. He'd learned that, learned to—

He was aware that someone was standing in front of him—expectantly, politely standing in front of him. Conscious of a sudden, overwhelming reluctance, aware that his whole world was turning, tilting, about to fall away, he lowered the magazine.

Fisher was a black man, probably in his early thirties, conservatively dressed in a blue blazer, gray flannel slacks, a white button-down shirt, striped red tie, everything in place, the pat picture of the upwardly mobile black on the make. His luggage, too, was part of the predictable package: matched saddle-leather cases, convincingly worn. His features were regular, classical Negroid. His eyes were shrewd and watchful: careful, cautious, calculating eyes. His hair was short. His voice was quiet, urbanely modulated: "Mister Carter?"

Silently, Powers nodded. His eyes, he knew, were beyond control, in helpless flight from the impassive brown face before him to the nearby faces of random passersby to the doors leading out of the terminal—

—the doors he wished he were walking through, free.

The black man was sitting beside him, eyeing him expectantly. Familiarly, and expectantly.

"Did you bring it? The money?"

"Yes, I—" With his eyes still betraying him, aware that his voice was a stranger's, he nodded, took out the envelope, handed it over.

"Thank you." The black man nodded calmly, slipped the envelope into an inside pocket, the money uncounted. "Twenty-five thousand. Right?"

"Y—yes. Right."

"In old bills."

"Yes."

"And I'll collect another twenty-five, right here, when the job's done. Me and you, here, just like now. Right?"

"Yes." Powers nodded, blinked, finally managed to keep his eyes steady, holding the other man's gaze. "Right."

"Okay—" The single word was soft and silky, the first suggestion of a Negroid patois. Was it intentional? Getting down to business, was Fisher deliberately evoking the dark, deadly menace of the ghetto, subtly threatening a black man's vengeance if their bargain were breached?

"Now," Fisher was saying, "what's the situation, the rundown? Where is he?"

"He—" Involuntarily, Powers glanced cautiously aside, licked his lips, lowered his voice. "He's traveling with a woman. It—it's all in there—" He gestured. "In the envelope, with the money. I made a note of everything. And their pictures're there, too. They're staying at the Starlight Motel, in Santa Rosa. That's an hour and a half north of here, by car. I put down their room number, too. Number twelve."

"Have you got someone watching them?"

Powers nodded. "A private detective. He found them this afternoon, just this afternoon."

"Is he staying at the same motel?"

"I—I don't know."

"This Santa Rosa—what kind of a place is it?"

"I—I don't know what you mean."

"I mean," Dodge said pleasantly, "what's it like? Fancy? Not fancy? Give me the rundown."

"Well, it—" Powers frowned, "it's neither one. I mean, it's a nice, quiet place. About a hundred thousand people, I'd say."

"What about black faces?"

"Black—?" Still frowning, Powers shook his head. Then, as realization dawned, he slowly nodded. "Oh, yes. I—I see. I see what you mean."

Dodge's full, purplish lips upcurved in a slow, contempt-twisted smile. "It's called protective coloration, Mr. Carter. That's what it's called in the jungle." As he spoke, he rose to his feet, picked up the two saddle-leather suitcases. "Tonight's Wednesday. Why don't we figure on meeting here—right here—at noon on Friday. That's assuming I've got the job finished, by then. If you watch the Santa Rosa papers, you'll read about it, probably, when it's finished. Or maybe you won't read about it, with luck. But, either way, you'll be bringing the rest of it, the other twenty-five thousand. Right?"

"Y—yes. Th—that's right. Friday. Yes. Fine."

"You won't forget, will you?" This, too, was said softly, a smooth, silky threat. "You wouldn't do that."

"N—no, I—I wouldn't do that."

"Good." Dodge nodded politely, smiled pleasantly, and walked away, softly whistling.

THURSDAY
September 13th

1

Willis Dodge yawned, bunched his shoulders, rotated his head, gripped the steering wheel with both hands, using the wheel to push and pull against, doing aerobics, keeping the muscles loose. He'd been working the neighborhood for almost five hours, sometimes parking, sometimes driving, trying to disappear into the scenery, just another citizen, minding his own business. Because, like he'd told "Carter," protective coloration was what it was all about: like animals, in the jungle. You didn't stick out, you had an edge. You could get closer, without the mark suspicioning anything. Or you could just wait, until the mark came to you. If you looked like you belonged, wherever you were, played the part, looked like the part you were playing, then you could just wait, take it slow and easy, do the job, get the money, go home, get laid, go to sleep, forget.

Kill or be killed. Jungle law. Ghetto law, too.

They always waited upwind, the jungle killers, lying in the tall grass, watching, waiting. For hours, they waited. Protective coloration: the right clothes, the right car—the right time, the right place—and you were home free.

In eight years, he'd played a lot of characters. He'd played a messenger once, and once he'd played a rock musician. That had been a good one, that part. He'd really gotten into it, bought leathers, a two-hundred-dollar cowboy hat, with a snakeskin band. Mostly, though, he played the simplest part of all: an ordinary hoodlum who'd kill for whatever he found in the mark's pockets. Because if the cops thought it was a mugging that misfired, they forgot about it. But a hit, a professional job, they never forgot, because they could sniff the headlines, the ink. So, whenever he could, he pretended to be a hood, robbing on the street. Meaning that he had to go through their pockets, turn them out, pull off the rings, the gold chains. Sometimes he found something, sometimes he didn't. Once he'd found nothing. Absolutely nothing. The mark had been rich, too: a union official, with a Coupe de Ville. A fancy car, a fancy house, a fancy wife—but nothing in his pockets. Zero.

And then once, in New York, on a skinny mark who'd looked like a bum, he'd found thirteen thousand dollars, in an envelope, stuck down the front of the mark's pants. And he got to keep it all, part of the deal.

So it averaged out. Whatever he could take, that was his commission, plus his fee.

Fifty thousand dollars, Nick Ames was worth.

Fifty thousand—his biggest fee ever.

The first time, that bookie who was holding out, he'd done it for five hundred dollars. And he'd almost died. On bad nights, he could still see it: that gun barrel, pointing at him, with the hole so big, so black, filling the whole world. And the click, when the gun misfired. He could still hear the click, the difference between living and dying, a defective firing pin, or a cartridge that wouldn't fire.

That first time—those first years—protective coloration hadn't been a problem. He'd operated where he'd spent his whole life, in Detroit, the whole city a slum, all of them killing or getting killed, all of them black, animals feeding on animals, living off garbage, pissing in doorways, breeding like maggots, fucking like dogs, everywhere.

Then he'd gotten the assignment in Kansas City. Venezzio had put him in line for the job, coached him, given him the plan, told him the moves, then given him the money: a thousand up front, another five, when the job was done. Later, he'd discovered that Venezzio had taken half, his fucking commission, he'd said.

In Kansas City, he'd learned about protective coloration, learned how it felt, a black face in a lily-white suburb, sticking out like a snake on a rock.

It had taken him a week, to get the job done—a week until he'd finally figured it out, finally bought some jeans and a workshirt and a floppy hat, and posed as a gardener, while he staked out the mark, memorized the mark's schedule, like Venezzio had told him.

A snake on a rock—Kansas City, so many years ago—Beverly Hills, only two years ago. They'd been the same, those two. The same problem.

And now Santa Rosa, the smallest town he'd ever worked. He'd arrived five hours ago. He'd slept last night at a hotel near the San Francisco airport. He'd left a call for seven o'clock. He'd had breakfast, rented a car, made the drive to Santa Rosa in exactly an hour and forty minutes.

And so far he hadn't seen one black face. Mexicans, yes. Lots of Mexicans. But not a single black face. Meaning that, wherever he went, whatever he did, they'd remember him. He'd seen it in the motel manager's eyes, seen that look, the look you always lived with, the look you never could quite forget.

He'd picked the Holiday Inn, always a good choice, probably with the most rooms in town. He'd washed up, changed into a sweater, took the heavy suitcase, went out the back way, to his car. He'd put the case in the trunk and driven to the Starlight Motel, on the other side of the city. His first drive by, his first trip around the block, had told him a lot—told him that it would be very simple, to keep track of the Toyota.

And very difficult, very goddam difficult, to get to them, get to the mark and the woman, get the job done. Because the motel was in a residential neighborhood: one-story houses built lot line to lot line, white picket fence to white picket fence, with no gaps, no vacant lots between, no alleys, even, that he could use. Meaning that, to get to unit twelve, he'd have to hop a fence, risk barking dogs, risk lights coming on, even husbands in pajamas, with guns.

He glanced in the mirror, checked his watch: 3:15 P.M. In Detroit it was 5:15, less than twenty-four hours since "Carter" had called. No question, jet airplanes had changed the world. The telephone, the jet engine, communication satellites, they were changing everything. And computers, too. In a few more years, everyone would be hooked into a computer: big brother watching them all.

In Sacramento, they had a fingerprint computer that could make a matchup in minutes, a matchup that would take months, by hand. Meaning that, if he left fingerprints, they could make him before he got back to San Francisco, if they were hooked into the FBI's computer, in Washington.

The police had the computers—and he had the twenty-five thousand dollars, safe in the suitcase with the guns, and the silencer, and the ice picks, and the ammo—and the two pairs of surgical gloves, to take care of the computer.

Three-thirty, now. Three-thirty on September thirteenth. In four hours it would be dark, or almost dark: seven-thirty, time to go to work.

But in those four hours, they could leave, the woman

and the man in unit twelve. They could check out, get in their Toyota, take off.

Possible, but not likely. Checkout time had come and gone. If they hadn't left by now, checked out, they probably would stay the night. Probably. But not for certain. Meaning that, if he didn't want to lose them, he had to keep watching the entrance to the motel.

Meaning that, to a dead certainty, he'd be noticed: a black man in a maroon Oldsmobile, hanging around. He could—would—keep moving. He could park a block away, and still see the entrance. Or else he could move forward a block, and see the entrance in the mirror. But that was as far as he could go: a hit man on a string, tied to his own stakeout.

Was "Carter's" private detective on the scene now? Right now, watching? He should've asked more about the detective. It had been a mistake, not to ask more. But in "Carter's" place, he wouldn't have answered. Or, if he'd answered, he would have lied.

So, to be safe, he had to figure that someone was watching. A white man, probably. A white detective staying at the motel, probably. Watching.

And some of them, some private detectives, they carried guns.

Everything you get, his mother used to say, you pay for. Meaning that everything was a tradeoff. It was another law of nature, another jungle law. Or, more like it, the same jungle law, the *only* jungle law: pay or get paid, kill or get killed.

His mother had paid. God, how she'd paid. The polite name was B-girl. But the bedroom walls had been thin, and the men had been loud.

He'd been seventeen, when he moved out. He'd been working up on Twelfth Street, spotting for Clarence Brown. Right from the start, Clarence had liked him, let him ride with him sometimes, making the rounds, keeping the pushers on the ball, off the shit. "You're a smart kid," Clarence told him. "You watch. You remember. You got a future." And when the wars started, for territory, Clarence had given him a gun, a Colt .45 automatic, army issue. He'd been in the car behind Clarence when the Beachum brothers had come up beside them, a van and two cars, with machine guns, fucking Mark 16s, the papers said. Clarence's car had skidded to a stop against some parked cars and Clarence had rolled out, rolled behind some trash cans, told him to get out, too. He'd been riding beside the driver, with the .45 stuck in his belt. He could still remember the weight of it, the feel of it, pressed against his young belly. Nothing had ever felt so solid, so important.

He'd rolled out of the car, like Clarence did, dodged low, got behind the trunk of Clarence's car, started shooting. He'd seen Alvin Beachum, right over his sights, lined up. He'd pulled the trigger, kept pulling it, felt the gun buck in his hands, saw Beachum fall.

They'd left him in the street, Beachum's soldiers. They'd left him, and they'd left Alex Saugis, too, dead, both of them dead.

That night, Clarence had called him in, given him two thousand dollars, told him how good he'd done, told him that he was in now. Only seventeen, and in. "You're a killer," Clarence had said, smiling at him, saying it so they could all hear, some of them who'd rolled under the cars, not shooting, just protecting themselves. "You're a natural killer, swear to God."

Two thousand dollars . . .

He'd never have money like that again, money that meant so much, made so much difference. Never before, never again.

Almost four o'clock—almost an hour, parked in one place. Already, a police car had passed, cruising: a new-looking car, neat-looking cops, looking him over. On their next round, maybe, they'd stop, get out of their car, ask questions.

2

Bernhardt answered the telephone on the second ring.

"How's it going?" Dancer asked. "Any change?"

"No change. Why?"

"I've just heard from the client. You can come in. Have you had dinner?"

"No."

"Well, have a good dinner, on the expense account. Then come in."

"Maybe I'll stay here tonight, come in tomorrow. There's something I want to see on TV. And the room's paid for until noon tomorrow."

"Suit yourself," Dancer answered. "Got to go. Shall I wait for your expenses before I authorize the check? Or would you rather have your time now, and your expenses later?"

Bernhardt smiled. To Dancer, he would always be a charity case. So, to make a statement, he answered, "Why don't you wait, write one check? Make it simple."

"Fine. Got to go, another call." Abruptly the line went dead. As Bernhardt cradled the phone, he looked out across the courtyard of the Starlight Motel. Dusk was falling: a soft, warm September evening. The Toyota was parked in front of unit twelve, where it had remained since noon, when Betty Giles and Nick Ames had driven to a nearby Mexican restaurant for lunch. Bernhardt had parked around the corner, walked to the restaurant, and sat at the counter, covertly watching them while he ate a taco and drank dark Mexican beer. Added to the few times he'd seen them together during the past twenty-four hours, and remembering Tuesday's conversation with Nora Farley, the half hour's surveillance in the restaurant had solidified Bernhardt's estimation of Betty Giles. Certainly, she was intelligent. The economy of her gestures, the quickness of her glance, everything about her suggested a high level of intelligence, of awareness. But her gestures and her glances had also revealed a certain tentative uncertainty, a failure of essential self-esteem. Somehow, somewhere, Betty Giles had been damaged. She'd lost her way, perhaps permanently, become one of those women who didn't think she deserved better than second best. Because, certainly, she and Nick Ames were a mis-match. Her mannerisms were reflective; his were abrupt, often truculent. She dressed with conservative good taste; he dressed to imitate the macho male. She was quietly polite; he sometimes sulked, sometimes blustered.

But, with all those obvious dissimilarities on one side of the equation, there remained on the other side the sexual component, nature's wild card. And whether or not he would have picked up on it without Nora Farley's cues, it nevertheless seemed clear to Bernhardt that Nick Ames was a bad habit that Betty Giles couldn't break. So she—

Across the courtyard, the door to number twelve was swinging open. Wearing a gray sweater and navy blue slacks that clung to the contours of her hips and buttocks, Betty Giles walked to the passenger door of the Toyota—and waited while Ames got in behind the wheel, finally reached across to unlock her door from the inside.

Tempted to get into his car and follow them to dinner out of simple curiosity, Bernhardt decided instead to walk to the entrance of the motel's driveway. He watched them as they turned north, toward downtown Santa Rosa. Seeing the Toyota slow for a stop sign at the first corner, he was about to turn back to the motel when he saw a maroon Oldsmobile approaching from the south. Years of surveillance suggested that the Olds was following the Toyota: Dancer's anonymous client, taking over the surveillance—or the pursuit. Instinctively, Bernhardt stepped into the deepening shadow of a huge Monterey pine that grew close beside the motel entrance. To his left, the Toyota was still stopped, for cross traffic. Meaning that, yes, the maroon Olds was slowing to a crawl as it passed the motel entrance. Even in the gathering twilight, still standing in the shadow of the pine tree, Bernhardt had a clear view of the driver: a young black man, remarkably good-looking, his profile classically Negroid, his manner suggesting a certain pride of bearing, even arrogance.

Thoughtfully, Bernhardt watched as the driver of the Oldsmobile allowed another car to turn behind the Toyota before he proceeded across the intersection.

If Bernhardt had been conducting a single-handed moving surveillance, considering the hour of the day and the frequency of the traffic, he would have done exactly what the black man was doing.

3

"I can talk to him," she said. "I *know* I can talk to him. *We* can talk to him. I'll talk to him first. Then you can talk to him, tell him you're sorry you did it. That's all it'll take, Nick. I swear to God, that's all it'll take."

"Jesus, Betty—" Ames sharply shook his head. "He tried to *kill* me."

"You *say* he tried to kill you. But you're not sure. There's no proof."

"That's not how you were talking when we left Los Angeles."

"We could've been wrong, though. Both of us, we could've been wrong. We've been assuming that he was behind it. But we don't—"

"A week after I called him," he said, "someone tried to kill me. Use your head, for Christ's sake. I can't afford to think anything else, except that he was behind it. And if you think about it, quit trying to make excuses for him, you'll see I'm right. It *had* to be him."

"But even if it *was* him, I still say we can—"

"Do you think he's going to forgive and forget, just because I say I'm sorry? Is that what you think?"

"Have you got a better idea?"

"As a matter of fact, I do. I've been thinking about it. All day, I've been thinking about it. And we've got two choices. Either we come back at him, fight him, or else we run—go where he'll never find us, start all over again."

"You'd pump gas and I'd find a job in a dime store. Is

74

that it?" She spoke bitterly. "I did that when I was in high school, worked in a dime store. I didn't like it."

"Listen, Betty—" His voice lowered, his face darkened. With a thud, his boots came down from the edge of the coffee table.

"Christ, Nick, you didn't even tell me, before you did it. And now you want me to change my whole life. Everything I ever worked for, you want me to give up. You didn't even consult me. You just—"

"You didn't have to come with me, you know. I didn't make you come."

"Oh, Jesus—" She shook her head, slid off the bed, went to stand close beside his chair. "Look around you, Nick. We're in a second-rate motel room. We're scared, and we're snapping at each other. And it's going to get worse, not better. Don't you see that? Don't you see how it'll be?"

"I see how it could be if we had a million dollars in the bank, that's what I see. He thinks he can handle me. But if the two of us did it—called him, told him what we'd do, that'd make all the difference. He'd have to give in, if he knew you were with me."

"But it's a crime, Nick. We'd be committing a crime."

"Like robbing from someone who robbed a bank, that's what it is. The man's a crook, for God's sake. A goddam criminal."

"Two wrongs don't make a right."

"Christ—" He got to his feet, facing her. His jaw was tight, his eyes were snapping furiously. Behind him, with the sound turned down, the TV offered a car chase through slum-blighted city streets. "Christ, that's all we need now. Sweet little sayings. Words to live by, for God's sake." Rigid at his sides, his arms were muscle-bunched, his fists clenched.

Would he hit her?

This time, would he hit her?

"So now what, Nick?" Standing squarely before him, she spoke softly, quietly contemptuous. Her dark eyes were steady, challenging him. "Are you going to slam out again?" She pointed to the revolver lying on the bureau, a blue-steel obscenity. "Are you going to take your gun and go out and find a bar, and start drinking?"

She saw his mouth thin, saw his body tighten, felt the full force of his furious frustration. But then she saw uncertainty tug at his mouth, saw his eyes falter. She could sense his body slackening as fear diluted his fury, robbed him of the hostility he took for assurance.

"Oh, Jesus—" Raising his unclenched hands, he took a single step forward. "Jesus, why don't we—let's both of us go out, have some drinks. What'd you say?"

Smiling now, responding to the small boy's fear that she sensed he was revealing to her, she shook her head. "You go. Have a couple of drinks. When you come back, we'll talk." She reached out, touched his chest with her fingertips. Because, when she touched him, she felt better. So far, anyhow, she'd always felt better.

Sheepishly, friends again, he shook his head, then nodded—then smiled. "Okay—" He touched her arm in return. "Okay. Bring you anything?"

"Nothing, thanks."

4

He'd already slipped the ice pick into its leather scabbard, already thrust the .357 into the holster at his belt, already put the surgical gloves in the side pocket of his jacket when he saw it: the Toyota, coming through the motel entrance, signaling for a left turn. He closed the lid of the saddle-leather suitcase on the Woodsman and the UZI. As he started the Oldsmobile, switched on the headlights and pulled out into the street, an oncoming car's headlights revealed a single head inside the Toyota—a man's head, unmistakably.

The bird was on the wing: fifty thousand dollars for a few second's work, more than most men made in a year, a whole year.

At the thought, he could feel it beginning: the rush, the certainty that he was a person within a person, the invisible hunter, a man like no other man, ever. Soon, he knew, the rush would carry him far beyond himself, setting him free. Already, images were flashing: snatches of random memory, some of them wild, some of them sad, all of them shattered pieces of some strange, mysterious puzzle. Sometimes he saw two people, a man and a woman, naked, locked together. The woman had his mother's face; the man's face was featureless, black but blank. Sometimes he saw Alvin Beachum's face, flattened against bloodied brick.

Ahead, the Toyota was slowing, pulling to the curb, stopping just short of a neighborhood bar, the Boots and Saddle. In the interior darkness of the Oldsmobile, Dodge smiled. When people drank, they got careless.

5

The bartender was about forty years old, two hundred pounds, totally bald. He wore a checked gingham shirt and blue jeans. The flesh of his face was pale and flabby; the bulge of his belly overhung a wide, silver-buckled cowboy belt. His disinterested eyes were colorless, his nose misshapen, his mouth indeterminant. His voice was hoarse: "Help you?"

"Bourbon and water," Nick answered. "Bar brand."

Grunting, the bartender made the drink, put it on the stained mahogany bar. Nick laid down a five-dollar bill, swallowed some of the bourbon, set the glass aside, and turned on the barstool. Like the sign outside, the Boots and Saddle was tacky: a few split rails, a few dusty saddles hung from fake rafters, several rodeo posters tacked to the barnwood walls. Of the four booths, only one was occupied. Five customers sat at the bar: three men, two women. The two women were talking quietly together; the three men, scattered along the bar, were silently drinking. Watching himself in the mirror behind the bar, Nick drained half his glass, felt the welcome warmth of the liquor. At two dollars a drink, he could buy the beginnings of forgetfulness for a ten-dollar bill.

As he drained the glass and signaled for a refill, he caught one of the women's eyes in the mirror, a quick, appraising glance. Just as quickly, she looked away. But, still, she'd let the suggestion of an invitation linger. She was a brassy blonde, probably in her late twenties, early thirties. If he'd been with someone, another man, and if they could agree on who wanted who, they could probably move in on the two women, the blonde and her friend. Several drinks later—thirty, forty dollars later—they might leave together, one couple in the women's car, he and the blonde in his car.

No. Not his car. Betty's car.

No, not his apartment. Her apartment.

And the money in his pocket, that was hers, too.

He was aware that he was avoiding the thought, pushing it aside, consciously blanking it all out, especially the awareness that he was eyeing a woman in a bar while he was paying for a drink with another woman's money. There was a name for men like that— a name he couldn't allow himself to remember.

The mind, they said, was like a computer: an incredibly complex computer, millions of electrical terminals switching on and off. But computers could be controlled, and so could the mind. And he'd learned, long ago, the secret of mind control, of complete, utter concentration. So, even now, even here, he was able to control his thoughts, able to plan, able to see the big picture.

The big picture . . .

God, it was one of his father's favorite expressions. His father the salesman—the bowling ball salesman.

Even today, remembering, he smiled at the expression. "What's your dad do?" a friend would ask, usually a high-school friend. And he'd smile, playing it cool, and he'd say his dad sold bowling balls. They'd smile, too, his friends. Because they knew his father must make good money, better money than he could make just selling bowling balls. Their house was split-level, and their car was always new. And in Milwaukee, at Central High, if you played football, that was all you needed: a split-level house and a new car you could get on Friday nights and parents who knew enough to stay upstairs, whenever his friends came over to play records in the recreation room.

But then came the merger.

And, surprise, his father wasn't selling bowling equipment anymore, wasn't selling much of anything, really. Drinking a lot, and playing around, probably— and disappearing for days at a time, sometimes. But not selling much of anything, not bringing in much money.

Their house had never been a happy place, not really. But it hadn't been unhappy, either, not until the merger.

He finished another drink, put a dollar bill beside the one already lying on the bar, signaled for another drink. It was time to begin with the switches again, arranging his thoughts, getting himself aligned. He'd let his thoughts wander away, off the leash, back into the past. And so, as they so often did, his thoughts had betrayed him, left him high and dry, trapped by ancient defeats, puzzles without answers.

But it was the future, not the past, that could betray him now. Defeat lingered in the past, a constant, bitter goad. But danger threatened in the future—

—danger, and death.

Lifting the drink to his lips—his third drink—he caught the blonde looking at him again. This time he smiled.

6

Dodge pushed the light button on his digital watch, checked the time. Exactly an hour had passed since the mark had first entered the bar. Once Dodge had gotten out of the Oldsmobile, crossed the street, walked slowly past the bar, looked casually inside, made sure of his man. And once—no, twice—he'd reparked the Olds. He'd checked the guns, too: five cartridges in the revolver, with the hammer resting on an empty chamber. A full clip of high-speed hollow points in the Woodsman, but nothing in the chamber, for safety. He'd made sure the silencer was tight on the Woodsman, made sure the ice pick was free in its scabbard, under his arm.

Now he made sure the surgical gloves were smooth over fingers and palms.

If he'd been somewhere else—in Detroit, or New York, or Los Angeles—he'd have more choices. The more people, the more choices, the better chance of getting close, getting the job done. He'd have a chance to use the ice pick, his favorite weapon, in a big city. He could take his time, pick his place, step in close, do the job: a jab at the base of the neck, from behind, or a thrust up into the heart, from the front. No fuss. No noise. No blood. With luck, he could be walking calmly away before the mark hit the sidewalk.

But here, in Santa Rosa, he couldn't get in close, not without sticking out, being remembered. And, anyhow, with the mark's car parked so close to the bar, there'd be no time for the approach, no room to maneuver.

So it had to be the Woodsman: two, three hollow points in the brain box. For the Woodsman, he was in perfect position, diagonally across from the Toyota, with half a car's length between the Oldsmobile and the car ahead, plenty of room to get out, without backing up. From this position, he could see the mark just as he came out of the bar. When that happened, he'd start the engine, make sure the transmission was in park, make sure the brake was set, make sure the engine was idling smoothly, so it wouldn't stall. Then he'd lift the lid of the suitcase, take out the Woodsman, jack a round into the chamber. He'd make sure the—

The door to the bar was swinging inward, the first time it had opened in fifteen, twenty minutes. Without realizing he'd done it, his fingers were on the ignition keys, ready.

Good. His mind was ahead of him, taking care of him.

"You're smart, Willis. You're truly smart."

81

It was Miss Redmond talking, his fourth grade teacher, the only teacher he'd ever liked, ever brought anything to, from home.

"And you're—"

The door of the bar was fully open now. And, yes—God, yes—it was the mark, alone.

And, yes—God, yes—the engine was turning over, catching, running smoothly.. The transmission was in park, the brake was set, firmly set, double checked. And now the top of the suitcase was coming up. As he watched the mark begin walking toward the Toyota, toward the front, his right hand closed on the familiar shape of the Woodsman's walnut grip. Keeping the gun low, he gripped the slide with his left hand, drew back the slide, let it thud closed. With his left hand free, he found the door handle, released the latch, pushed open the door.

Timing, now—everything was timing. The years had come down to hours, and the hours to minutes—

—and now the seconds were beginning: long, lengthening seconds, time within time, one long, silent scream.

Yes, the door was fully open. And, yes, the engine was running, not overloading, not stalling, like one of them had done once, in Boston. And, yes, he was standing beside the Oldsmobile, with the Woodsman down at his side. He'd practiced this, practiced in front of a floor-to-ceiling mirror, like a dancer.

Across the street, the mark was rounding the front of the Toyota. The mark's right hand was reaching into his pocket, for his car keys. From the left, up the street, came the sound of an engine, a flash of headlights. And from the right, too: another engine, another pair of headlights—two cars, coming at the same time, from opposite directions, against the odds he'd calculated so carefully for this quiet residential street.

"Don't forget the odds," Venezzio had said once. *"If they aren't for you, they're against you."*

Range, thirty-five feet, at least, an impossible shot in the darkness, with a pistol. The car from the left passed, a Datsun Z loaded with kids. The mark was at the Toyota's door, bending slightly at the waist, fitting key to lock. To the right, the second car was still a half block away, coming slowly. From the Z car came the trailing sound of teenage laughter.

The Toyota's door was slowly coming open. The mark was swinging his right leg into the car.

At his side, the Oldsmobile's engine was still idling strongly. Without that, the engine running, he'd never make it, never get away.

"A wheelman is good," Venezzio had said. *"But then he knows, he's your weak link."*

Quickly, he looked to the left, then to the right, up and down the dark, deserted sidewalks. Except for two dogs, trotting side by side beneath a streetlight, the sidewalks were deserted. Across the street, the mark was inside the Toyota, behind the wheel, with the door closed. In seconds, the mark would start the engine.

—for you, or against you—

A hundred feet—fifty feet—the headlights from the right were coming slowly, steadily closer—

—past. Finally past.

He was moving ahead, quickly crossing the street. Each step was a century, the total of everything: the schoolyard fights, won and lost, the .45, bucking before his eyes. Even the women, wild beneath him. Everything.

And nothing, too.

If fear ever caught him, nothing was left.

"Think of the money," Venezzio had said once. *"Just the money."*

The Toyota's engine was turning over on the starter,

finally catching. Range, fifteen feet, and closing. The mark must first back up, before he could go forward, get out of the parking place. Was the driver's window up or down? Did it matter? Had it ever happened before, that he'd shot through glass with the .22, a hollow point .22?

The money: a stack of hundred-dollar bills—five hundred of them.

Ten feet. Five feet. The Woodsman was coming up. And now, magically, it was the Colt .45. They all became the .45, lined up on Beachum.

Behind the glass, the mark's head was turning—eyes wide, mouth open. On the trigger, his finger curled, tightened. The muffled explosion hardly moved the barrel, with the weight of the silencer holding it down. Instantly, the glass was crazed, turned milky-white, thousands of tiny cracks surrounding one small black hole—

—surrounding the hole, concealing the face behind, protecting the mark behind.

Another shot—another hole, an inch from the first hole.

Not enough. Not nearly enough. For fifty thousand dollars, not nearly enough.

Seconds, now—it all came down to seconds.

With his left hand, he reached for the door handle. Thank God, he'd remembered to put on the gloves. Once he'd forgotten. Just once.

The door was coming open, swinging wide. From his left, he could hear another engine, see another pair of headlights, coming fast. Was the Oldsmobile's engine still idling? If he could pray, he would.

Inside the car, the mark lay on his right side, across both front seats, facing forward. Still alive, still breathing, softly moaning. Good; the eyes weren't turned on him, begging for life. That had happened once, too—

another time long ago, more money in the bank. Hard earned money. Nobody knew, would ever know, how hard it came, all that money.

Moving now with a mind of its own, the Woodsman came close to the skull, just behind the ear. Until now, this instant, he'd done it all, guided them both, himself and the gun. But then the gun came alive. It was always so surprising, this final moment, when he gave himself to the gun, finally to free himself.

The first explosion rocked the head, already bloody. And the second explosion, and the third, muffled by both the silencer and the car, all of them made the head move loosely, like the mark was shaking his head, arguing about something.

He straightened, struck his head on the doorframe, ducked, saw the headlights pass—saw the two dogs, standing side by side on the opposite sidewalk, watching him.

In his whole life, he'd never had a dog. Even with all the money, he'd never had a dog.

FRIDAY
September 14th

I

Yawning, Bernhardt stretched his hands high over his head, bent smartly at the waist, touched his toes, yawned again, scratched himself, considered repeating the exercise fifty times, decided he could skip the regimen today, since he was, after all, on an out-of-town assignment, a break in his normal routine. Instead, still reflectively scratching, he switched on the TV at random and opened the floor-to-ceiling drapes, taking care to stand clear of the window, since he wore only shorts.

Across the courtyard, a black-and-white police patrol car was parked in the space reserved for room number twelve, where the Toyota had been parked last night. A second police car, unmarked, was drawn up behind the first. Inside number twelve, indistinctly, Bernhardt saw a man dressed in plainclothes standing with arms folded, staring at something—or someone—inside. Even though the man's features weren't readable, his air of quiet authority marked him as a detective.

On the TV, anchorwoman Jane Farley, with her striking face and exciting mane of dark brown hair, was beginning an interview with Akira Kurosawa. Quietly, tastefully, she projected the deference due the maestro in his seventy-fifth year. Bernhardt turned up the volume, listening to the interview as he slipped into fresh underwear, clean socks, and corduroy slacks. Still listening attentively through the open bathroom door, he washed his face, shaved, combed his hair. Back in front of the TV, he took a sports shirt from the back of a chair, slipped into it, buttoned it, sat on the edge of the bed, and tugged on running shoes as he watched the pretty young American television personality and the elderly Japanese director. Plainly, the woman was struggling to bring the interview alive for the American housewife. Just as plainly, Kurosawa had come to talk about the art of the cinema.

With the interview mercifully ended, Bernhardt switched off the set, put his wallet, keys, and change in his pockets, then stepped out into the sunny warmth of the bright September morning. Across the courtyard, the door to number twelve was swinging open. A uniformed officer emerged, followed by the plainclothesman. At the same time another plainclothesman emerged from the motel office, equidistant from number twelve and Bernhardt's room. Sauntering, Bernhardt walked toward the motel coffee shop as the second detective joined the other two men, all three of them standing between their two cars as they talked quietly, seemingly abstracted, each man staring off in a different direction. Three newspaper vending boxes lined the narrow sidewalk beside the door to the coffee shop: a box each for the *San Francisco Chronicle*, the *Los Angeles Times*, and the *Santa Rosa Record*. About to drop a quarter in the *Record* box, Bernhardt checked the dateline, realized that the box contained yesterday's newspapers. He bought a *Chronicle* instead, pushed open the coffee shop's door and chose a seat at the counter. Three of the coffee shop's dozen-odd tables were occupied, but only one man sat at the counter. Wearing a Caterpillar cap and a tight-fitting yellow T-shirt with the sleeves rolled up to display aggressively bulging biceps, the man sipped coffee as he stared out across the courtyard at the three officers, still closely conversing. Also staring at the policemen, ignoring Bernhardt, an overweight waitress stood with one hip wedged against the counter, her freckled arms folded beneath large breasts. The easy familiarity of customer and waitress suggested that the man with the bulging biceps was a "regular," not a guest of the motel.

"A little action, eh?" the man was saying. "Someone get robbed?"

As Bernhardt reached for a menu, the waitress raised beefy shoulders, ponderously shrugging. "Who knows?"

"Those're detectives. See the badges, pinned to their shirts?"

"I know they're detectives, Charlie. More coffee?"

"Fine." Charlie drained his cup. As he waited for his refill, he glanced briefly at Bernhardt, then glanced indifferently away. *I'd Rather Be Truckin'* was stenciled across the front of Charlie's yellow T-shirt. With the coffeepot in her hand, the waitress turned away from the window to face Bernhardt.

"Coffee?"

"I'm going to have a Denver omelette," Bernhardt said. "And coffee with the omelette, please."

"Right." She put the coffeepot on the counter, flipped open her pad, wrote out the order, clipped the slip to a revolving drum, and spun the drum to face the fry cook. Now she moved sluggishly to the cash register, meeting a man who laid a check and a ten-dollar bill on the counter beside the register. Looking past them, Bernhardt saw the uniformed officer opening the patrol car's passenger door for Betty Giles, who had just come out of her motel room. Eyes straight ahead, head rigid, plainly numbed, the woman moved as if she were sentenced to death, and was approaching the gas chamber. Solicitously, the patrolman closed the door, tested it, then moved briskly around the front of the car, getting in on the driver's side. In their unmarked car, the two detectives backed up, let the black-and-white patrol car precede them out of the motel's courtyard.

"When does today's paper come?" Bernhardt asked.

"Should be here by now," the waitress answered shortly. "If you're in a hurry, you can probably get one downtown. We're at the end of the line, out here."

"Thank you."

"There they go," said the man in the Caterpillar cap, moving his jaw toward the window. "Whatever it was, it couldn't've been very important."

• • •

"A *Record*, please," Bernhardt said, putting a quarter on the drugstore counter and displaying the newspaper's logo, for the proprietor of the newsstand to see.

"Right." The proprietor didn't look up.

Bernhardt's Ford was parked at the curb, with his suitcase on the rear seat. He got in the car on the right side, opened the paper, and scanned the front page.

MYSTERY SLAYING
ON SOUTH STREET

It was a brief one-column story at the bottom of the page:

Responding last night to reports of shots being fired in the two thousand block of South Street, police discovered the body of a man tentatively identified as Nicholas Ames, 36, a resident of Los Angeles. No additional details of the slaying are immediately available from official sources, but witnesses at the scene believe that Ames had spent some of the evening at a nearby tavern, and had just returned to his car when an unknown assailant approached the car and fired several shots through the window of the driver's side. The victim was pronounced dead at the scene, and was taken to the county morgue for positive identification. Detective Sergeant Clifford Benson promised to reveal more details of the slaying as they become available.

Bernhardt reread the story, refolded the newspaper, then sat silently for a moment, staring at nothing.

They'd been together, Betty Giles and Nick Ames. It had always been a given, that they'd be together.

Someone had hired Dancer to find Betty Giles. Dancer had assessed the client, decided there was enough money in the job to show a profit, and made the deal. Playing the potentate, his favorite role, Dancer had deigned to pass the job on to Bernhardt. As always, keeping his edge, Dancer had supplied only the details needed to get the job done, nothing more.

Thirty-six hours later, defying the odds, Bernhardt had located the woman. Of course, she'd been with Nick Ames; she couldn't help herself. Find Betty, find Nick, a star-crossed package deal.

Case closed.

For Nick Ames, permanently, the case was closed. And for Dancer, too, the case was closed: bills rendered, check received, reports filed and forgotten.

Grimly, Bernhardt dropped the newspaper on the floor of the rear seat, clambered impatiently over the Ford's control console, started the engine.

Driving a steady sixty, he could be in San Francisco by eleven o'clock. He'd go to his apartment first, to get his messages, make at least one phone call.

Then he'd see Dancer.

2

Somehow she couldn't remember the two detectives' names. The patrolman's name was Henderson. His name, she could remember. Henderson had been the first to knock on her door. He'd been surprised to learn that he was the first one—surprised and distressed, that no one had told her Nick had been killed last night. "Are you Mrs. Ames?" he'd asked, holding his uniform cap awkwardly in his big-knuckled hands. "Mrs. Nicholas Ames?" When she'd said she wasn't Mrs. Ames, he'd been plainly relieved. A wife's grief would have pained him, added to his policeman's problems. But a girlfriend—possibly a pickup for the night, shacked up in a motel room—this was something Henderson could handle.

"Here we are—" One of the detectives, the Chicano one with the soft brown eyes, was gesturing to a door marked "Viewing." Politely, he pushed open the door for her, waited for her to enter first. It was a very small room, dimly lit, with two chairs and a wall phone. The chairs were canary yellow, the wall phone was institutional white. The room was lit by a single panel of fluorescent lights. From waist height to the ceiling, a brown curtain was drawn entirely across one wall. She knew why she was there, knew what waited on the other side of that curtain. Yet, incredibly, she didn't believe it would really happen, didn't believe he was dead, his body pale and cold, laid out in the next room.

All her life, she'd been able to keep some part of herself separate from shock, protected. She could still vividly remember the night her stepfather left, could still remember the sounds of their voices: her mother, screaming, her stepfather shouting. But she'd heard other sounds, too: a cacophony of white sound, a stifled, secret lament: her soul, protesting, protecting her. This barrier of sound was her only defense.

It was the same sound she heard now, her only hope.

And, indistinctly, the other sound: the detective's voice, saying something indistinguishable on the telephone. Now, with the phone still held to his ear, he was nodding, signifying anonymous agreement. He replaced the phone in its white plastic bracket and turned to face her. His expression was both regretful and compassionate. He was a kind man, a conscientious man, probably. A caring man.

"—you're ready?" he was asking, stepping to the curtain. His nut-brown hand was reaching behind the draperies, searching for the cord that would draw the drapery back. He'd done this before, then.

A dirty job, he was probably thinking. But someone had to do it.

She was aware that she was nodding, was moving a half step forward, closer to the curtain.

Why was she nodding? Of what was she approving— or disapproving? Could she comprehend it, what had happened? Could anyone comprehend it? God, perhaps?

Slowly, inexorably, the drapes were moving, revealing a large plate-glass window. Behind the window was a tiny rectangular room, brightly lit, painted a blinding white. A stainless steel gurney had been wheeled into the center of the tiny room. Covered by a green sheet, a body lay on the gurney. Only the face was exposed: Not the hair, not even the ears, only the face. Nick's face, as pale as white marble, a perfect profile of death.

The pale face was changing its relationship to the sill of the plate-glass window, which meant that she was nodding. The detective was speaking, asking his detective's question as the drapes slid back. She could read the question in his soft brown eyes, even though his voice was indistinct, obscured by the secret white sound within, still silently raging. But, small miracle, she could clearly hear her own voice: "Yes, that's him. That's Nick Ames."

Immediately, the drapes moved, returning their viewing room to its previous dimness. The detective was opening the door for her—one door, followed by a hallway, followed by a second door. Now they were outside, in the sunshine. From the position of the sun, she knew it was not yet noon. The policemen had come a little after eight, to tell her what she'd already known, that something had happened to Nick. All night, lying awake in the queen-size bed, she'd realized that there were only three possibilities: either he was dead, or he'd been arrested, or he'd decided to—

"—take you home," the detective was saying, unlocking the door of his car. "Back to the motel, I mean." He waited for her to settle herself, closed her door, got in behind the wheel, started the engine, pulled away from the curb.

"We'll want you to stay in town for a couple of days, at least for the inquest," he said. "Will that be all right?"

"I—I guesso. Yes." She nodded. It would be stupid, she realized, to say anything else. Then, because it was suddenly very important, she turned in the seat to face him. "Excuse me," she said. "But I—I'm afraid that I've forgotten your name. I'm sorry."

"It's Ochoa," he said, adding with a touch of modest pride, "Sergeant Ochoa."

"Thank you, Sergeant Ochoa. Thank you for being so kind to me."

3

Bernhardt dropped his bag on the floor beside the couch, rewound the answering machine's tape, pressed the start button, listened to one short message from Dancer, a longer message from Dave Falk saying that tonight's read-through of *The Buried Child* must be postponed because the rehearsal room had been fumigated yesterday, instead of the day before. The room, Falk said, still smelled. And no other room was available. The third message was from Pamela Brett, saying that she wasn't sure what time the rehearsal started. Bernhardt played Pamela's message twice, once to verify the phone number, once to listen to her voice. It was a quiet voice, self-possessed, with an easy, melodious lilt—an ingenue's voice, pleasing to the ear. Listening, he realized how often he'd thought about her, these last four days.

But, tragedy before comedy, business before pleasure, he checked his address book, punched out the police department's switchboard.

"I'd like Homicide, please. Lieutenant Peter Friedman. This is Alan Bernhardt."

A long, tedious silence followed. Then: "Sorry, Mr. Bernhardt. Lieutenant Friedman is out in the field. Can anyone else help you?"

"How about Lieutenant Hastings?"

"Just a minute."

Moments later, Hastings came on the line. His voice was the male counterpart to Pamela's voice: also pleasant, also melodious. At the instant's thought, a wayward image intruded: Pamela and Frank—yes, they shared certain similarities, the two of them. Both were quiet, thoughtful—handsome, too. Would they be drawn to each other, if they ever met?

"Alan?"

"Frank—yes. Listen, I'm sorry to bother you. I know Pete's out, so you're probably busy. But I think I might've gotten myself into something, and I wonder whether you could help me out. All it'd take is a phone call to Santa Rosa."

"Dancer strikes again, eh?"

Reluctantly, Bernhardt nodded, folding his long, lean body into a chair. "It could be. Yeah."

"What's the problem?"

"I was hired to find a woman named Betty Giles, who's running from some problem down in Los Angeles. She was traveling with a man named Nick Ames, her boyfriend. Thanks to Pete, I found them in Santa Rosa. They were staying at a motel up there. The Starlight Motel. I located them Wednesday afternoon, and called Dancer. The next day—yesterday—I was pulled off the case. And last night, Nick Ames was killed. Shot."

"Do you think you were hired to set him up?"

"I don't know. But if I had some idea of the particulars, how he was killed, and why, I'd feel a hell of a lot better."

"Do you know who's handling the investigation?"

"No. That's it—I don't know a damn thing. Nothing, except that he was shot." As he spoke, he glanced at the Santa Rosa newspaper, open beside the telephone. "It happened on South Street. The two thousand block of South Street."

"Where are you now?"

"I'm at home—" He gave Hastings the number.

"I'll see what I can do. Will you be there for another hour?"

"I'll stay here till you call."

"Right. Talk to you soon."

Before he could thank the other man, Bernhardt heard the line go dead. He broke the connection, and was about to dial Pamela's number when the phone came alive in his hand, warbling shrilly.

"Hello?"

"Is this Mr. Bernhardt? Alan Bernhardt?" It was a woman's voice, tentative, indistinct, unsure.

"Yes."

"This is Nora Farley. Betty's mother. Betty Giles."

To mask a surge of sudden excitement, he let a beat pass. "Yes, Mrs. Farley—" Another beat, for pacing. Then: "Have you heard from Betty?"

"Yeah. I—she called a couple of hours ago. And I'm worried, Mr. Bernhardt. I'm worried sick." Her voice was low, clogged with emotion. "Nick Ames was killed. Murdered, last night. Did you know that?"

"Yes, I did. I've got a call in to the police right now, trying to find out what happened."

"They were up in Santa Rosa. And I remember that you asked me about Santa Rosa, so I had to call, to ask you. He was shot, up there."

"What did Betty say, Mrs. Farley? Tell me what she said, her exact words. Can you remember?" Trying to calm her, he spoke slowly, deliberately, at the same time glancing at his watch. He'd give her ten minutes, then he'd hang up, clear the line for Hastings' call. *"Think."*

"Well, she—she's kind of numb, I guess you'd say. In shock, I suppose. Still in shock. She said that they'd tried to kill him before. That's why they left L.A., she said—because someone tried to kill him. He was scared, she said, because he thought they'd try it again, try to kill him, if they stayed in L.A. So that's why they left, see, left L.A. It was just like I thought. It wasn't a vacation at all, that they took. It was—"

"*Who* tried it again? Did Betty say *who*?"

"No," she muttered. "I asked her, but she wouldn't say."

"Did she say what Nick had done, why they wanted to kill him?"

"No, not that, either. I asked her, but she wouldn't say. She didn't agree with it, though, what he did. She told me that. She begged him to give it up, not do it, whatever it was."

"Is she worried for herself, Mrs. Farley—worried that she could be in danger?"

"I asked her that. But she didn't even answer. I asked her twice. And it—" She broke off, drew a deep, unsteady breath. "And it worried me, that she didn't answer."

"Why?"

"Because she didn't seem to care what happened to her. It—it scared me, the way she said it."

"Did she say what she intends to do now? Is she coming here, coming to San Francisco?"

"No—" Her voice was hardly audible. "No, she didn't say, wouldn't tell me where she's going. And that scared me, too."

"Why?"

"Because Betty said she was going to make them pay. For killing him."

"Did she elaborate on that, say what she meant?" As he spoke, he glanced at his watch. They'd been talking for almost fifteen minutes.

"No. I asked her what she meant, but she wouldn't say, except that they'd pay. But that's why she won't tell me where she's going next—because she'll be in danger, if she tries to make them pay. I know it. I just *know* it."

"Is that what she said—exactly what she said, that she'd make them pay?"

"No. But that's what she meant. I know that's what she meant." Her voice trailed off into an emotion-choked silence.

Bernhardt let the silence lengthen, then spoke gently: "I've got to go now, Mrs. Farley. I don't want to miss the call from the police. But I'll keep in touch with you. And if you hear from her again, call me. Try here first, then call the office—Herbert Dancer, Limited. Have you still got the card I gave you?"

"Yes."

"Well, hang on to it. And try not to worry, Mrs. Farley. If they wanted to harm her, they'd've already done it."

"Do you think so?" He could hear hope in her voice—a hesitant, tremulous hope. It was his responsibility to somehow keep that hope alive.

"I'm sure of it. Absolutely sure. I'll get back to you in a few hours. Okay?"

"You're the only one I called, Mr. Bernhardt. You—you seemed kind, seemed like you cared. And—and there's no one else, that I can call. I—" Suddenly she began to sob.

Conscious of the sheer weight of responsibility he could incur, he nevertheless knew he must say it, must make her believe that, yes, he cared: "I'm glad you feel like that, Mrs. Farley. You're right, to feel like that. Exactly right."

"It's just that—" Loudly, wetly, she snuffled. "It's just that I'm alone, you know. All alone."

"I know," he answered. "I know how you feel. Because I'm alone, too."

• • •

Bernhardt was pouring boiling water over the instant coffee in his favorite mug when the phone warbled. He took a moment to stir the coffee, then carried the cup into the living room, put it beside the phone.

"Hello?"

"This is Frank, Alan. You've been on the phone."

"I'm sorry. It was about this same case, in Santa Rosa. I couldn't shut it off." As he spoke, he reached for a pad and pencil. "Any luck?"

"That's for you to decide, I guess. I talked to Sergeant Ochoa, in Santa Rosa. He says that Ames was staying at the Starlight Motel, with Betty Giles. You know that."

"Yes."

"Ames went out last night to a bar—a neighborhood bar, the Boots and Saddle. He stayed there for a couple of hours, drinking. There weren't any problems. No fights, no words exchanged, nothing. He just sat on his stool, apparently, not saying much. Then, about eleven, he paid the bill, went outside, got in his car—Betty Giles' car, actually. All the interrogation reports aren't in yet, but apparently there was a car parked across the street from Ames' car, maybe on stakeout. That part isn't clear, how long the other car was there. But, anyhow, Ochoa has a witness who says that, as soon as Ames left the bar, the driver of the other car got out, and walked across the street, and started shooting. The witness says he shot twice through the driver's window, then opened the door and shot several more times. And that pretty much squares with the facts. There were two holes in the window glass—and six holes, altogether, in the body. All of them in the neck or head."

"Good shooting."

"There's more."

"Oh?" Bernhardt sat up straighter.

"The witness says the guy used a silencer. He swears to God."

"Is he a qualified witness?"

"Who knows? He says he heard a kind of sharp splatting."

"Did he actually see the gun?"

"No. But there's something else, that supports what he said."

"What's that?"

"The weapon was a .22. And the bullets were probably hollow points. Tell you anything?"

"A hit man's weapon. Is that what you're saying?"

"That's what I'm saying," Hastings answered. "Exactly. At close range, a high-speed hollow point .22 does more damage than a jacketed .38. And there's no ballistics. Then there's the silencer. Ruger and High Standard and Colt—they all make .22 automatics with a barrel that isn't enclosed by a slide, which means they're perfect for a silencer. File off the front sight, and you're in business. Of course," he added, "this is all theory."

"It sounds like pretty good theory, though."

"I think so."

"Anything else?"

"As a matter of fact," Hastings said, "there is. First, the witness says he thinks the killer was a black man. He's not sure. It was dark, and a streetlight was out, apparently. But that was his impression."

Instantly, the street scene outside the Starlight Motel returned: the black man in the maroon Oldsmobile, following Betty Giles and Nick Ames, in their white Toyota. Something about the black man's presence, his haughty aloofness, had remained firmly fixed in Bernhardt's memory.

A black hit man . . .

Hired by whom? For what reason?

"What else?"

"The woman," Hastings said, "Betty Giles. They took her downtown, to identify the body. Then they took her back to the motel, and told her to stay put. But she didn't. She packed her bag, and paid her bill, and took a cab."

"A cab to where?"

"They're still checking. It hasn't been more than a couple of hours since she split."

"She left her car behind," Bernhardt said thoughtfully.

"She didn't have any choice. It was impounded, for forensics. If she wanted to get out of town in a hurry, she had to leave the car."

"Maybe she'll be back to claim it."

"Maybe. But she also disobeyed Ochoa's order not to leave town, as I said. So, technically, she's a fugitive, if he swears out a complaint."

"She panicked."

"Obviously."

"Is there more?"

"That's it," Hastings answered. "Except for one thing."

"What's that?"

"Ochoa wants you to call him, give him what you've got. I said you would. Right?"

Responding to the unmistakable note of command in the other man's voice, Bernhardt concentrated on maximum projection as he answered, "Right." He broke the connection, drew a long, deep breath, then sat silently for a moment, staring with unfocused eyes at his small rectangular view of the landlord's garden, visible through the living-room window. He'd always resisted organized activities, including the current fad for meditation. But an actor's stock in trade, after all, was his command of moods. So before he called Pamela, he wanted to draw back from the darkness of murder. He wanted to remember the particular quality of Pamela's voice, wanted to recall, again, their moment at Mike's, sitting across from each other, smiling, their eyes searching.

He let the memory linger, drew another deep breath, touch-toned her number.

"Hello?"

"It's Alan Bernhardt, Pamela. Guess what?"

"What?"

"They fumigated the rehearsal room, and then didn't let it air out, apparently. And there's no other space available."

"*Fumigated*? Why?"

"Do you really want to know?"

She chuckled. "I guess not. So is the read-through off?"

"I'm afraid so. There's a Friday night performance, obviously, in the theater itself."

"What about someone's house?"

"I don't think Dave Falk would want to do that. He's very big on theater mystique, even if it's just a rehearsal room."

"The smell of the greasepaint coming under the door?"

He smiled. "Something like that. But listen—if the read-through is off, what about the two of us getting together? Would you like to have dinner?"

A short silence followed. What was she thinking—feeling—deciding? Did she realize that, if she put him off, he wouldn't ask again? Some men, denied, redoubled their macho efforts, eventually prevailed.

But some men—the vulnerable ones—would turn aside, retreat within, get back behind those inner defenses, so carefully erected over the years. Some men . . .

". . . don't you come over here?" she was saying. "I've got a casserole in the freezer."

"A casserole? Great. What time?"

"How about seven?"

"Seven is perfect."

As he cradled the phone, he realized that he was smiling: a wide, spontaneous smile, a smile from other times, other places—other dreams.

4

When she saw Bernhardt, Marge Ferguson smiled, opened her center drawer, withdrew an envelope, handed it to Bernhardt.

"Happy September fourteenth, Alan."

"Thanks, Marge." He slipped the unopened envelope in an inside pocket and gestured toward Dancer's office. "Is anyone with him?"

"No. But he doesn't want underlings disturbing him. Listen, Alan, I've got a date next week with a very intellectual guy. He went to Harvard, in fact. Any chance of a deal on tickets?"

"Probably. I'll see what I can do. Right now, though, I want to see him—" He gestured again. "It's important."

"Now, Alan, you know how it goes. What seems important to mere mortals doesn't even register on Dancer's—"

"How about murder, Marge? How about homicide detectives, knocking on his door? Think he'd like to have a little advance notice?"

"I get your point." As she reached for the phone she raised a forefinger. "Don't forget those tickets."

"No problem."

Dancer's desk, usually uncluttered, was covered with stacks of miscellaneous papers.

"The IRS," Dancer said, gesturing to the mis-matched stacks of receipts and charge slips. "I'm being audited, and my goddam accountant is in the hospital."

"Can't you get an extension?"

"I've already had two extensions. What is it, Alan? What's so important?"

"It's the Betty Giles thing—Betty Giles and Nick Ames. He was murdered last night, in Santa Rosa. He was murdered, and Betty Giles is running."

Eyes narrowed, mouth pursed, Dancer pulled at an earlobe. "Any particulars?" As he spoke, he gestured Bernhardt to a chair. Ignoring the invitation, Bernhardt leaned forward, placing the fingertips of both hands on Dancer's desk. Making long, hard eye contact, he spoke softly:

"Yes, Herbert, there are particulars. Several particulars. Would you like to hear them?"

Resigned, Dancer rolled his chair back from the desk and turned to face the view window. The message: Bernhardt's audience with his superior had begun—and the clock was ticking.

"I found them on Wednesday," Bernhardt said, "about four o'clock in the afternoon. About twenty-four hours later, you called me off the case. And that night— last night—Nick Ames was killed. It looks like he could've been killed by a hired gun—a hit man."

Frowning, Dancer swiveled in his chair to face Bernhardt. Uncharacteristically, Dancer wasn't wearing a jacket, and his tie was loosened. His improbably cherubic face was thoughtful. As always, his eyes were cold, revealing nothing.

"Why do you say it was a hit man?"

"Because the murder weapon fired .22 high-speed hollow points. And it probably had a silencer. That's a hit man's weapon."

"Have you ever seen the ads in some of these *Soldier of Fortune* magazines? Silencers—machine pistol conversions—anyone can get anything."

Ignoring the response, Bernhardt said, "There's only one way the facts add up, Herbert. Whoever hired you wanted Nick Ames dead. He knew Ames and Betty Giles were together, so he said he wanted us to find the woman, as a cover. As soon as I found them, you called the client—and he got on an airplane. When he arrived in Santa Rosa, you relieved me. He took over the stakeout—and killed Ames. Which means that we're accessories to murder."

Elaborately long suffering, Dancer sighed. His manner was condescending as he said, "Alan, you're dramatizing. Do you realize that you're dramatizing?"

Grimly choosing not to reply, Bernhardt asked, "Is the client a black man?"

"No, he's not a black man. And he's not a hit man, either. That, I can guarantee."

"Who is he?"

Once more Dancer sighed, pointedly consulting his wristwatch. "Alan, we've had this conversation before. I'm not going to tell you who he is. And you know it."

"I talked to Betty Giles' mother. She says Betty is running. She's scared, and she's running. I think she's in danger."

"Why do you say that?"

"Because I think she knows why Nick Ames was killed—and I think she knows who killed him. She told her mother she was going to make them pay, whoever did it. And if she goes after them, she could get killed."

"She's upset. It's understandable. She'll cool down."

"Of course she's upset. She's also breaking the law, leaving Santa Rosa. She was told to stay for the inquest."

"That's her problem, Alan. It's not your problem."

"Listen, Herbert, I'm going to find Betty Giles. I'm going to try and square this."

Slowly, meaningfully, Dancer shook his head. "No you're not. You're going to forget about it, Alan. You're going to let it die. We're clean now. That's the way I want to keep it. We were hired to do a job, and we did it. Maybe the client lied to me, maybe he didn't. Maybe the whole thing is a coincidence. But, whichever way it comes down, we're clean. Which means that we aren't going to ask questions."

"You might feel clean, Herbert. But I don't feel clean. I feel dirty. And it's your fault."

Abruptly, Dancer hitched his chair closer to the desk, dropped his eyes to the small, scattered piles of papers that littered his desk. The audience was ended. Bernhardt remained motionless for a moment, standing rigidly before the desk. When he spoke, measuring each word, he was conscious of his actor's craft: "I'm going to find her, Herbert. And that's a promise."

Reluctantly, Dancer raised his cold, colorless eyes. For a moment he held Bernhardt's gaze. Then, as if he pitied the other man, he shook his head. "If you do that, Alan—go looking for her, poking around—you're through here. You understand that."

In reply, Bernhardt unclipped his pager from his belt, laid it on Dancer's beautifully burnished walnut desk. Next he withdrew his wallet, took out his plastic-coated private investigator's license, laid the license beside the pager.

"I'll keep the gun permit," he said. "That's in my name."

"Alan, for God's sake. You're—"

"This could turn out to be one of the best moves I ever made," Bernhardt said. "Already, that's what it feels like."

"You'll go broke."

"I've always been broke. I survived. Good-bye, Herbert. Watch the newspapers."

5

"That flight leaves in two hours and ten minutes, Miss Giles." The ticket clerk handed her the ticket folder. "Gate six." He pointed to his left.

She stood for a moment with the folder in her hand, watching her suitcase moving on the conveyor belt, one suitcase among many. Most of the suitcases contained enough clothing for a weekend, or a week.

Her suitcase could contain everything, all that was left of her life.

Aware of an impatient cough from the traveler behind her in line, she moved aside, slipped the ticket folder in her purse, made sure the purse was fastened. At five o'clock in the evening, the Burbank terminal was crowded. Conservatively dressed businessmen hurried from their shuttle flights to waiting cars, or cabs. Young people laughed together, their voices clear and clamorous. Just ahead, an attendant pushed a middle-aged man in a wheelchair. The man's head lolled nervelessly against the chair back; his hands were crossed in his lap, inert. His eyes were empty.

As empty as Nick's eyes: dead eyes in a cold, dead body.

Riding in the police car from the morgue to the Starlight Motel, the detective had tried to talk to her, tried to comfort her—and tried to pump her, too. Why had she come to Santa Rosa, she and Nick? Where had they planned to go next? She'd tried to be polite, tried to answer him. But, as if they were tethered, her thoughts had returned again and again to Nick's face. They'd tucked the green sheet close beneath his chin, and arranged another sheet like a nun's habit, concealing the hair, revealing only the face—the face so incredibly pale in the piteous white light, the eyes so utterly empty.

Finally, because she couldn't think of anything else, she'd asked the detective—Ochoa—why they hadn't closed Nick's eyes. It was only civilized, she'd always thought, to close a dead man's eyes. Embarrassed, Ochoa could only apologize. It was necessary, he'd said, that they take pictures, for identification. Several pictures. And for the pictures, he'd said, the eyes must be open.

And then he'd gone back to his questions, patiently probing. Like her tethered thoughts, returning again and again to Nick's dead eyes, Ochoa's questions constantly came back to the gun. Why had Nick been carrying the gun? The gun had been on the floor beneath the Toyota's seat. Did she know that it was illegal to carry a gun out of sight—even if the gun was duly registered, which it was.

She realized that she was standing near the entrance of one of the airport's restaurants. Was she hungry? Had she eaten today?

The uniformed policeman—Henderson—had knocked on her door at eight-thirty that morning. He'd told her that Nick had died. Just that, nothing more. Then, later, Ochoa had arrived. He'd stayed inside with her, waited until she'd finally mastered herself, quit crying. Ochoa had asked her to dress, while he waited outside. There's been a bag of fruit on the closet shelf, beside the bottle of bourbon that Nick had always taken when they traveled. She'd eaten a banana, she remembered. And later, back at the motel after the trip to the morgue, stuffing clothing at random into her suitcase, she'd eaten an apple. Curiously, though, she hadn't been conscious of the taste. She'd chewed, and swallowed, and felt the food swell in her throat. But there'd been no taste, no sensation of pleasure.

Neither would there be a sensation of pleasure tonight, alone in a strange bed. Whenever they traveled, every night, they made love. They'd talked about it once, how erotic they felt, in motel rooms. Forbidden games, she'd said, that must be part of it, part of the erotic pleasure. Nick hadn't responded, not in kind. He'd simply smiled his slow, knowing, stud-in-heat smile, moved close to her, put his hands on her where he knew she liked it most.

Without realizing it, she was standing near the cashier's stand, waiting to be seated. And, yes, a hostess was approaching, smiling, gesturing for Betty to follow her. The hostess was Chicano, like Ochoa.

She ordered at random: a turkey sandwich, soup, salad, and, after some thought, a glass of wine.

When he'd left her at the Starlight Motel, Ochoa had told her not to leave town, warned her not to leave Santa Rosa. But as soon as he'd gone, she'd started to pack. In minutes, she'd phoned for a cab, paid the bill with her VISA card, and lugged her suitcase out to the curb, where she'd waited for the cab. It hadn't occurred to her that she was probably breaking the law. Her only thought was that she must get out of the motel room, where Nick's things were still scattered around. She couldn't look at his things, and she couldn't bear to touch them, either, not then. She hadn't given a second thought to her car, which had been impounded, Ochoa had said—adding that, after they'd finished examining the car, they'd "do their best" to clean it. Only then did she ask him how Nick had died, how he'd been killed. Reluctantly, Ochoa had answered that Nick had been shot while he sat behind the wheel. And then, doggedly, Ochoa had come back to the same refrain, transparently rephrased: Who would have wanted to kill Nick? Why? What were they doing, really doing, in Santa Rosa, she and Nick? Why had they come? Were they really on a vacation? And what about the gun? Why had Nick carried a gun?

Within minutes of arriving at the station, she'd been on an express bus to San Francisco, less than two hours away. Only then, with the bus under way, its tires singing on the pavement, did she realize that she shouldn't have left his things behind. Rather than leave them to strangers' hands, she should have packed his bag—packed his shirts and trousers, his underwear, his socks. She should have taken his suitcase with her, taken his things, kept them. She realized that now, realized that she'd made a mistake.

She was intimately familiar with his things; she did his laundry, sometimes. And sometimes he did her laundry. It was part of living together, doing each other's laundry. She knew that now, knew what it meant, really meant, to live with a man. She'd been thirty-two when he'd moved in. Except for weekends, she'd never lived with a man before. Vividly, she could remember the first time she'd done their laundry. He'd stained his shorts: small brown stains, at the crotch. This, she'd thought, was reality. The movies, the magazines, that was one thing. This was something else.

At the Greyhound station in San Francisco she'd been lucky: immediately, she'd connected with a bus to the airport. Only then, it seemed, during the ride to the airport, had she begun to think, begun to plan.

Plan?

No, not plan. Except to call her mother from the airport, tell her mother what happened, she had no plan. She'd known it wouldn't help, to call her mother. She'd known how her mother would react, even known what her mother would say, the phrases she'd use. But there'd never been any question, that she must call her mother.

Because her mother was all she had. The two of them, they were alone. All alone.

As she sampled the soup and nibbled at the sandwich, she realized that she was staring through the restaurant window at a bank of telephones.

It had started with a phone call. Nick had discovered DuBois' number in her phone book, identified only as "D.D." He'd told her that much, confessed that much. And, yes, he'd been drinking when he'd made the call, doubtless goaded by his persistent, pernicious dreams of glory—and goaded, too, by the suspicion, festering more virulently with every passing year, that his dreams weren't coming true, might never come true.

They were both products of their past, she and Nick. She and Nick, and everyone else. For better or worse—better for her, worse for Nick—they were cast in the mold their parents had fashioned. Her father had left them, left her and her mother, just the two of them, with no house, no money, no hope. Yet, doggedly, blindly, instinctively, her mother had done her best—worked hard, and cried into her pillow.

From earliest memory, she'd been ashamed of her mother. Whatever the ceremony—the National Honor Society, high-school graduation, college graduation—she'd wished her mother wasn't there.

Only later, much later, had she realized that her mother, too, had wished she wasn't there.

In contrast, Nick had always admired his father, admired the new cars, the flashy clothes, the booming salesman's laugh. In high school, Nick had it all: a car during his senior year, girls calling constantly, parties in the downstairs "rec room," Cokes served by his mother with her bouffant hairdo—even an honorable mention on the all-state football team.

For Nick, it had all been too much, too soon—too easy. Because, when the house of cards suddenly tumbled down, and his father had shriveled before his eyes and his mother's voice had shrilled, Nick began to lose his way. He'd struggled, of course, done his best. But always, it seemed, he'd confused style with substance, appearances with reality. First he'd tried stock car racing—until he'd crashed. Next he'd gone back over the same ground, selling performance auto parts, drinking and bullshitting with the customers, as his father had done. Then, finally, there'd been the get-rich-quick schemes, each one a failure, each one leaving him a little less of a man inside himself.

And then there'd been the phone call . . .

She pushed the food away, and looked at the glass of wine, half full. Should she finish it? If she did finish it, she might not make her own phone call. To the extent that she knew herself, she knew that a small amount of liquor could blur her thinking, cloud her resolve.

Almost reluctantly, she pushed the glass away. She looked at the check, opened her purse, dropped some money on the table beside the check. She rose, left the restaurant, walked to the bank of open phone booths. She put her purse on the shelf beneath the phone, opened the purse. She found her address book, verified that, yes, she still remembered the number. She opened her coin purse, took out two quarters, deposited them in the telephone's coin slot. She stood motionless for a moment, receiver to her ear, hearing the buzz of the dial tone.

In the eleventh grade, she'd acted in the school play, an avant garde production called *Jaguar*. On the opening night, waiting in the wings for her cue, she'd felt numbed, suddenly immobilized, her throat dry, her limbs useless. For the first time in her life—and the last time—she'd seemed to exist apart from herself, a terrified stranger.

Until now, the last time . . .

Until now, when it was all happening again: the same slackness of the limbs, the same clenched throat, the same sense of helpless disembodiment as she touchtoned the numbers, heard the phone begin to ring. As she listened, she could clearly see the large, lavishly furnished room with its magnificent view of the ocean, the room she knew so well.

Three rings. Four.

"Yes?"

"This is Betty."

A pause. Then, without changing inflection: "Yes, Betty. Where are you?"

"I can't tell you that."

"I see. I'm sorry to hear it, Betty. You believe that, don't you?"

"You had him killed. Didn't you? You tried it once here in Los Angeles. And yesterday—last night—you had it done. Didn't you?"

"We can't talk about it on the phone, Betty. You realize that."

She made no response.

"Will you come to see me, so we can talk?"

"No," she answered. "No, I can't do that."

"You won't, you mean."

"He said it was you, the first time. I thought he was wrong. I told him he was wrong. But he knew it was you—knew you gave the order."

"Are you coming back, Betty? Eventually?"

"No."

"I see." He spoke softly.

In the silence, she could hear the noise of the telephone lines, a gentle sizzle. Was it possible that he could have the call traced? Could he have sworn out a warrant for her? Would he do that? She couldn't imagine. She'd never been able to imagine what he'd do. Which was the reason for his success, his incredible success. No one could predict what he'd do. Ever.

She realized that she was nervously clearing her throat, as if she had been called upon by a teacher, required to recite a lesson she'd only half prepared: "I'm going to tell them what you did—and why."

"No, Betty. You can't. When you think about it, you'll realize you can't. It's important that you think about it. Very important."

"I've got to go. I can't talk anymore."

"Will you promise to think about it? Will you call me again, in twenty-four hours?"

"No, I won't promise that." She raised her forefinger, broke the connection. In the receiver, she heard a small, decisive little click—possibly the most significant sound of her life.

6

Daniel DuBois replaced the handset on its console. He remained motionless for a moment, staring thoughtfully at the phone. He was a small man, totally bald, with a large head and a shriveled body. The flesh of his face was sallow, cross-hatched by countless lines. The muscles on the left side of his face had slackened, leaving his mouth sagging and the lid of his left eye half closed. He wore a blue business suit, and sat in an elaborately appointed wheelchair, his partially paralyzed body angled slightly to the right. Fingers permanently crooked, his left hand lay helplessly in his lap.

The right side of the wheelchair was drawn close to the Regency table that served as DuBois' desk. Except for two telephones, both within reach of DuBois' right hand, the top of the table was uncluttered. Now, slowly, DuBois lifted the console phone with his right hand, set it aside, used a palsied forefinger to touch a single button on the console. He put the phone in his lap, pressed one of three buttons on the wheelchair's right armrest. The chair pivoted to the left, allowing him to look out through the floor-to-ceiling window, with its panoramic view of the ocean. Today the sky was overcast: long, leaden, low-lying clouds, roll upon roll out to the horizon, casting the water beneath a sullen gray.

When he lifted the phone to his right ear, the connection had already been made.

"Justin?"

"Yes, sir."

"You'll have to come over."

"Right away."

"Thank you." He turned the chair again, pressed another button, spoke again into the phone: "Mr. Powers will be coming. Show him right in. And no more calls, please, unless they're critical." He listened, then nodded. "Yes, thank you."

He replaced the phone, and again sat immobile for a moment, once more staring at the phone, a modern-day electronic miracle. The push of one button connected him with his secretary. Press another button, and he was talking to Justin Powers. With equal facility, other buttons connected him to New York, and London, and Bonn, and Tokyo.

In an earlier age, the measure of a nobleman's power was the number of courtiers who attended him, or the number of swordsmen he commanded. Today, the telephone, not the sword, was the symbol of power. A touch of a button, a few words exchanged, and fortunes were made—or lost. In moments, lives were ruined—even lost.

He'd been eighteen years old—a brokerage clerk—when he'd gotten his first phone. A year later, he'd gotten a second phone, his first tangible talisman of success: two phones on his desk, one for outside calls, one for inter-office calls. It was 1929, the year of the crash—the year he'd first experienced sex. Looking back, remembering, it was plain that of the two—the second phone or Florence LeMay—the second phone had been infinitely more significant, more definitive. And secretly, perhaps, more satisfying.

At the thought, he smiled: a twitching of his mouth on the right side, making the sag on the left side more grotesque.

He touched a button on the chair's armrest, backed away from the Regency table, turned again to the window that framed the distant seascape. He would remain here until Powers arrived, in about twenty minutes.

Telephones and women . . .

If he chose to reduce his life to its symbolic essences, certainly a telephone and a woman would be primary. Years ago—twenty years ago, at least—when he'd been less stringent about his contacts with the outside, a man named David Griffin had gotten in to see him. Griffin had been recommended by Jack Curtis, whose instinct for the bizarre had always been amusing. "Give him fifteen minutes," Curtis had urged. "You'll never forget it, I promise."

Griffin's card had described him only as a "Heraldic Scribe." He'd been a young man, energetic and smooth-talking, with a quick, engaging smile. He'd come directly to the point, saying that he sought a commission to execute the DuBois coat of arms. He'd already done considerable research, he'd claimed, already discovered that an ancestor on DuBois' mother's side had been an aide to Louis the Fourteenth. Then, getting briskly down to business, pencil poised over a pad of paper that he'd taken from an expensive attaché case, Griffin had inquired as to DuBois' primary "life interests." Amused, he answered that he enjoyed power, paintings, and women, more or less in that order. Apparently Griffin had taken him seriously. A week later, unsolicited, he'd received a rough sketch of the "DuBois coat of arms." Along with the obligatory knight's helmet and stylized battlements, the elements had included—yes—a moneylender's scale, crossed paint brushes, and the outline of a woman's body.

Could one vicariously experience the pleasures of the flesh once erection was no longer possible, and the body was infirmed? Sometimes, in his sixties, he used to wonder. And now, in his seventies, bound in his wheelchair with a safety belt, alone with his view of the ocean, with the best of his French impressionists hung on the walls, he knew the answer. Too late, he knew the answer.

Once, in his eighties, Montaigne had been asked whether he regretted having lost his sexual desires. Theatrically, the old man had raised a forefinger to his lips, dramatically demanding silence. "Do not speak so loudly, young man," Montaigne had said, "lest the gods discover my bliss."

Florence LeMay . . .

She'd be seventy-six now, if she were still alive. Her body would be shriveled, her voice cracked. Like him, she would lie awake in the night, chronicling her infirmities, wondering how the next day would differ from the day just past. Did she remember him, as he remembered her? Of course, in later years, she would have heard of him. Everyone who read newspapers would have heard of him. But, before she'd read about him, Florence could have forgotten him—as he had forgotten, long ago, so many others, so many anonymous women, in so many darkened rooms.

Had Florence LeMay forgotten those few minutes in her living room, on the couch, the two of them coupled so urgently, so artlessly? It was, he knew, a possibility, a distinct possibility. Because, for Florence, it hadn't been the first time. So, like him—like everyone else on earth—she could have forgotten. She could have—

The console was buzzing. From a small holster on the left arm of the wheelchair he took a cordless phone.

"Yes?"

"Mr. Powers is here, Mr. DuBois."

"Thank you. Send him in, please. No calls."

"Yes, sir."

He propelled himself behind the desk, maneuvering into position just as Powers came through the door, which Katherine closed soundlessly behind him. As always, Powers wore a dark suit, gleaming white shirt, perfectly knotted regimental tie. And, as always, his manner was stiff and studied, a second-rate actor who'd played one part so long that he'd finally managed a limited credibility.

"Sit down, Justin—" He gestured to one of two antique armchairs, placed to face him across the Regency table.

"Yes. Thank you." Powers placed his attaché case on the floor beside his chair, sat down, crossed his legs, arranged his trouser creases, absently tugged at his shirt cuffs—all without looking directly at DuBois.

"Did everything go smoothly last night?"

"I—ah—" Simultaneously, Powers seemed to both nod and also shake his head. Finally: "Yes. Th—there weren't any problems, that I know about."

"Good. Has the second payment been made?"

Powers swallowed, then nodded: a single ill-at-ease inclination of his head, a mannerism that evoked a child's discomfit, compelled to perform in the presence of adults.

"I don't mean to press you," DuBois said. "I'm not asking for details."

"I know—" Powers nodded again, then raised an uncertain hand. "It's just that this, all this, it's—" He broke off, searched for the words. His eyes, DuBois saw, were hollow, his gestures ineffectual, an embarrassment to behold. "It's unsettling."

DuBois permitted himself a small, half-paralyzed smile. "I always enjoy your choice of words, Justin. Understatement, it's a gift—" Ironically appreciative, he nodded. "'Unsettling,' indeed. Very good."

This time, Powers made no response. At his temple a vein had begun to throb.

"The reason I asked you to come," DuBois said, "is to tell you that Betty just called, not more than an hour ago. She was upset. Very upset. Which is understandable, of course. One reason for the, ah, exercise, after all, was to make her think, shake her up. But it's impossible to limit these reactions, once they're started. That goes without saying. So—" Regretfully, he shook his head. "So we may have to deal with Betty, too."

"Deal with—?" As if he couldn't comprehend it, Powers frowned fretfully, moved forward in his chair, focused his gaze intently on DuBois. "You mean—?"

Clenched on the arms of the chair, his hands were knuckle-white.

DuBois nodded. "It's possible. It was always a possibility. For now, though, I want you to find her, keep her under surveillance. I have reason to believe that she's here, in fact. In Los Angeles."

"Here?"

DuBois nodded. "Perhaps it's the moth and the flame—the victim drawn inexorably to his fate. It's a phenomenon that's always interested me, the extent to which each of us is preprogrammed, governed by an elaborate set of psychological reactions that is incredibly predictable. Science is learning more and more about genetics—physical traits that are immutable. I suspect the same predictability is applicable to psychological traits. Day to day, we think we're free to make choices. But I suspect we may be deluding ourselves. I suspect that one's persona is immutable, formed partly by genetics and partly by experience, otherwise known as habits. And habits, I submit, are actually nothing more nor less than well-worn electrical pathways embedded in the circuitry of the brain. That's not stated very precisely, I admit. But when we consider that, more and more, science is discovering that electricity is actually the elemental component of all matter, then I think the theory holds up."

"But—" Powers was shaking his head now, transparently denying that which his cowardness wouldn't allow him to face. "But we can't do it again. I—I can't. I simply can't."

As if he hadn't heard, DuBois spoke reflectively, his eyes soft-focused: "People like Betty have their destiny—and people like us have our destinies. Betty is destined to be used by others. She's a victim type. That's the way her experiences have programmed the circuitry of her brain, if you accept my previous premise. But people like me—" He paused to consider. "People like me are the predators, the manipulators of lesser men. And you, Justin—" His eyes came into sharp focus, fixed on the other man. "You are a lesser man. People like you depend on people like me. It's bred in the bone. Or, if you like—repeating myself—in the circuits of the brain."

A brief, desperate flicker of dissent showed in Powers' eyes. "If you're talking about business, then that's true. But this other, it's—" He broke off, visibly shaken, struggling to find strength enough to pronounce the word that, finally, must be spoken between them. When he finally summoned the strength, the word was only a whisper: "It's—it's murder." For a moment Powers sat mute, his hollow eyes staring at nothing. Then, mutely, he shook his head. "I—I still can't believe I did it, actually did it, had it done."

"You did it because you were paid to do it, Justin. You depend on me. We've already established that. And, conversely, you are an extension of me. I am the brain, you are the instrument—the arms, the legs, the voice. You are the visible me, one might say. And Nick Ames was a threat to me. Possibly a very serious threat. So it became necessary—vital—that he be eliminated. I made the decision. And you executed the decision. It's as simple as that. In olden times, I suppose I would have cleaved Nick Ames asunder with my broadsword. Or, to continue the analogy, you would have done it, to oblige me. But we live in a complex society. Things are managed differently now. However, the elementary fact remains that, occasionally, someone becomes so dangerous that he must be killed."

"I know that. And I never questioned what you—"

DuBois raised his right hand a few inches above the arm of his wheelchair. The gesture was enough to silence the other man in mid-sentence. "This has happened before, Justin. In fact, it's happened several times, before your, ah, tenure. *Fortune*, after all, calls me the world's third richest man. My net worth is more than many nations of the world. And when one operates at that level—when one does what's necessary to parlay a few thousand dollars into billions—people sometimes die. It's regrettable, of course. Richard the Third, I'm told, often wept, surveying the dead after a battle. But that didn't mean there wouldn't be another battle, even though it might be fought for nothing more substantive than pique. The point being, of course, that it was royal pique. And the truth is, Justin, that for centuries, lesser men have always died to avenge royal pique."

"But I don't—"

"Nick Ames, of course, was nothing more than an insect—a bug—waiting to be squashed. And to that extent, I regret the necessity for all this. He wasn't a fit adversary, wasn't worth the risk. But, through a fluke, he became a problem, as I've already said. He stumbled on a secret—on a carefully concealed vice, to be accurate." DuBois shook his head: a pale, skin-covered skull, a death's head rotating on a sagging column of waxen cords. "And we must be prepared to pay for our vices, Justin. Major or minor, we must be prepared to pay. And that imperative, that immutable law, is the reason it was necessary to do what we did." He paused, allowing himself a moment of compassion, even a sympathetic smile, as he stared at the other man. "This is hard for you, Justin. I realize that. You're not in complete possession of the facts, and that's always a difficult position. But suffice it to say, for now, that I made a mistake when I decided to surrender to a vice. Not a minor vice, but a major vice. And Nick Ames, through a fluke, caught me up. It's as simple as that. I gambled, and I lost. So now I must redress the balance." He smiled again—benevolently, he hoped. "Does that make it easier for you, Justin?"

"I—ah—" Predictably, always predictably, the other man shook his head. "I—ah—"

"When we become older, Justin, we give ourselves the pleasure of surrendering to our vices. It's part of our reward. However, in the process, we can become vulnerable, even to insects like Nick Ames."

Powers waited a moment, until he was sure DuBois had finished speaking. Then, tentatively: "You've never told me the reason—never told me why Ames had to be—" He broke off, swallowed, moistened his lips. "You didn't tell me what he did, what he tried to do."

Gently, DuBois nodded. "That's correct. I didn't. And when you think about it, Justin, you'll realize that we should leave it like that. Don't you agree?"

Hesitantly, Powers nodded. "I agree to a point, of course. But I also think that—"

"It's for your own protection, Justin. When you think about it, you'll see that I'm right." He paused, watching the other man's face as the words registered. "You're in an exposed position. So the less you know about motivation, the safer you'll be. Don't you agree?"

This time, the purpose of Powers' answering nod was plain: in defeat, he could only hope to hide the despair that registered so plainly on his face. So he sat inert, head cravenly lowered, eyes averted. Patiently, DuBois waited for the other man to finally lift his head. Then DuBois nodded in the direction of Powers' attaché case. "Since you're here, let's do a little business. There's a coup brewing, I understand, in Zimbabwe. I think we'll go long on palladium. Don't you agree?"

Powers frowned, pretending to consider the point. Finally, he nodded. Cordially, DuBois returned the nod.

7

Sipping Chardonnay, Bernhardt let his eyes wander idly around Pamela Brett's apartment. The building was a restored turn-of-the-century San Francisco mansion that had been remodeled into apartments. Her living room was vintage Victorian, featuring a cupola with three curved glass windows that offered a sweeping view of downtown San Francisco, with the bay beyond. The high ceilings were coved; the woodwork was intricately carved. The floors were parquet. The fireplace was framed in marble, its mantel supported by plaster cupids. The kitchen was small but efficient, built in a room that might once have been a wardrobe closet. The bedroom had a view of the Golden Gate Bridge. Like the kitchen, the tiny bathroom had been fitted into a small space that had originally served another purpose.

Rent, Bernhardt estimated, at least fifteen hundred a month. Maybe more.

If the apartment was classic upscale San Francisco, the modern, squared-off furniture was typically Los Angeles: Coldwater Canyon, Bernhardt guessed, or Malibu. The chairs and tables were made of oiled teak or rubbed walnut; the covering of the sofa was expensively nubbed, probably handwoven, aggressively natural. The coffee table was fashioned of thick glass, magnificently supported by a weathered, twisted crotch of mountain juniper. On Rodeo Drive, Bernhardt calculated, the table would cost thousands. A small Danish teak dining table stood in an alcove. The table was set for two, with sparkling glassware and gleaming silver.

"Can I come in the kitchen and watch you cook?" he called. "Carry anything in?"

"Actually," she called back, "it's almost ready. Why don't you open the wine?" She appeared in the doorway, bottle in one hand, corkscrew in the other. As he took the bottle, their eyes met—and held. Slowly, gravely, they exchanged a smile. It was a serious smile, both tentative and trusting, a smile that neither asked a question nor offered an answer. As Bernhardt worked with the bottle's lead seal and the corkscrew's stubborn levers, he considered the significance of the smile they'd just shared.

Reduced cues . . . It was one of those half-remembered phrases left dangling in his consciousness, a leftover from some long-forgotten course in elementary psychology. Yet, over the years, the phrase had constantly recurred as he'd tried to pick his way through the thickets of human relationships, personal and professional. In the mating game, the suggestion of a smile could mean everything—or nothing. In the theater, his stock in trade was subtlety: raised eyebrows, deep sighs. Working the streets, sorting out the good guys and the bad guys, an uneasy glance could make a case—or break it. Reduced cues, then, were what his life was all about.

Bringing him here, now, to Pamela Brett's apartment, struggling to draw a reluctant cork as he remembered the smiles—his smile, and her smile.

What had she seen in his face, exchanging their smiles?

What had he seen in her face? Did she—

In the doorway again, smiling a hostess' smile, no longer a tentative lover's smile, wearing two oven mittens, she held a steaming casserole in both hands. Stepping back, giving her and the hot dish room, he watched her set the casserole on an ornamental tile. She returned to the kitchen, came back with a salad bowl. As she left the kitchen, she switched off the light behind her.

In the mating game, light management was important, too—another reduced cue. A darkened kitchen, softened light in the dining alcove, it could all mean something—or nothing.

As she sat across from him, he raised the bottle of wine. "Shall I pour?"

"Please."

Forgetful of cork fragments, he filled her glass first, then his. She raised her glass. "To the play."

"The play."

They drank, smiled companionably, served themselves, began eating. The September evening was warm, and he'd taken off his jacket. With her fork in her hand, she pointed to his waist. "You're not wearing your pager."

"I turned in my pager today."

"Meaning?"

"I quit. It's a long story. And not very interesting."

"Oh." She nodded, dropped her eyes. He'd said it too abruptly, then, shut her out too harshly. He could see it in her eyes, the same vulnerability he'd seen Monday night. She'd picked up on the hostility he felt for Dancer, transferred it to herself—the actress' sensitivity, misdirected, turned inward.

Watching her, he sipped his wine. Then: "But if you're interested, I'll tell you."

She smiled, lifted her shoulders. The smile said she was interested, the shrug said she didn't want to pry, didn't want to intrude.

"I've quit before," he began. "We've always had our differences, the boss and I. But this time it's serious. This time he screwed me good."

"Was it money?"

"It's not the money." He let a beat pass. Then, because the alliterative line was too good to waste, he said, "It's murder."

Yes, her eyes were widening—those dark, solemn eyes, the eyes he'd been thinking about, these last several days. And, yes, on cue, she was swallowing. "Murder?"

"He sent me to Santa Rosa, to find a woman. Her name is Betty Giles. But I think I was really hired to set up a man for murder. His name was Nick Ames, and he was traveling with her. I'm not sure that's what happened. There's no real proof. But Dancer—the boss—won't tell me what I need to know, to make sure I'm in the clear. So I quit. I should've done it before. Long before."

"Murder . . ." She spoke incredulously, her food forgotten.

"Am I spoiling the dinner? I don't want to do that."

"No, it's just—I mean—" At a loss, she shook her head. "I mean, murder is something you read about, hear about. It—somehow it doesn't seem real."

"It happens, though. People are murdered every day. Usually it's pretty elemental stuff—a wife hits her husband with a cast-iron skillet during their standard Saturday night fight, or one dope pusher shoots another dope pusher, for business reasons. But other things happen, too—more complicated, exotic things."

"This murder in Santa Rosa—what'll you do? Tell the police?"

"I've already told the police. Maybe they'll find the murderer, maybe they won't. But there's more to it than that." Once again, he was self-consciously aware that he was building the suspense, playing the role of the grim, stoic private eye. Leaning across the table, she waited for him to go on.

"What I've got to do now is find her."

"Why?"

"Because I want to find out what happened—what really happened. That's the only way I'll know for sure whether Dancer used me to set this guy up. I've got to see Betty Giles, talk to her. I've got to know."

"It could be dangerous, though, couldn't it?"

"I'm not sure. I don't think so, though." He smiled. "If I thought it was dangerous, I wouldn't do it. I don't believe in looking for trouble."

"Do you—" She hesitated, then asked, "Do you carry a gun?" Her voice was hushed, as if the answer could frighten her.

"Pam—come on—" He gestured to her plate, then ate a large forkful of the casserole: seafood and artichokes in cream sauce, delicious. "Eat your dinner. Drink your wine."

"You *do* carry a gun. Don't you?"

"Usually not, as a matter of fact. Someone carries a gun, he gets shot at. Now come on. Eat. Drink."

Obediently, she sampled the salad and the casserole, then sipped the wine. But he could see determination in her face. She wasn't through with him, wasn't finished asking questions. He couldn't deflect her, not permanently. Since they'd been talking, he'd seen the two sides of Pamela Brett: the hesitant, sometimes vulnerable, often pensive side, and this quiet, willful, determined side.

"I have another question—" She looked at him, tentatively smiling: that small, shy smile, the one he'd remembered last night, just before he went to sleep. "It's a—" She hesitated, visibly embarrassed. "It's an impertinent question, this one."

"Shoot." His smile, he knew, was free and easy, gently teasing her. "No pun intended. You talk. I'll eat." As he spoke, he lifted the lid of the casserole, ladled out another serving for himself, replaced the lid. The ladle was heavy: sterling silver, probably, not stainless. The place setting's pieces were heavy, too. Later, he would check the trademark.

"The question is," she said, "won't it be expensive, trying to find her? Won't it cost a lot of money? Or is someone retaining you?"

"No one's retaining me. And, yes, I suppose it could get expensive. But the fact is—" Now it was his turn to hesitate. Should he tell her the whole story? Everything?

He drained his wineglass, reached for the bottle, topped off her glass, refilled his own.

Yes, he would tell her. Last night, just falling asleep, he'd thought of her, thought of her smile. That was reason enough to tell her.

"The fact is, I've got a secret stash, in the bank. I've never touched it, until now." He sipped the wine, finished his salad. Now he reached for a French roll, which he would break in pieces and use to sop up the sauce left on his plate from the casserole. "Would you like to hear about my stash? If you'd like to hear about it, I'd like to tell you. But I warn you, there's an introduction. A long introduction."

"I'm crazy about long introductions. Ever since I first read Shaw."

"Well, I told you, I remember, that all my family's gone. My father was killed in the Second World War, and my mother died of cancer, several years ago." As he spoke, he saw remorse shadow her eyes; she hadn't meant to reopen these old wounds, the same wounds he'd already revealed to her Monday night. Briskly, he continued: "My mother was a dancer. That's all she cared about—modern dance, and left-wing politics. If she wasn't dancing, she was marching, or volunteering to lick stamps."

"The way you talk about her," she said, "it sounds like you cared for her."

"I did care for her. She was a standard type, I guess you'd say—a typical New York Jewish intellectual, very serious about everything, very intense. She was also very well informed—a Vassar graduate, in fact. And she was a very passionate person, a real rabble-rouser, when she got started. She could've been a politician, if she hadn't been so hooked on dancing."

"Did you live in Manhattan?"

"Sure. Greenwich Village, of course. In a loft, naturally. It was great, I loved that place. I could fly model airplanes, in there. And my grandfather—my mother's father—owned the building, which obviously helped. Which brings me to the stash—my grandfather. He was a clothing manufacturer—and my mother was an only child, a much loved only child, maybe a Jewish princess, let's face it. From the time my father was killed, my grandfather subsidized my mother—and me, too, later. I don't mean he completely supported her. She always taught dance, always had all the students she could handle. But my grandparents took care of the big ticket items—my schooling, vacations, trips to Europe, things like that."

"Did you go to private schools?"

He nodded. "Not fancy private schools. But good private schools. My great-grandfather was a tailor who lived over the shop, and my grandfather started out selling women's wear. So even if I'd wanted to go to Choate or Andover or Exeter, which I didn't, they wouldn't've let me in, probably—not without a pedigree. And, for sure, my grandfather wouldn't've paid, even if they had let me in. He was a rabble rouser, too—one of those vintage Max Lerner-style left-winger

Jewish intellectuals. To him, the Choate crowd was the enemy, oppressors of the working class."

"So where'd you go to school?"

"The Bancroft School, in Manhattan. And then Antioch College."

"Antioch—impressive."

He smiled, nodded, shrugged.

"Theater arts?"

"English. But I spent all my time in the theater. And writing, too. I wrote a lot of short stories, started a couple of novels—the usual." He hesitated, then decided to say, "Mostly, though, I fell in love, when I was in college. Every three months, regularly, I fell in love."

"You, too?" Remembering, she shook her head. For a moment they held each other's gaze, silently confirming that, yes, they'd both loved often and well, in earlier years. Then, dropping his eyes, he spoke more concisely, finishing the story:

"I got married, two years out of college." Because he didn't want her to think that the horror of Jenny's death still possessed him, he said it calmly, dispassionately. "We both wanted to act. We lived in New York, not far from my mother's place. We made the rounds, hit the casting calls. Finally we started to connect. Jenny connected first, then I started to get small parts. And I started writing plays, too, learning the craft, learning how tough it is.

"And then, Jesus, my grandparents died, in a car wreck. I think my grandfather had a heart attack. By that time, his business had started to go sour, no one knows why. There was still some money left, but nothing like he used to have. He'd even had to put a mortgage on his house, to keep his business going. But, anyhow, he left my mother about fifty thousand dollars—and he left me twenty thousand. And, like a fool, I used the money to back a play. It was a can't-miss play, supposedly. And there were other backers, too—big-time Broadway backers. The deal was that even if the play didn't do more than make expenses, I'd still get my money back. But it didn't even come close to making expenses—plus there was some pretty creative accounting, I've always suspected. But, basically, it was my fault. I was twenty-five—I can't believe it, how dumb I was about the world—how naive I was."

"Actors are innocents, most of them. Either innocents, or sharks—the successful ones, I'm beginning to suspect."

Nodding reluctant agreement, he refilled their glasses, finishing the bottle. He could feel the mild buzz of alcohol beginning. His speech, he knew, was slurring slightly.

"The reason I'm telling you all this, giving you all this background, is that when my mother died, sixteen years ago, she left everything she had to me—mostly the fifty thousand, from her father. And the memory of the twenty thousand I'd lost was so strong that I decided—swore—I wasn't going to touch any of the money she left me until I was forty, at least. I didn't even put it in stocks, blue chips or otherwise. Because I swore, you see, that I wouldn't speculate with it. I put it in the bank—right in the bank, at six percent, or whatever. And it's been there ever since—compounding. When I turned forty, I thought maybe I'd buy a house, take some of the money for a down payment. But instead I bought a car—a second-hand car, for fifteen hundred dollars, which was more than I'd ever paid for a car in my life. I bought the car, and then forgot about the money—until now, today."

"So the money's been compounding for years," she said thoughtfully. "Fifty thousand dollars."

Gravely, he nodded. "That comes to a hundred thousand, now."

"So now you've quit your job . . ."

He nodded. "You've got it. I hadn't gone farther than the elevators before I'd decided to go in for myself—start freelancing, doing investigations. I've had lots of chances in the past. A lot of people—friends, acquaintances—have asked me to work for them. But, like a fool, I always passed them along to Dancer. He charges fifty dollars an hour, and pays me thirty. So I'm going to charge thirty-five, maybe forty. I've already ordered the calling cards and stationery from one of those quickie overnight printers. I'll get a permit from the state, no sweat. And I'll be in business."

"You won't be getting forty dollars an hour to find Betty Giles, though."

"That's unfinished business."

She raised her glass. Over the rim, her eyes came alive. Her voice was richer now, lower, more intimate. "Here's to business, unfinished or otherwise."

He smiled, sipped the wine, then raised his glass to hers. "Here's to friendship. Ours."

He'd expected her to drop her eyes: the maiden, demuring.

Instead, meaningfully, she let her eyes linger with his.

MONDAY
September 17th

1

Bernhardt switched off the engine and sat behind the wheel for a moment, looking across the street at Betty Giles' apartment building. The building was almost exactly what he'd expected: probably about ten years old, plainly planned for profit. The construction was stucco, three stories high. The color scheme was beige and pink. *La Canada Arms*, in raised letters, was featured prominently above the lobby's aluminum-framed glass doors. Three palm trees were planted in a small grassy area in front of the building. White-painted rocks described a circle around each tree, and redwood chips filled the circle. Three spotlights sprouted from the redwood chips, one spotlight for each tree. The grass was improbably green, immaculately trimmed. A small vacancy sign was propped on the low brushed aluminum sill of the lobby's plate-glass window.

He locked the car, walked across the street, and studied the apartment listings. There were twelve apartments in the building. Opposite number nine, "B. Giles" was listed. Opposite number one, he saw "E. Krantz, Mgr." After a moment's thought, he pressed the button for number nine. He waited, tried again, then pressed number one. Standing in the midday heat of hazy, smog-sulphered September sunshine, he took a clean handkerchief from his pocket and blotted his damp forehead. The handkerchief came away wet and grimy, one infinitesimal tracery left by millions of automobiles confined in an airless basin of land that should have been left a desert.

"Yes?" It was a woman's voice, loud and brassy, coming from a small speaker set into the wall beside the building directory.

"My name is Alan Bernhardt," he said, speaking into the perforated disc. "I'm a private investigator, and I'm inquiring about Betty Giles. It'll just take a few minutes. Ten, at the most."

"A private *investigator*?" She spoke on a sharply rising cadence, as if she were registering a complaint.

"It won't take long. I promise."

"Just a minute."

The glass door allowed him to see into the ground-floor hallway, where the first door was opening. E. Krantz was a small, thin woman. She was middle-aged—and desperately resisting. Her hair was dyed a dark, muddy brown. Her purple toreador pants were skintight. Her face was aggressively overdrawn: too much bright red lipstick, too much iridescent purple eye shadow, too much eyebrow pencil. Over the toreador pants she wore a large, loose-fitting, off-the-shoulder sweatshirt that fell to her mid-thigh, according to the latest teenage fashion whim. As she came closer to the outside door, the penciled eyebrows drew together in a suspicious frown as she looked Bernhardt over twice, head-to-toe. Finally, grudgingly, she half opened the door. Bernhardt was ready with an outdated plastic identification plaque and a business card. She examined the plaque, squinting suspiciously as she compared Bernhardt's face with the picture. Next she examined the business card, newly printed.

"You can keep the card," Bernhardt said.

"About two months ago," she answered, "some guy

came around saying he was a private detective. It turned out he was a bill collector."

"Some private investigators collect bills," Bernhardt answered. "I don't." He smiled.

Still studying him, transparently suspicious, she stood with her thin body aggressively blocking the entrance. Plainly, E. Krantz was a person who would welcome a confrontation. But when Bernhardt continued to simply smile, offering no resistance, she finally asked, "Is Betty in some kind of trouble? Is that it?"

"No," he answered, "that's not it. But she's traveling, and apparently can't be reached. Her employer's got some questions—things they need to know, about her job. They want to talk to her, but they don't know where to look."

Accusingly, she raised his card. "This says you live in San Francisco. So what're you doing in Los Angeles?"

"The last contact we had from her was in San Francisco. Her mother lives there."

"Hmmm—" As E. Krantz pondered, a man and a woman, laughing together, excused themselves as they left the building, walking between them. The diversion seemed to help E. Krantz come to a decision. Grudgingly she stepped back into the foyer, gesturing for Bernhardt to enter. The all-glass entryway was decorated with a life-size pink plaster Venus and a white-and-gilt Grecian-style bench. E. Krantz sat on one end of the bench, abruptly gesturing Bernhardt to a seat on the other end.

"I haven't got much time," she said. "The pool man's coming in about a half hour. And an upholsterer, too." She shook her head. "It's always something with a job like this. There isn't an hour, I swear to God, that there isn't something to do. Yesterday one of the tenants asked me to walk her dog. Honest to God."

Projecting a broad, bogus sympathy, Bernhardt dolefully shook his head. "People take advantage, there's no question. Aren't there dog walkers? Have you looked in the Yellow Pages?"

"In Van Nuys?" Scornfully, she snorted. "You must be kidding. Beverly Hills, maybe. Malibu. But not Van Nuys."

"There's nothing wrong with Van Nuys," Bernhardt protested, keeping the smile resolutely in place. "It's nice, here. Very quiet."

She snorted again, shrugged, laid his business card on the bench between them, absently plucked at the folds of her sweatshirt. "Personally," she said, "I've about had it, with L.A., I mean, everywhere you go, you've got to drive. And I've got asthma, too. When there's smog, I can't breathe. Like now. Today. There's a first-stage smog alert, today. Or hadn't you noticed?"

Elaborately sympathetic, Bernhardt fervently nodded. "I noticed, all right." Then, tentatively: "About Betty Giles . . . Do you remember how long she's lived here?"

"Two years and three months," she answered promptly.

"Was—is she a pretty good tenant, would you say?"

Grudgingly she nodded. "Yeah, she was—is. Like, when she went away, she left a note saying that she expected to be gone about a month. And she left a post-dated check, for the next month's rent. Most people wouldn't do that. At least, not these tenants here." Resentfully, she glanced over her shoulder. "Los Angeles—" Petulantly, she shook her head. "You can have it."

"Do you have the note that Betty left?"

"No. I've got their check, not the note. It didn't say much, just that they were going away, and asking me to—you know—pick up newspapers from in front of her door, take packages, things like that. See—" Exasperated, she gestured. On the third finger of her left hand, a large diamond ring sparkled. Or was it a zircon? "See, that's what I mean, about being a servant. I can't tell you how much time I spend, just picking up after people."

"You say 'they' were going away. She and Nick Ames, you mean."

"Right." Scornfully, she accented the single word. "Nick Ames." Contemptuously, she grimaced.

"You don't like him, I gather."

"Well," she answered, pursing her mouth, "I can't say he ever gave me any problems. It wasn't that. In fact, to be fair, he was better than most, around here. He and Betty, they're the best tenants I've got, except for the MacLeans, and maybe the Finks. But he was always hanging around. You know what I mean?"

"He didn't work. Is that what you mean?"

"Right," she answered heavily. "That's it exactly. He's one of those men that just don't like to work, I guess. He said he used to drive stock cars, until he crashed. And maybe he did, I don't know." She considered, then added thoughtfully, "He's a good-looking devil, though. I'll give him that."

"Betty works, though," he prompted.

"Oh, yeah. Sure." Quickly she nodded. "She has irregular hours, sort of. But she must have a good job. A real good job, judging by her furniture, and everything."

"What's her work? Do you know?"

E. Krantz shook her head. "No. I never found out. She's pretty closed mouth. Nice, but closed mouth. You know?"

Bernhardt nodded. "Yes, I know." He let a beat pass, hoping that she would elaborate. When she offered nothing more, but instead looked pointedly at her wristwatch, he asked, "When did they leave, exactly? Do you remember?"

"It was, lessee—" Frowning, she touched the tip of a pink tongue to the bright red of her upper lip. "It was eight days ago. Or maybe nine, depending on how you count."

"You didn't actually see them leave, then."

"No."

"Did anyone else see them, do you know?"

She shook her head, then shrugged. "Not as far as I know, no one saw them." She looked again at her watch. "That pool man's due any minute." She rose to her feet.

Rising with her, he said, "Can I ask you just one more question, Ms. Krantz?"

"What's that?" Once more, suspicion puckered her eyes, pulled at her mouth.

"You say they left in the night. So I was wondering, did you get the impression that they left in a hurry?"

"As a matter of fact," she answered, "I did. The kitchen was clean, and they took the garbage out, and everything. But the place wasn't picked up—and the bed wasn't made. Which wasn't like Betty, at all. She's always been—" She broke off, looked quickly at Bernhardt. As if he hadn't noticed her landlady's lapse, he blandly continued to smile encouragement as she caught herself, explaining: "Sometimes, you know, apartment managers have to enter the tenant's place. If there's—you know—running water, anything like that. It's the law." As she said it, her voice hardened defensively.

"Oh, sure," he answered, turning toward the outside door. "You're right, it's the law. Absolutely."

"Absolutely," she repeated vehemently.

2

Like the office, the receptionist was impeccably high styled: every gesture, every glance, every nuance, was carefully calculated for its urbane effect. Standing in front of the receptionist's desk, Bernhardt was aware that, for this particular mission, he'd miscalculated both the character he'd intended to play and the costume he'd chosen for the role. He'd imagined that a smooth, knowing, with-it character, casually dressed, would maximize his chances for success in the sunny southland. He'd obviously been wrong. Without doubt, all the males at Powers, Associates wore ties—and all the females wore heels.

Holding his newly minted business card with manicured fingers, the receptionist was frowning slightly as she looked at Bernhardt.

"What is it, exactly, that you want?" she asked. "And why do you want it?"

He wasn't comfortable with the story he'd concocted, but neither had he been able to improve on it:

"There's an illness in her family. When her mother tried to reach Betty, to tell her, she discovered that Betty had left town for a month. Betty's apartment manager couldn't help me. So this is the next logical place for me to try."

Without producing a single crease in the receptionist's flawlessly made-up face, the frown remained in place. "I haven't seen Betty Giles for weeks," she said. "Maybe months."

145

"But—" As if he may have wandered into the wrong office, Bernhardt looked quickly around. "But she works here."

Condescendingly, she shook her head. "Not really. Not steady. I've been here six months. And I've only seen her two or three times."

"Two or three—?" Incredulously, he looked at her. "Are we talking about the same Betty Giles? About thirty, thirty-five? Small, dark brown hair? Pretty? Good figure? Smart?"

"We are indeed," she said. "That's definitely Betty."

"So you *do* know her."

"I know her, yes. She does business with Mr. Powers, occasionally. But that's it. She comes and goes. I always thought she was a consultant."

"Then I'd like to see Mr. Powers." As he said it, Bernhardt instinctively switched to a brusque, decisive persona, giving orders, not asking for favors.

"I'm sorry—" Smoothly, she shook her head. "That's impossible, without an appointment."

"Listen, Miss"—he looked down at the etched-glass nameplate on her desk—"Miss Fairchild. Betty Giles' mother is desperate to find her. Otherwise she wouldn't've gone to the expense of sending me down here from San Francisco, which is where she lives. She's not a wealthy woman. Now—" He let a slow, solemn beat pass. "Now, I don't know the particulars. I don't know who's sick, who's dying. But I think that, if you'd talked to Betty's mother"—he let another beat pass, let his voice dolefully drop, let his face forlornly sag— "you'd want to help. Because this one day is the whole shot. Everything."

Vexation deepened Miss Fairchild's frown. "I don't understand what you're saying."

"I'm saying," Bernhardt intoned, "that Betty's mother

can only afford to hire me for one day. That's it. Period. The end."

Miss Fairchild's mannequin-perfect face registered no emotion as she studied him. In the lengthening contest of silence, Bernhardt concentrated on keeping his expression balanced: not too confrontational, not too maudlin. It was, after all, just a job—at least to the character he was currently playing.

Finally he saw her come coolly to a decision: "I suspect, Mr. Bernhardt, that you're not giving me the whole story. But if you're lying, you're very good at it." Suddenly she smiled: a slow, knowing smile, a speculative, woman-to-man smile. "And I've always admired chutzpah." She let the smile linger, let her eyes linger a little longer with his before she lifted her phone and touched a button on her console.

"Julie, this is Kay. Have you got a few minutes? There's a gentleman here who's trying to locate Betty Giles. I thought you might be able to help him." She listened, nodded. "Fine. I'll tell him." She broke the connection and replaced the receiver just as a buzzer sounded.

"She'll be right out," the receptionist said, speaking quickly, mindful of the buzzer's summons. "Her name is Julie Ralston, and she's just going on her break. You can buy her a cup of coffee. If you're around at five o'clock—" Perceptibly, her smile warmed. "You can buy me a drink." As she watched his reaction, she lifted the phone. Her "Yes?" was richly spoken, perfect for its corporate purpose.

• • •

"We have to talk fast," Julie Ralston said, diligently spreading butter on her hot croissant. "I've only got twenty minutes, portal-to-portal." She smiled at Bernhardt. It was a wide, cheerful smile, utterly guileless.

Just as Julie Ralston, Bernhardt had decided, was probably utterly guileless, perfect for the girl-next-door part: the brash, bouncy second female lead in a fifties "B" picture, the sunny, freckle-faced post-tomboy who never quite got the guy.

"You're a friend of Betty's," Bernhardt said. "Is that right?"

Promptly, she nodded. "Right. We used to see each other every week or two. Lately, since she's been with Nick, we haven't seen each other so much. But we always talk on the phone, a couple of times a week."

"What's her job, at Powers, Associates? Do you know?"

"No," she answered, "I surely don't. We've told each other everything, Betty and I. Or, anyhow, most everything. But Betty never talks about her job." She bit into the croissant, sipped some of her steaming coffee, and smiled: another cheerful, candid smile. Her voice, Bernhardt realized, was softened by the suggestion of a southern accent.

"Did you two meet at Powers, Associates?"

She nodded. "That's right, we did. And Betty does stop by the office, here, every once in a while—every two or three weeks, I'd say. But it's usually just hello and good-bye, at least where I'm concerned. She goes right in to see Mr. Powers. They talk for a half hour, maybe, and then she leaves. And that's it." She shrugged, drank more coffee, smiled again. Then, as the smile faded, she said, "Why're you asking? Is something wrong? Is there trouble?"

He'd expected the question and had already decided how he'd answer.

"Yes," he said, "there's trouble. A lot of trouble, maybe. That's why I'm trying to locate her, to warn her that she could be in danger. That's not what I told the receptionist. But that's what I'm telling you." He spoke quietly, evenly, looking at her squarely. Here, with Julie Ralston—now, with time running out—there was no leverage left but the truth. And there was no role left to him but the real one: Bernhardt, playing himself.

"What kind of trouble?"

"I'm not sure. That's what I'm trying to find out from you."

"I don't understand."

"I'm trying to talk to people, piece together what they know about Betty. Her mother helped, and so did her landlady, a little. I'm hoping you can help, too."

"But I don't know anything. Not really." As she spoke, apologetically, she looked at her watch.

"Tell me what kind of a person she is. What kind of things does she like? What doesn't she like? What frightens her?"

Eating the last of the croissant and drinking the last of her coffee, she considered. Then: "Betty is a quiet person. That's what I like about her. She's quiet, and she's considerate, too. She's one of those people who always remembers your birthday. She's a good friend."

"I'm glad to hear it," Bernhardt said, nodding appreciatively. His first time out on his own, *pro bono*, it would be sad to think that he was operating in the red on behalf of a dud or a deadbeat. "Is she a secretive person, would you say?"

She shook her head. "No. She's not secretive about anything but her job. I had the feeling that she was sworn to secrecy about her job, what she does. It was part of the deal, I think."

"She makes good money, I understand."

"Yes—" Judiciously, she nodded. "Yes, I think she does make good money. She sends money to her mother, I know. Regularly. And she buys things for cash. Even cars."

"What about Nick Ames? Do you know him?"

Regretfully, she sighed. "I met him a few times. We didn't have much to say to each other."

"Betty obviously likes him."

Still regretfully, she nodded. Then, after a short pause, she decided to say, "Betty is one of those women who always seems to end up with the wrong man. And I've never understood why. She's got everything. She's very intelligent, and very well educated, too. And she's pretty. She's got a pretty face, and a great little body. But she doesn't—" Julie Ralston shook her head, searching for the phrase. "She doesn't *act* like she's pretty. Do you know what I mean?"

Gravely, Bernhardt nodded. "I think I do. It's called a negative self-image."

Relieved, she nodded, briskly bobbing her head. "I think you've got it." She began sliding out of the booth. "I'm sorry. But I've just got to go."

He slid out with her, dropping money on the table. "I'll go up with you. I want to give you a card, and write on it where I'm staying in Los Angeles, what motel. If you think of anything else, I'd appreciate you giving me a call."

"Oh, I will," she answered. "I promise I will."

"I believe you," Bernhardt answered.

• • •

Entering the elegantly furnished reception room, Bernhardt said good-bye to Julie Ralston, then turned to Kay Fairchild, the receptionist with the provocative smile and the challenging eyes. Riding up in the elevator, he'd speculated on Kay Fairchild—and on what she'd meant, exactly, when she'd mentioned a drink after work. Was the high-styled Ms. Fairchild prepared to grace his debut as a free-lance investigator with the offer of her languidly exciting body? What would the high-styled Ms. Fairchild be like in bed, climaxing?

What would it take to find out—how many drinks, how many dollars?

Facing her across her desk again, neither Kay Fairchild's words nor her manner offered any clues. Instead, coolly, she said, "Mr. Powers has made some time for you." Without lifting her telephone, she touched a button on her console. Then, sotto voce, she added, "Next time, Alan, wear a tie. Okay?"

Before he could reply, the inner door opened to reveal another high-styled woman, this one blonde.

"Mr. Bernhardt?"

"That's right."

"Will you come with me, please?"

"Gladly."

3

Thank God the receptionist had thought to mention the man from San Francisco to his secretary—who, in turn, had mentioned the man to Powers. And, thank God, Powers had reacted exactly as he should, pretending nothing more than a mild curiosity as he wondered aloud why a private detective would be inquiring about innocuous, mild-mannered Betty Giles. Then, pretending to find some unexpected room in his schedule, he'd told his secretary to tell the receptionist that he could see the man. Briefly.

Then he'd told his secretary to delay the man—Alan Bernhardt—for ten minutes. On principle, he'd learned it was better to let unpredictable visitors wait, hopefully to make them more maleable, more manageable.

But no sooner had he given the order than he'd realized it had been a mistake. He should have had Bernhardt shown directly in. Because, instead of disconcerting Alan Bernhardt, the delay was deepening his own anxiety.

So, for ten minutes—nine minutes, now—he must clear his mind, compose himself, take firm control of his own thoughts, his own emotions. Sylvia had been amused when he'd studied the book on the efficacy of thought control. But he'd persisted. Diligently, he'd practiced the process. Three times a day, at regular intervals, the same time every day, seven days a week, he'd practiced. So that now, at will, he could transport his thoughts back in time to any point he chose, and thus liberate himself from tension in the present. That was the secret: concentration on past pleasures, past achievements, past fantasies. Even driving back from the interview with DuBois, with his nerves screaming, he'd been able to lose himself in the half-forgotten pleasures of the past. Surprisingly, he'd decided to fix his thoughts on the stamps he'd collected as a boy. Clearly, he could remember the satisfying heft of the albums, and the sweet taste of the adhesive on the stamp hinges. And, yes, he had learned about foreign countries, from the stamps he collected. After school, while the other boys played at their foolish games, chasing a ball, manfully colliding with each other, beating up on each other, he'd worked at his stamp collection, fixing the stamps in his albums, cataloguing them. He'd traded, too. Even as a child, he'd been a talented trader. At nights, in bed, he would plan his next acquisition, calculate the terms of his next trade.

Just as now, lying in bed, he planned his next move in the market, or in real estate, or commodities. But now he lay beside Sylvia, whose acquisition he had also carefully planned.

Give us the child until his sixth birthday and he'll always be ours, was the popularly conceived axiom of the Catholic church.

As the bough bends, so grows the tree.

Human affairs, he'd finally come to realize, could be summed up by its platitudes. Birds of a feather *did* flock together. And, yes, the early bird *did* get the worm.

Until a few days ago, an eternity, it seemed, his nocturnal calculations—yes, his grownup fantasies—had centered solely on the markets, on the constant ebb and flow of human events, and the financial trails they left. Many of these calculations, of course, were artful dodges, chronic exercises in amiable self-deception. Only rarely did he permit himself to face the inescapable, admit to himself that he was Daniel DuBois' faithful retainer, nothing more. For every ten dollars that he invested for DuBois, as directed, he invested a dollar for himself, on the side. He bought when DuBois bought, sold when DuBois sold—and prospered when DuBois prospered, much as the chauffeurs of capitalists were reputed to prosper from scraps of market information overheard from the backseat.

Until a few days ago, acquisitions and concomitant divestments had been the entire focus of his thoughts, of his adult fantasies.

Now the focus was murder.

In Santa Rosa, a man lay dead, beginning to slowly decompose. His body had been eviscerated, and the results had been duly recorded. With a small electric saw, the coroner would have taken the top of his skull off, removed the brain, examined it, put it in formaldehyde, as evidence. The vast machinery of law enforcement would have recorded the coroner's conclusions, and added information of their own: fingerprint evidence, ballistic evidence, computer printouts. Inexorably, that machinery was—

His secretary was knocking. The time had come, a possible prelude to utter disaster. The doorknob was turning; the door was swinging inexorably inward.

Alan Bernhardt was a tall, lean, Lincolnesque man with a deeply etched face and dark, alert eyes. The clothes were wrong, but the manner was calm, confident. There was no smile. The voice was quiet, scholarly: "Mr. Powers?"

"Mr. Bernhardt." Without rising from his leather chair, without offering his hand, Powers motioned the other man to one of two matching chairs placed to face the desk. The matching chairs were two inches lower than his own chair, a trick he'd learned from Daniel DuBois—yet another trick.

The opening was diffident—deceptively diffident, Powers suspected.

"Your secretary told you, I guess, why I'm here."

"You're trying to locate Betty Giles, she said." Powers smiled encouragement. "I'd like to find her, too. So if you do find her, I'd appreciate it if you'd give me a call." He opened his center desk drawer, selected one of three business cards, slid it across the desk. "That'll get you through to me here and at home. Hang on to it. Both the numbers are unlisted." He broadened the smile. "Is it ethical for you to represent two clients? If it is, I'll be glad to chip in, do my share. In fact, lately, I've been thinking about hiring someone to—" Suddenly it flared across his consciousness: dark as death, blinding as the flash of Armageddon, a swift, terrible incandescence that revealed his mortal danger, a self-inflicted wound. Because Bernhardt could know he'd hired Dancer to find Betty Giles. Bernhardt could also know that Nick Ames had been murdered. Meaning that Bernhardt could connect him to the murder.

So if he denied it, and Bernhardt knew the truth,

knew he'd hired Dancer, therefore knew he was lying, then Bernhardt's suspicions would be aroused.

Only silence could protect him.

Or incriminate him, attract attention, perhaps arouse suspicion. Because his face, his eyes, were out of control, betraying him. He knew it, could feel it.

Across the desk, attentively, the other man was watching him. Silently.

Ominously?

"Miss—ah—Miss Fairchild says you're working for Betty's mother, that she retained you. There's illness in the family, Miss Fairchild said. And Betty doesn't know. Is that true?"

Now, slowly, the detective was smiling. It was a pleasant smile, almost a shy smile.

Deceptively shy, falsely pleasant. Because this man was a hunter. A predator, who lived off the misery of others, exploited their vulnerabilities, their miscalculations.

"No," Bernhardt answered, "it isn't true. Nobody's sick. But somebody's dead. And Betty Giles has disappeared. I'm trying to find her. I can't tell you why."

"But will you take a retainer? Betty's associated with me, a business associate. I'd like to be kept informed."

"Why?"

"Because," he answered quickly, "she's important to us—to me. She left on short notice. She's got answers I need."

"What kind of answers?"

Powers shook his head. "I can't respond to that, I'm afraid. This business—my business—is multinational investments. *Big* multinational investments. We need information on a vast array of subjects. And Betty has some expertise that's valuable to us. Very valuable. In fact—" He hesitated. Without realizing it, he'd made his decision.

When he was eleven years old, at summer camp, he'd taken a dare and jumped from a high riverbank into a stream. He'd never forgotten the terror, falling so far through the air.

"In fact," he continued, "I hired a competitor of yours to find her, in San Francisco."

"Oh?" Alan Bernhardt seemed interested. Politely interested. "Who?"

"Herbert Dancer, Limited. Do you know them?"

"Oh, sure. They're big. Very big. I'm just a one-man operation." The diffident, disarming smile returned.

He'd played blind man's bluff, as a child. He'd always hated it, the groping in the dark. And the fun house, at the amusement park—the pitch-black room at the fun house—it had always terrified him.

"You're not—in touch with them, then. With Herbert Dancer."

"No," Bernhardt answered. "Not really."

To mask a sudden wild surge of relief, Powers dropped his eyes to the desk. Like a balm, he could feel assurance returning, a calm, sustaining warmth.

"You say someone's dead? Who?"

"A friend of Betty's. A man named Nick Ames. Did you know him by any chance?"

Powers frowned, elaborately considered, finally shook his head. "No, I'm afraid not. Should I?" He smiled, then glanced at his watch.

"No," Bernhardt answered. "Probably not." He rose to his feet. Cordially, Powers rose with him.

"Where're you staying, Mr. Bernhardt? If I hear from Betty, I'll call you. And, as I've said, I'd very much like to hear from you if you find her, whether or not you want to accept a fee."

"I'm staying in Santa Monica." Bernhardt produced a

card, which he placed on the desk. "I've written the name of the motel on the card."

"Thank you. And good luck." He waited for Bernhardt to leave, then took a business card from his wallet, placed the card beside Bernhardt's, on the desk. Quickly, he touch-toned a number.

"Yes. Mr. MacCauley, please. This is Justin Powers calling." As he waited, he swiveled in his chair to face the window. With offices on the twenty-first floor of the Sinclair Building, his view included the San Fernando Valley, and the range of mountains to the east. The day before yesterday, with Santa Ana winds blowing, visibility had been unlimited. Today, the mountains were hidden behind a pall of yellowish gray smog.

"Mr. Powers?"

"Yes. How are you?"

"Fine, sir."

"Any progress yet?"

"Not yet, Mr. Powers."

"Well, I have some information that might be of help to you."

"Oh?" MacCauley's voice was politely skeptical. "What's that?"

"There's a man named Alan Bernhardt. He's a private investigator from San Francisco, and he's looking for Betty Giles, too. It's not related to me, the reason he's looking for her. He's working for someone else, entirely. He won't say who. But it occurred to me that if you assigned someone to follow Bernhardt around, you might make it easy for yourself."

"It's possible, I suppose. And if you want us to put him under surveillance, we will. We'd normally put an electronic bug on his car, and assign a man to follow him that way. It'd mean an extra man, though. More expense."

"Don't worry about the extra expense. I want her found. The sooner the better. And remember, don't report to anyone but me. You've got my private lines."

"Yes, sir, I have. And you'll be hearing from me. I'll put someone on Bernhardt, too. Immediately."

"Good. Very good."

4

"Miss Giles—" Cordially, the motel manager smiled. His name was Farnsworth, she remembered. Norman Farnsworth. "How've you been?"

"Fine, thanks. How've you been?"

"Very well—considering that the season hasn't started yet. But you don't mind the heat, I seem to remember."

"It's a dry heat. And I've missed the desert."

"Well, you can pretty much take your pick of cabins—at summer rates. Would you like one with a kitchenette? The price works out to be the same as a single room, in season. And there's only a couple of restaurants in town that're open."

"All right. Fine."

"How long'll you be staying?"

"I'm not really sure."

Ruefully, he chuckled. "Not that it matters. You can stay the whole month of September, or what's left of it, no problem." As he spoke, he filled out a registration card and presented it to her, along with a pen. She signed the card, copied the license number of the rental car from its plastic key fob, and gave him her VISA card. As he took an impression and filled out the blank form, he said, "I should tell you that the phones in the cabins aren't working. We're changing the system, putting in a better one. But it won't be ready until next week, maybe longer. They have to come from San Diego, the installers. That's a problem. And there's a problem with getting the new equipment, too. Or so they say. But there's a phone booth by the road. And there's another one here—" He pointed. "Just around the corner from the office."

"That's all right. I'm not expecting any calls. A booth is fine." She took her VISA card and a key, thanked him, and left the small air-conditioned office. As she opened the door, the desert heat met her with a force that was almost palpable. Walking to the car, she looked at the pool, so clear and cool, so infinitely inviting, somehow so reassuring. She would go to her cabin, change into her bathing suit, and give herself to the water.

• • •

She signed the chit, slipped her VISA card in her wallet, and drank the last of her wine, a better-than-average Cabernet Sauvignon. She'd ordered a bottle with her dinner, something she seldom did. When she rose from the table, she momentarily lost her balance, steadied herself against the table, then began walking toward the door. On a September night in the desert, off-season, mid-week, the restaurant was almost deserted. The only diners were two tables of "townies": local, year-round residents who traded on the winter residents who began arriving in mid-October—and began leaving in mid-May. Whenever she'd come to Borrego Springs during the season she'd felt like an outsider, with no entrée to either the affluent winter residents or the ordinary citizenry. But the desert itself had always called to her, for reasons she'd never been able to fully understand, but which had little to do with people, either the tourists or the townies. Words like "vast" and "elemental," and "irreducible," had always surfaced when she thought of the desert, but she'd never been able to work the separate words into a meaningful whole.

Outside, at seven-thirty in the evening, the heat was less intense than it had been just an hour before, when she'd entered the restaurant. Her car was parked close by, a blue Nissan, rented at the Los Angeles airport. She stood beside the car, then leaned against it, her head lifted, looking up into the sky. To the east, the horizon was lightening; soon the moon would rise. To the west, only a few miles distant, mountains rose rank upon rank, diminishing shades of purple against a sky still blushed a fading orange by the setting sun. Farther to the west, beyond the mountains, the Los Angeles Basin began, that enormous smog-shrouded network of freeway-linked communities that crowded the shores of the Pacific from San Diego in the south to Newhall in the north: millions upon millions of people living in a shallow depression that, without Colorado River water brought over the mountains, would hardly support a few hundred thousand, herself probably not included.

She'd left the Nissan's windows open, as most people did, in Borrego Springs. She got in the car and sat motionless for a moment, looking out at the desert night. The year-round population of Borrego Springs was about two thousand, tripling or quadrupling when the winter residents arrived. The town was laid out around a central circle, the circular hub of four roads. One road led to the east, out to the town's small airport, and then across the desert to the Salton Sea. Another road led west from the circle toward the mountains, passing an upscale motel and two small shopping malls. Both of the malls were upscale, too, catering to the affluent "snowbirds" that came from as far away as New York and Chicago. The roads to the north and south led out from the circle to the town's residential districts. Some of the houses were small; others were elaborate desert haciendas, most of them Spanish-styled. A few miles out of town, both north and south, developers had built planned desert resorts: high-styled, high-priced condominiums clustered around the obligatory golf courses, tennis courts, swimming pools, and artificial lakes, all kept perpetually green by water pumped to the surface from an aquifer that, some said, could be depleted in a hundred years.

She started the car, made a U-turn in the middle of the deserted street, entered the central circle, and turned out to the right, heading south. Aware that the wine had dulled her reflexes, she drove slowly, with exaggerated care. Her motel, the Ram's Head, was almost a mile south of the circle, where the townspeople's small stucco houses thinned out and the haciendas began, each one built on more than an acre of desert land. Except for an illuminated roadside phone booth built close beside the motel entrance, the discreet blue of the Ram's Head's small neon sign was the only blemish of commercialism that local ordinances had allowed to intrude into the gathering darkness. The juxtaposition of the sign and the phone booth set against the dark, starry vastness of the desert night was provocative, evoking the subtleties of a Hopper painting, a comment on the uneasy coexistence of commerce and nature.

She drove slowly past the motel and continued south toward the open desert, the only car on the wide, string-straight county road. Occasionally she passed house lights set back from the roadside and scattered among the trees that grew so dramatically once water was brought up to the desert floor. Ahead was an intersection: a gravel road angling into the hard-topped road from the west. The graveled road rose gently, climbing a rise that lead to the mountains, only a few miles away. She slowed, turned, drove up the gentle rise for perhaps a mile before she pulled the Nissan onto the shoulder of the road. She switched off the engine and headlights, set the brake, got out of the car. Yes, her timing had been perfect. To the east, just visible above the far horizon, a new moon was rising. She would stand here in this vast, elemental silence, in this place she'd come to so often before, searching for the eternal illusion of inner peace that, sometimes, she had seemed to fleetingly find. Beneath these stars, she would wait for the moon to rise, Shakespeare's celestial orb, connected so mysteriously to life on earth. She would give as much of herself as she could to the soul-settling silence of the vista—and take as much as she could, in return.

Then she would return to the motel. And make the phone call.

5

She'd read the books, seen the movies, knew that, in a minute or two, it was possible to trace a phone call. So when the connection was made, after she pulled the door of the phone booth closed, she checked her watch: twenty minutes to nine, plus thirty seconds.

"This is Betty Giles," she said. "I want to speak to Mr. DuBois. Now. Right now. Otherwise, I'll hang up. In thirty seconds, I'll hang up." As she spoke, she watched the wristwatch's digital numerals change, one digit a second. In twenty seconds, she heard the husk-dry voice: "Yes, Betty?"

She didn't really know what she intended to say, hadn't rehearsed it. She knew only that she wanted to hear a tremor of fear in his voice, the same fear she'd seen him inflict so effortlessly, so dispassionately, on others—so many others, over so many years.

"I've told you that I'd make you pay for having him killed. And now I've decided how. Just now, just this minute, I've decided how."

"Betty—" She heard him sigh: a deep, condescending, exhausted exhalation. Had she ever heard him speak quite like this? Had she ever heard him sound so fragile?

"Betty, it's a cliché, but you were like a daughter to me. You know that, don't you?"

She made no response.

"It's not too late to make this right," he was saying. "Is it money? Is that what you want?"

"I want you to be afraid. I want you to beg."

"You can't make me afraid, Betty. And you can't make me beg, either. You should know that." His parched, cracked voice was mildly reproachful. He'd always talked to her like this—like she was a child. A talented, tolerated child.

"Then I'll tell the newspapers. I've given you your chance. But now I'm going to call the newspapers."

"They won't believe you, Betty. They wouldn't dare to print what you tell them."

"You had him murdered. You're not above the law. I'll tell them you had him murdered. And I'll tell them *why* you had him murdered. I'll tell the police, too—the newspapers and the police, both of them."

A silence followed. Suddenly she remembered the time, looked at her watch. How many minutes had—?

"If you do that, Betty—if you tell the police this story—then I can't help you. If you'll think about it, you'll see that I can't—"

Her finger on the receiver hook cut off the rest. She stood for a moment slumped against the glass side of the phone booth, staring at her finger on the hook. The booth was stifling. She replaced the receiver and pushed open the bi-fold door. Immediately, the cool night air rushed in. She was perspiring—sweating, really. Her face, her neck, her body, were wet, and the cool air was a mild, welcome shock: evaporation, a physical law, working to stabilize her body temperature, keep her healthy—keep her alive.

But scientific fact was one thing; her mother's axioms were something else. And her mother believed that drafts caused colds. If you were inside a house—or a phone booth—and you were in a draft, then you'd certainly catch cold. Especially if your hair was wet, or you were sweating. Wind, though—natural, undirected, open-air wind—was less dangerous, her mother believed, less likely to produce a cold.

So she was leaving the phone booth. She was standing aimlessly a few feet from the blue neon motel sign. A dutiful daughter, she was minding her mother. From the south, out of the desert darkness, a car was coming, traveling fast. She turned, watched the headlights grow larger. It was a pickup truck, with rock music blaring louder than the sound of the engine. As it swept past, she saw two dirt bikes secured in the bed.

Nick had ridden dirt bikes, he'd once told her, in competition. A motocross accident had broken his leg, given him his slight limp. His body was a map of scars, a visual history of his life on the racetracks. When he'd first detailed his scars for her as they lay naked in bed, sated, she'd reacted as a properly educated young woman might be expected to react, with a certain prim fastidiousness, hesitant to look fully, frankly, at his naked body, hesitant to touch the scars with timid fingertips. Yet she'd also been aware of something more elemental: the tribal woman lying with her mate, her defender, the man who bore on his body the scars of the warrior, his badges of ancient honor.

Where was he lying now, her warrior, the man who challenged the titan? Tonight was Monday. He'd died—been murdered—on Thursday night, four days ago. How long did they keep bodies in the morgue—in cold storage? A week, they'd told her, possibly more. Because, in a murder investigation, the body was evidence. Like a bloodied length of pipe, or fingerprints found at the scene of the crime.

Would he have left her, if she'd been the target? Would he have run away, terrified, as she'd run away, leaving her dead on a stainless steel table, refrigerated in a stainless steel drawer?

At the thought, she heard herself moan: a long, wordless keening, an inarticulate protest at this self-inflicted pain. Yet it was necessary that she think about him, lying dead in the morgue. Because, yes, she must punish herself, must atone for the sin of leaving him alone, abandoning his body.

His only living relative, she knew, was his father, a ruined hulk of a man, a drinker, still a fast-buck salesman—except that the bucks were fewer now. His father had visited them once in Los Angeles. When he left, he'd asked Nick for money.

In the airport at San Francisco, she'd spent an hour on the phone until she'd finally located his father. He'd cried when she'd told him Nick was dead. They'd always been pals, he said. Always.

Now a car was coming from the north, from town. This one was a large car, a Cadillac, sedately driven. So, standing beside the road, she'd seen the two phases of

Borrego Springs: dirt bikers returning from riding through the desert, and the tourists, so-called, comfortable in their Cadillacs, doubtless returning from dinner at the elegant French restaurant north of town, a millionaire's retreat that rigidly enforced a starchy dress code, even off-season.

She watched the Cadillac's taillights grow smaller in the darkness, heard the sound of its engine grow fainter, until finally both were lost in the desert to the south. Then, irresolutely, she turned to face the motel. It's twenty-odd cabins, some single, some double, were scattered among low-growing desert trees and high-growing cacti, all of it artfully planned, doubtless, for its studied naturalism. Her cabin was located roughly in the center of the motel's sizable tract, probably several acres, just beyond the southern edge of town. At nine o'clock there were only three other cabins lit, besides hers. In the off-season, on a weekday, the Ram's Head was certainly operating at a loss.

Earlier, she'd seen something in the *TV Guide* that interested her, an old movie. So she should return to her room, switch on the TV, try to lose herself.

Or else she should return to town, go to the bar adjacent to the restaurant, have a few drinks.

Unless, instead, she went to the liquor store, across from the restaurant. She could buy a bottle of brandy. She could take the bottle of brandy back here, to the motel. She could double lock the door, and switch on the TV, and drink the brandy while she watched the movie.

But first, before she decided, she would surrender herself to the telephone, for one more call. Because the television and the telephone were all that were left to her, now—one offering the balm of forgetfulness, one offering human contact once removed, her only real hope, her last illusion.

6

Shoes off, pillows propped behind his head, Bernhardt lay on top of the bedspread on the queen-size bed. On the TV screen, Robert Mitchum was threatening Gregory Peck in the opening scenes of *Night of the Hunter*. Whenever he could, he watched Mitchum, certainly one of the best actors the Hollywood star system had ever produced. Like Bogart and Lee J. Cobb, Mitchum made it look easy.

Sometimes he wondered how he would have fared in Hollywood. Years ago, he'd auditioned for a soap opera pilot that would have been shot in New York. He hadn't gotten the part, but the producer liked what he saw, and offered to introduce Bernhardt to some people "out on the coast." He'd already decided to leave New York, either for Los Angeles or San Francisco. So he'd thanked the producer and bought an airplane ticket for Los Angeles. He'd stayed almost three weeks, making the rounds. The producer's name opened a few doors, and one agent had been interested enough in him to invite him to lunch—in a restaurant that, he'd later discovered, was habitually used for second or third echelon lunches. The agent had been a shrewd, aggressive, quick-talking barracuda of a woman, grossly overweight. Over coffee, she'd looked him squarely in the eye and told him that, frankly, she didn't think he was motivated enough to make it in Hollywood. Years later, he'd learned she'd committed suicide, because of a—

Beside the bed, the telephone rang. As he turned

down the TV volume and answered the phone, he glanced at his watch. The time was almost eleven-thirty.

"Mr. Bernhardt?" It was a woman's voice: a soft, tentative, anxious voice, a young voice.

"Yes."

"This is Julie Ralston. We talked earlier today, had coffee."

"Yes, Miss Ralston. What's up?"

"Well, I—I heard from Betty, just about an hour ago. I'm sorry I didn't call sooner. But I've—" She hesitated. "I've been thinking whether I should tell you—call you."

"You're doing the right thing, Miss Ralston. Believe it."

"Well, I—I'm not sure. I mean, she told me not to tell anyone that she'd called. But she—she sounds terrible. Really terrible. And when you and I talked, I thought you were—you know—pretty sympathetic, pretty honest. So—" Her voice faded into an uncertain silence. He could visualize her, could imagine her frowning as she tried to decide what was best for her friend. What the world needed, Bernhardt decided, was more people like Julie Ralston: honest, conscientious people, with most of their illusions still intact.

"Tell me what she said, Miss Ralston. I think she's in trouble, and needs help. I've already told you that."

"Will you help her?"

"If I can, I will. First, though, I've got to find her."

"What'll you do, when you find her? I mean—" Once more, she hesitated. "I mean, will the—the police be involved?"

"I'm not sure. But if they do get involved, it won't be because I call them. That's all I can tell you."

For a moment she didn't reply. Then, in a low, awed voice, she said, "Nick Ames—she said he was killed. Murdered. Up north, she said. In Santa Rosa."

"Yes."

"You knew that, then. When we talked today, you knew he'd been killed."

"Yes."

"You—you didn't tell me."

"No," he answered, "I didn't tell you. If you think about it, that's how it should be." He let a beat pass, then said, "If you'd hired me, you wouldn't want me telling everything I knew. Would you?"

"No, I guess I wouldn't."

He let another beat pass while she considered. Then, quietly, he said, "Tell me what she said, Miss Ralston."

"Well, it—it wasn't what she said, so much as the way she said it. I mean, it was like she was just about at the end of her rope, you know? Like she didn't care what happened to her. At least that's the impression I got."

"Are you saying that she sounded suicidal?"

"Well, I—" She broke off, thought about it. "I don't think I'd go that far. But, see, Betty is thirty-three, you know. She's never been married, never had any children. So she—you know—she has the feeling that life was passing her by. So now, with Nick dead—well—it pretty much wiped her out, I guess."

"Did she tell you how he died?"

"She said it was robbery. He was shot during a robbery, she said."

"Did she say anything else, about his murder? Anything at all?"

"No," she answered slowly, "not that I can remember."

"Did she seem worried? For herself, her own safety?"

"It didn't seem like she was. At least, she didn't say she was worried. But—" She hesitated: a short, tentative pause. "But I asked her—you know—whether she was making arrangements. Funeral arrangements. And she said that, no, she couldn't make the arrangements because she couldn't stay in Santa Rosa—that she'd be in danger, if she stayed. So that's when I thought about what you said today, about there being trouble. And that's when I decided to call you."

"Do you have any idea where she is now?"

"Well, not really. But she said something about how she felt just as empty as the desert, something like that. I forget exactly how she put it. But then I got to thinking, and I remembered that she's been going to a place called Borrego Springs, in the desert. She loves it there. And so when she said something about the desert . . ." Her voice trailed off into a speculative silence.

"Where's Borrego Springs? Do you know?"

"I've never been there, but I know where it is—about fifty, sixty miles south of Palm Springs, maybe a hundred fifty miles from here, from Los Angeles."

"If you were me, and you wanted to find her, would you go to Borrego Springs?"

"Yes," she answered slowly. "Yes, I think I would. Definitely."

TUESDAY
September 18th

1

"A beer, please." Bernhardt put a five-dollar bill on the bar. "Do you have Heineken's?"

"Sure do," the bartender answered cheerfully. He was a small, quick-moving, middle-aged man with a face like a ferret and a thick head of brown hair that was almost certainly fake. Except for two men and a woman talking quietly at a nearby table, the barroom was deserted. The time was 3 P.M. The temperature in the street outside was almost exactly a hundred degrees.

Bernhardt waited for the bartender to make change, then asked, "How many places in town are there to stay?"

"Three," the bartender answered promptly. "There's the Casa Portola, just a hundred yards from here. It's bigger than it looks, goes back from the street quite a ways. Then there's Granger's about a mile west. They're pretty posh—" As he spoke, he looked Bernhardt over, obviously having concluded that Granger's might be beyond his means. "Then there's the Ram's Head, about a mile south of town. That's a nice place, clean, good management, kind of rustic. It's got separate cabins."

"How about restaurants?"

"You mean fancy restaurants? Or just plain eating restaurants? Because, see, there's a real fancy restaurant

173

north of town. *Real* fancy." Once more, dubiously, he looked Bernhardt over. "You gotta wear a tie even during the summer, give you some idea."

"How about the plain ones?"

"Two," he answered promptly. "There's ours—" He pointed to a door with *The Circle* spelled out in red neon script. "Then there's The Crosswinds, out east of town, at the airport. We're just open for dinners, though, both of us. If you're looking for something to eat now, you'll have to settle for pizza, across the street, between the liquor store and the grocery store." As he spoke, one of the two men sitting at a nearby table got up, came to the bar, and held up three fingers. While he set out three bottles of beer and made change, the bartender continued: "After October fifteenth, though, it's a different story. There's a real good restaurant called Hopkins, in the mall. The mall's across the street and down to the right—that fancy place, where the bank is, and those other shops." Mischievously, he grinned. "We're primed to say 'shops,' you see. Not 'stores.' Or, if we really want to play the chamber of commerce game, we say 'boutiques.' But Hopkins won't be open until October fifteenth, like I said."

"The reason I'm here," Bernhardt said, "I'm looking for a friend. Her name is Betty Giles. We missed connections in Los Angeles, and Borrego Springs was her next stop. She's in her middle thirties, dark hair, small, good-looking." He swallowed some of the beer, smiled. "Ring a bell? I don't think she's been here more than a couple of days."

"Doesn't ring my bell," the bartender said cheerfully. "If I was you, I'd just make the rounds of the motels. Wouldn't take too long."

"Thanks." Bernhardt finished the beer, laid fifty cents aside, pocketed the difference. "I'm traveling on a budget. If I miss her, what motel should I stay at?"

"I'd stay at the Ram's Head," the bartender answered promptly. As he spoke, the mischievous grin returned. "I'd stay at the Ram's Head, and I'd eat at The Circle—" He gestured again to the door leading to the restaurant. "And I'd drink here. Right here."

"That sounds like good advice." Bernhardt nodded, slid off the barstool, and walked to the door.

• • •

The Ram's Head Motel office had windows on two sides, and Bernhardt was signing the register when he saw her. She was wearing a one-piece black bathing suit, and was walking across the lawn toward the swimming pool. She was barefooted, and had a white towel draped around her shoulders. Plainly, beneath the towel, her breasts were full and firm. Her buttocks and hips were solid, her legs and thighs generous. It was an exciting body—a peasant's body, once or twice refined. She walked to a chaise, where she'd left a paperback book face down on the concrete apron of the pool. The pattern of her movements was contradictory, somehow both self-effacing and self-sufficient. As Bernhardt watched her, he remembered his first conversation with Julie Ralston, and his suggestion that Betty Giles might suffer from a negative self-image. The intellectual's throwaway line might have been more accurate than he'd suspected, because most women with a body like Betty Giles' would calculate that they had a decisive edge in the mating game, and would display their assets accordingly. They would arch their backs to display their breasts—not let their shoulders slump, as Betty Giles was doing. Most women would move their hips and buttocks more provocatively, more invitingly. If body language was the name of the game, Betty Giles had chosen to sit on the sidelines.

"I'll give you cabin eight," the manager was saying, handing him a key. "It's close to the pool."

"Good. Thanks." He took the key, pocketed his wallet.

"If you want to stay longer than just the one night," the manager said, "there's no problem. No problem at all."

"Thanks," he answered. "I'll remember that."

2

On the third ring, he rolled to his left side, regretfully withdrawing from her.

"Ohhhh . . ." It was a soft, sated protest. "Oh, no. You can't—"

"Shhh. Wait." He laid a forefinger on the parted curve of her pouting mouth. "Lemmee hear the machine."

As, from the living room, he heard his own voice, recorded, followed by the caller's voice: "Yes, this is Mr. Carter, calling from California. I wish you'd give me a call as soon as—"

Quickly, he snatched the phone from the bedside table. "This is Fisher. Hold on a minute, please. Just a minute." And to the woman: "When I pick it up in the living room, I want you to hang this up. Then I want you to get your ass in the bathroom, and close the door."

"But—"

"Save it. This is business. Someone listened in on me, once, and I never forgot it. And neither did she, I'll guarantee you that. She didn't forget, and neither did anyone who ever looked at her, after that. You follow?"

As he spoke, he gripped her naked shoulder, felt her
spasm of pain, heard her gasp. Then, quickly, he got
out of bed and walked into the darkened living room.
He winced as his bare buttocks touched the cold leather
of the couch, then picked up the phone. With his palm
over the mouthpiece, he called, "Okay, hang it up.
Then do like I told you." Into the telephone he said,
"Just one more minute, Mr. Carter. Just hold on." He
waited until he saw her briefly in the hallway: a slim
white body moving languidly in the darkness. When he
heard the click of the bathroom door closing, he spoke
again into the phone: "Yes, sir. Sorry for the delay.
What can I do for you?" As he spoke, he could visualize
the other man's face, with its pursed, prissy mouth and
its narrow, pinched nose. He could visualize the eyes,
too: coward's eyes, always moving. And it was the eyes
that told the story. Always. Venezzio had told him that,
told him to watch the eyes. Always.

"Are you alone?" the other man was asking.

"I'm alone enough to talk. You can talk, too. Nobody
can hear you. Don't worry."

"Yes. Well, I—I've got another assignment for you."

Leaning gingerly back against the couch, he smiled.
Satisfied customers, that's what business was all about.
You did good work, you got called again, pennies from
heaven.

Be sure your umbrella,
Is upside down . . .

"Well, sir, I'm happy to hear it. What's the rundown?"

"It's—ah—" The voice caught, faltered, finally continued: "It's the woman. You know what I mean, don't
you—know the one I mean?"

"You mean—" He hesitated. How should he say it, to
be safe? "You mean the woman that was with him, out

there—the guy we did business about, last week? That woman?"

"Yes. That woman."

To himself, pleased, he nodded. A woman had to be easier than a man. And he knew her already, knew her by sight.

Satisfied customers . . .

Be sure your umbrella,

Is upside down . . .

"Is she at that same place?"

"No, she's not. She's down in Southern California, just about a hundred miles southeast of Los Angeles, maybe a hundred fifty. So I was thinking, we could meet at the airport, like we've done before. Not the San Francisco airport. The Los Angeles airport. LAX. Wouldn't that be simpler than going into all this on the phone?"

As he listened to the other man asking the timid question, as he heard the tremor of fear in the voice, he smiled. Because this moment, this feeling, was what it was all about. The money was wonderful. Every day, every single day, he charted his stocks, calculated the value of his CDs. But this was what it was all about, this small, secret rush of satisfaction, listening to them squirm. And the terror in their eyes, too, face-to-face, win or lose, live or die—that was something only he could experience: Willis Dodge, the best in the business.

"Yes, Mr. Carter, LAX, that'd be better. It'll be the same price—the same deal. Right?"

"Y—yes."

"Half up front, half afterward."

"Yes."

"Good. It's about a hundred fifty miles from Los Angeles, you say?"

"Yes."

"Okay. I'll get the first plane out of here in the morning, bright and early. Why don't you call me back in a half hour? I'll have a time for you, when I'll be arriving."

"Yes. Good. Thank you."

"Thank *you*, Mr. Carter." He let the mockery come into his voice now, let him hear the playful contempt. "Thank you very much, Mr. Carter."

WEDNESDAY
September 19th

1

"Here—" Powers took a map of California from his inside pocket, unfolded it, refolded it once, twice, finally flattened it across his knees. He pointed. "There it is. Borrego Springs. She's staying at a motel called the Ram's Head."

Dodge took the map, frowned as he studied it. "Is it a small town?"

"I think so," Powers answered. As he spoke, he shifted uneasily in the chair. They were sitting in one of Los Angeles International's concourses, two among thousands, a flux of humanity. If someone recognized him, saw him talking to this well-dressed black man, they would remember. "It's in the desert, I think." He frowned. "I should've gotten an atlas."

"I'll get one. Well—" He glanced at his watch, then looked expectantly at the other man. "I'd better split. What about meeting here, right here, same time, three days from now? That way, we won't have to talk on the phone. If there's any problem, any delay, I'll have you paged here, at the airport, and we'll talk then. Three days from now. Okay?"

"Yes. Fine." He reached into another pocket, withdrew a plain white envelope. "Here's the—" He licked his lips. "Here's the first installment."

"Thanks." Dodge slipped the unopened envelope

into his own pocket, and rose to his feet. He picked up his matched suitcases, nodded pleasantly, and walked briskly away. As Powers watched him go, he realized that he was beginning to tremble uncontrollably.

2

Before he'd rented the Camaro, he'd gone to the airport newsstand and bought three California travel atlases, each one with a listing for Borrego Springs. He'd put both suitcases in a locker and taken the atlases into a restaurant, where he ordered a late breakfast. While he ate, he studied the atlases, then checked the road map "Carter" had given him. Conclusion: if Santa Rosa had been a problem for a black face, Borrego Springs would be worse. Because the smaller the place, the richer the place, the worse the problem got.

But for every problem there was an answer—two answers, to this problem. He could blend in, disappear into the background, play the part of a laborer, or a porter. Or else he could come on strong, play it big, stand out. He'd been in Palm Springs once, on vacation. He'd stayed at the Sheraton, in a suite. Played golf. Spent a hundred dollars for dinner, spent three hundred dollars for a girl, a white girl. He'd seen Flip Wilson at a club, not performing, just living it up, the big shot, people hanging around him, like he was a boxing champ. So Flip had fitted in, playing it big.

In Santa Rosa, he'd tried to blend in, disappear. He'd imagined he was a waiter who worked in a big hotel in San Francisco, made good money, decided to take a drive up north, maybe to see the redwoods. It was something else he'd learned from Venezzio, the importance of playing a part, being ready if a policeman ever pulled him over—ready with a story, ready with a gun, too. Decide who you are, Venezzio had said, and stick to it. If you're a garbage man, dress like a garbage man, act like a garbage man—*think* like a garbage man. Like an actor does, learning a part—or a football player does, psyching himself up for the game, visualizing himself in the end zone, spiking the ball.

During breakfast at the airport, studying the atlases, he'd thought about it, concentrating as hard as he'd ever concentrated in his whole life. He could have been a novelist, concentrating on a character he was creating. And finally he'd got it, settled on his story. He'd be a real estate salesman, from San Francisco—a smooth, cool real estate salesman who worked for a big company—Coldwell Banker, he'd decided, very upscale. He'd be their token black face, make about seventy-five thousand a year, selling big buildings, scheduled to move up into management, a real smooth operator.

He'd found a men's wear shop at the airport. He'd bought two pairs of Bermuda shorts, four lightweight sports shirts, and a thirty-dollar straw hat, narrow brimmed. After considerable thought, he'd decided on running shoes. He'd made sure the shirts had long, square-cut tails, and were cut full enough to cover whatever he'd carry in his belt. At the shop next door, he'd bought a pair of designer sunglasses, heavily tinted. Then he'd gone to Hertz, and decided on the black Camaro, for just a touch of flash. Because a black working for Coldwell Banker, making it big, he'd want a touch of flash, a little show.

Easing the Camaro into a turn on the two-lane road, he took his foot from the accelerator, slowed the car enough to look out over the desert, still several miles ahead. For most of the drive south from L.A., the smog had been so bad that his eyes had watered. Only when he left the freeway and began climbing the western slope of the low mountain range that separated the Los Angeles basin from the desert had the sky turned a true blue. And now, on the eastern slope of the mountains, the air was so clear he could see for miles across the desert looking east. One range of mountains, just four thousand feet high, had made a big difference in the terrain, too. The western slopes had been lush with thick-growing trees and bright green grass. But the eastern slopes were dry as dust, with sagebrush as far as the eye could see. Between the ridge of the mountains and the Salton Sea, according to the travel atlases, the only underground water was in Borrego Springs, just ahead. He was facing forty or fifty miles of desert. No water, just sand, sagebrush, cactus, and the strange, stunted trees that grew in the desert.

Still driving easily, rhythmically, he was conscious of the pleasure the Camaro gave him as he swung it smoothly from side to side, testing his skill in the curves. The highway ahead was straightening as it descended. Soon he would be on the desert floor, where there were no hills, and the roads were straight as strings.

The first car he'd ever owned had been a Camaro: a bright red Camaro with black striping, brand-new, bought right off the showroom floor. He'd been nineteen years old, just passed his birthday, when he bought it. And ever since, for nine years, every year, he'd bought a new car: another Camaro, then a Corvette, then a 280Z. All of them had been customized, some touch that was only his, even if it was just a striping job, with his initials on the doors. Every year, he used to buy a different car, never the same kind of car two years in a row.

But now he drove BMWs, only BMWs—conservatively painted BMWs, none of them customized, nothing flashy. When he'd bought the red Camaro—for cash, a big wad of cash—he'd gotten all dressed up: wide lapels, narrow tie, everything cool, lots of flash, like he was going out with the most beautiful woman in the world.

But when he bought his last car, the 633CSi, he'd worn a three-piece suit, everything button down. And he'd paid by check, just wrote out a check with his Cross pen. The salesman, too, had used a Cross pen. But the salesman's pen had been silver—and his was gold. They'd laughed about that, he and the salesman, one of them black, from the slums, the other one white, probably a Harvard man, the way he talked.

3

Aware that she'd read the same sentence twice, still without comprehending what she'd read, she closed the book and put it on her towel, folded beside her poolside chair. She'd bought the book in town earlier in the day, as an experiment. It had been almost a week since he'd been killed, a week tomorrow night, at about ten-thirty. In a week, she'd hoped, the worst of the wounds within would have begun to heal. So she'd bought the book, a copy of *Time and Again*, a book she'd always meant to read, hopeful that she'd be able to concentrate on the story, refocus her thoughts, tear them away from the memory of Nick, his face so still, so white, eyes open, lying on the gurney, draped in the institutional green sheet, only his face showing.

Was that particular color green reserved exclusively for the dead and the dying, some universal agreement, some immutable law? She'd once seen a traffic accident victim being loaded into an ambulance—covered with a green sheet, the same color green.

Why had she left him there? *Why?*

For a year, they'd lived like man and wife. So she should have waited for his father to arrive, to claim the body. They should have shared some special ceremony, she and his father.

But she'd run away.

Why?

Logically, because she feared for her life, feared that Nick's murderer would come looking for her. Because what Nick knew, she knew. What he'd known, he'd learned from her.

But if she'd been afraid—too afraid to return to her apartment—then why had she called DuBois, threatened him—challenged him? Everyone, she'd once read, had a death wish. Under certain conditions, given certain stresses, it was normal to invite death, either consciously or subconsciously. For every suicide, there were doubtless thousands who subconsciously invited death: the driver who wouldn't stop drinking, the woman who walked alone down dangerous streets, all of them rushing their appointment in Samarra.

At the far end of the pool, the shallow end, a man lay stretched out in the sun while his wife and their small children paddled happily in the water. The mother was teaching the daughter to float, supporting the little girl with her hand at the small of the girl's back, exhorting her to relax. The mother-and-daughter scene was classic, everything motherhood should be, could be—the laughter, the grace, the trust, and the love. And the young husband, watching and smiling, completed the picture: an American dream, the family at play, infinitely secure, unreasonably happy, candidates for a Norman Rockwell painting.

For as long as she could remember, she'd seen herself in a picture like this. She'd known it would happen; she'd never lost faith. Because all the promises had been made: the TV sitcom, the movies, the glossy four-color ads, all of them had promised her happiness: a sanitized, deodorized, homogenized future, she and her husband and their sanitized, deodorized children.

It had been in high school that the dream had begun to lose definition, like an old photograph, fading in the sun. It had happened quite suddenly, it seemed—on a Friday in April, perhaps, when there'd been a party, and no one had invited her. Until then, she'd always thought she was pretty, always thought that, when the time came, she'd find the right man, the one who fitted into the Norman Rockwell painting.

But something had happened to her on that Friday in April. Perhaps it had happened in her subconscious, between the time she'd gone to sleep and the next morning. Because it seemed that until one day, one specific, fateful day, she'd always thought of herself as pretty—just the one simple word, "pretty."

But then, the next day, she no longer thought of herself as pretty. She didn't think she was ugly. She'd never thought that. It was just that, from that particular day until this particular day, she'd never thought she was pretty.

And prettiness, she knew, was a state of mind. Prettiness, and everything else, everything that mattered, it was all a state of mind. Pretty was a code word—for a teenager, for a woman, any woman, pretty was the ultimate code word. In high school, "pretty" meant that the boys liked you, wanted to take you out—wanted to feel you up in the backseats of their fathers' cars. Later, after everyone had lost their virginity, "pretty" meant, simply, that you were a woman that men wanted to lay. The prettier you were, the more men wanted to lay you. And the more men wanted to lay you, the prettier you felt, therefore the more self-confident you felt of your sexuality. Meaning that you could pick and choose. Making you more inaccessible. Making you, therefore, more desirable. It was a simple supply-and-demand equation, really—elementary stuff, for first-year business school majors.

She shifted her gaze to the only other poolside person: the tall, lean, fortyish man with the dark, quick eyes. The man moved easily, smoothly, like an athlete. And he smiled like a shy schoolboy. She'd seen him yesterday, when he'd registered. Ever since, she'd been aware of him watching her, appraising her.

Yesterday, on her second evening in town, she'd driven out to The Crosswinds restaurant, located a few miles east of town, at the airport. Just as she was ordering, he'd arrived. He'd taken a nearby table, and nodded to her, and smiled. She'd returned the nod, but not the smile. She'd wondered whether he'd followed her from the motel to the airport with sex on his mind. It wouldn't've been difficult to follow her. In the desert, day or night, cars were visible for miles. But he hadn't followed up on the smile, and she'd left while he was still eating his entree. After dinner, in the twilight, she'd decided to drive east for a few miles, away from town, out into the desert. When she'd turned back toward town, she'd seen his car still parked at the restaurant.

Last night, late, after the TV movie, she'd unlocked her door and walked past the swimming pool and out through the motel's broad driveway to the county road and the phone booth that stood close beside the road, beneath the motel's blue neon sign. Without realizing it, she'd intended to call her mother, perhaps to reassure her mother that, yes, she was feeling better—or, at least, wasn't feeling worse. Yet she also realized that she was reluctant to make the call. While she was debating, standing a few feet from the sign, facing the phone booth, she was aware of a sound from behind her: a soft, furtive scuffling. Quickly, she'd turned—in time to see a shadow of someone standing beside a huge ocotillo bush that grew beside the driveway. Suddenly terrified, she'd darted to her left, putting the phone booth between herself and the bush. As she stood there, two cars had materialized out of the night, one pair of headlights coming from the north, from town, the other pair blazing out of the desert. Instinctively, she'd raised her hands, to signal. But something had prevented her, some irrational reluctance to make a scene, cause a fuss.

The cars had crisscrossed almost directly before the motel entrance, leaving her suddenly alone, in darkness again. And then, when she'd looked at the ocotillo, there was no figure, nothing. Watchfully aware that the man, whoever he was, must have come from the motel, she'd returned to her cabin, double locked the door, turned up the TV.

Could a killer have a shy smile and a pleasant, open face, and a manner reminiscent of an assistant professor of the classics?

He was just a few feet from her now, sitting shaded from the sun beneath a redwood lanai that ran the full width of the pool. He was sitting at a table. There was a briefcase on the table, and a clipboard. Frowning thoughtfully, eyes far away, he was sucking at a ballpoint pen. He'd been sitting like that, writing, for most of the afternoon, long before she'd come out to the pool with her copy of *Time and Again*.

She looked at her watch, lying beside the book on the beach towel. Three o'clock. She was more than halfway through the day; in eight more hours, with luck, she could sleep. It was the sixth consecutive day she'd gotten through alone, without Nick. So the hours had indeed turned into days. And tomorrow, the days would have turned into a week, one whole week, alone. And weeks would become months, and eventually the months would become years—until, finally, she would die, too. With or without another man, she would die, too.

It was natural, probably, that she should think of her own death, natural that she should even welcome the thought—accounting, perhaps, for the phone call she'd made, to Daniel DuBois.

But was it natural that, so soon, she should wonder whether she could find another man?

Was it natural that—yes—she'd begun to wonder how she would respond, if the man across the pool, the lean, intriguing-looking stranger, should make a move on her? Was it natural that, so soon, she was wondering what it would be like with a quiet, sensitive-looking man, after more than a year with Nick?

They'd come here once for a week in February, she and Nick. He'd never been to the desert, despite having lived for years in Los Angeles. And, sure enough, he hadn't liked the desert—didn't see the point of going to the desert when they could've gone to Hawaii, or Puerto Vallarta. She'd been wise enough not to try and make him see what she saw: the subtlety of the desert vegetation, the sense of timelessness, the feeling that life was reduced to its essentials, much of it scaled down to less than human size. Even the trees were hardly higher than a man's head, and cacti a hundred years old were only a few feet high, a world in miniature. In her imagination she could sometimes see a small arroyo transformed into a canyon where fist-size rocks were boulders, and thumb-size cactus husks were as large as fallen trees. At will, she could change the scale of the universe, with herself looking down, the creator.

Yet, when the setting sun turned the nearby mountains purple, a separate shade of purple for each range, and the desert sky turned yellow, and orange, and finally black, and the stars came out, and the desert vegetation disappeared in the night, she was transformed again, this time into something smaller than the smallest desert animal, awed by the vastness of the night sky, the eternal mystery of infinity.

At first, she'd tried to share it all with Nick, tried to show him what she saw, make him feel what she felt. But she knew he'd never really listened, never really looked.

But then Nick had discovered that he could rent a dirt bike and ride out into the badlands, so-called, east of town, where there were miles of off-road tracks, set aside for dirt bikers. So, the last two days they were here, Nick had ridden the badland trails while she read, or swam, or walked through the desert. She had a snapshot of him on his dirt bike, squinting into the sun, his nose wrinkled, smiling for the camera.

What would have happened to them, if he hadn't died? Would they have stayed together, she with her degree in fine arts, he with his stock-car racing trophies, and his scars to prove it?

She'd never known, really, how it had happened that she and Nick had gotten together. She knew the details, of course. He'd been visiting friends, a couple who lived in her apartment building, staying with them for the weekend. There was a small patio between the two halves of the building, with an even smaller pool. Wearing their bathing suits, Nick and his friends, the Kramers, had been sitting around the pool on a sunny Saturday afternoon, drinking beer. Nick had arrived in Los Angeles two days before, she'd discovered later, on a selling trip. Like Larry Kramer, the host, Nick sold performance auto parts. Both men had taken their lumps on the racing circuit, and they shared a rough and ready camaraderie that she'd found appealing for its bluff exterior that was obviously meant to conceal a genuine warmth.

She'd been wearing a bathing suit when they'd met, one that she knew was flattering—just as, now, she was wearing the same kind of suit, a black one-piece suit cut high on the sides. She'd been reading—just as she'd been reading now. And, yes, she'd been aware of the good-looking stranger. Just as, now, she was aware of this new stranger, still sitting hunched over his clipboard, brow furrowed, apparently deep in thought—the same man who, incongruously, last night, she'd suspected of wanting to kill her, for money.

But here, in the bright sunlight, the suspicion seemed preposterous, and as she watched him she wondered what he was so industriously writing, seemingly so oblivious to everything else. Could he be a writer? A fortyish student, working on his thesis? Or, probably more like it, he could be nothing more glamorous than the manager of a small branch bank, who happened to look a little like a poet as he puzzled over a contribution to next month's issue of *The Rotarian*.

Thinking about it, still speculating, she rose to her feet, stretched, and walked to the edge of the pool, at the deep end. With her back to him, she stood motionless for a moment, concentrating. Then she moved forward on the parapet until her toes could curl over, gripping the edge. She gathered herself, crouched, flexed, drew a deep breath, held it—and committed herself to the dive.

4

"How long'll you be with us, Mr. Fisher?"

"Why don't we say two days?" He slid the VISA card across the counter and smiled. "I've got to see about this heat."

The clerk was a small, middle-aged woman, skinny and dried out, with leathery skin, uneven teeth, and clear blue eyes. She didn't return the smile, but instead frowned as she examined the registration card he'd filled out. Now she looked up at him sharply, as if she were comparing his face with a passport photo. Finally, plainly reluctant, she put his VISA card in the impression machine. As she jerked the lever roughly back and forth, the muscles of her forearm flexed. He signed the VISA chit, put both the card and the receipt in his wallet, took the key to his room, and walked out into the afternoon glare of the desert heat. He would unpack, take a quick shower, change shirts. Then he would drive around town, get the feel of the place, check out the restaurants and the stores—and the local law enforcement. He'd find people who liked to talk—and he'd let them talk.

And then, when he'd gotten the feel of the place, gotten the roads in and out clear in his mind, he'd check out the Ram's Head Motel, a mile out of town to the south.

The entrance to the Ram's Head Motel was a wide, graveled driveway that narrowed as it curved in among the dozen-odd cabins that were visible from the road. The cabins had been built at random, in no particular pattern, mingled with wild-growing desert vegetation and trees, some of them low, feathery trees, some tall palms. Cacti grew between the trees, some small, some head high. A tall, white-flowered hedge screened the motel grounds from the road, but the driveway was wide enough to reveal a large oval swimming pool. The motel office was built across the driveway from the pool, closest to the road. Among the trees, Dodge could count three cars parked beside the three separate cabins. A waist-high split rail fence bordered the motel property on two sides, joining the flowering hedge at the road. The cabins were plain stucco, simply built. According to one guidebook, rentals began at forty dollars a day. And the guidebook mentioned twenty-one units, so the property must go back farther than he could see through the cacti and the trees. Beneath the small blue neon Ram's Head Motel sign, "Vacancy" was spelled out in red neon. Just to the left of the sign, maybe ten feet away, there was a telephone booth—an old-fashioned roadside telephone booth, with folding doors.

To himself he nodded, put the Camaro in gear, began driving slowly south, toward the open desert.

If he'd planned it, he couldn't have worked out a better layout. Never.

Some layouts were easy, some were hard. Some seemed impossible. Once, in Chicago, he'd spent a whole week working out a plan. He'd even made notes on when the mark came and went, when the patrol cars passed, when the mailman came, and the delivery boys, and the children coming home from school. And there'd been neighbors, too, neighbors all around, living in split-level houses. It had been very complicated, that Chicago situation.

But this situation was simple—deadly simple. There

was a woman in a cabin at the Ram's Head Motel. He'd seen her earlier, a lucky chance, when he'd driven past, still getting the feel of the town. He'd seen her walking from the pool to the motel office. She'd been wearing a black bathing suit, and she'd had a better body than he'd have thought. So she was there, in her cabin, one cabin among twenty-one, built so they looked like they were all natural, all part of the desert, with only a split rail fence that separated the fake Ram's Head desert from the real desert: no-man's-land, with only a few scattered houses nearby. Big, low, rambling houses, that had been built to look like they were part of the desert, too.

But all of them were faking it, pretending to be part of a desert they could never live in, not for a minute, not without their swimming pools, and bars, and air-conditioning. Because the desert was nothing but sand and rock and cactus and heat like an oven.

And anything that moved in the desert was notice-able. An animal, a car, a man—anything that moved would be seen—and remembered. And the town was no different: two thousand people, baking in the sun, marking time until the tourists began arriving to open their winter homes, start spending their money. Any new face, even a white face, would be remembered. Al-ready, he knew, people were watching him—and won-dering. The people he'd talked to—the woman at the motel, the man at the gas station, the man at the hard-ware store where he'd bought a few things, just for the conversation—they'd remember him. And they'd talk to each other, too. In small towns, they all talked to each other.

So the longer he stayed, the bigger the risk. Knowing what he knew now, it would have been better if he'd driven into town, found the Ram's Head, spotted her, knocked on her door, did the job in broad daylight, using the silencer, or else the ice pick, taking a chance. He could've been out of town in minutes—out in the desert. Or, better, he could've gone back the way he'd come, over the closeby mountains west to Los Angeles, or southwest, to San Diego. Even if he was seen doing the job, it would take the local sheriff a half hour to get organized, get together with the highway patrol, get it on the radio. And a half hour was all he'd need, even in daylight.

But already it was too late for that kind of a plan. Already he was known: a well-dressed black man driving a black Camaro—a real estate man, he'd told them, successful, just passing through, on his way to Mexico. So if anything went wrong, he could be identified. And in daylight, things went wrong. Unless everything was planned, carefully planned, things went wrong.

So he must wait until dark—four more hours, until it was dark. He'd wait, and he'd watch. Whatever it took, he'd do the job tonight.

5

As DuBois touched one green button on the arm, the wheelchair's motor whirred, the right wheel turned and the chair pivoted to the left, bringing him directly in front of the Utrillo. The painting was titled "The Marketplace," and represented the best of Utrillo's middle period. This was the time when Utrillo had been experimenting with the middle of his palette. Never had he been more successful with his close values and subtle textures, even though, in this period, it was possible to discern the beginning of the broader, bolder brush strokes that characterized his most productive, most evocative period, the period that continued until his death.

With the first two fingers of his right hand, he simultaneously pushed the two green buttons, lightly. The motor whirred again; the chair inched forward, letting him move close enough for his quadra focals to bring the details of the painting into sharper focus.

Specially designed wheelchairs, specially ground lenses—special bed, special food, a special communications network mated to a mainframe computer, they were the miracles of science that circumscribed his life.

Yet, half a glass full, they expanded his life, these mechanical and electronic miracles. Without the self-propelled wheelchair he would be immobilized, dependent on a servant to wheel him wherever he went: to bed, to the bathroom—and here, to his paintings, these masterworks, these magnificent painted fragments of men's lives, literally their souls expressed on canvas stretched over wooden frames. Without his gadgets, he would be denied this pleasure, this ultimate experience of his life.

Without the gadgets . . .

Without Betty.

If electrical gadgets circumscribed his life, then so did platitudes. *She's like a daughter to me* was one of the paler platitudes. *The child I never had* was another.

But, surprise, these pale platitudes were definitive. Because, surprise, ever since he'd given the order to Powers, he'd—

In its holster slung outside the chair's right arm, the wireless intercom phone beeped. As he touched the button beside the flashing red light he checked his watch: 5 P.M. exactly. As usual, Powers was precisely on time.

• • •

"Let's go out on the deck," DuBois said, turning the wheelchair to face the sliding glass door. With a kind of resigned contempt, he watched Powers come obediently to his feet, cross to the door, slide it open, step aside, wait for him and his wheelchair to whir out onto the deck. Without being told, conditioned to guard against drafts, Powers slid the door closed, then took a chair to face him. DuBois took a moment to admire the late afternoon vista: low clouds lying golden over a purpling ocean. When he spoke, his voice was soft: "What I want from you, Justin, is an update." He paused, faintly smiling as he saw anxious puzzlement cloud the other man's eyes, pucker his mouth, pinch at his nostrils.

"You mean—" The tip of Powers' tongue circled his pursed lips. "You mean an update about—" Unable to pronounce the name, he broke off.

"Yes," DuBois said gently, "I mean an update about Betty."

"But I—I thought we'd agreed that the—the less we knew, each of us knew, the better. You said—"

"I said the less you knew about the, ah, background, the better it would be for you. And as for me, as long as there aren't any problems, then there's no reason I have to know any of the, ah, operational details. And that's still true. However, since the last time we talked, I've been reconsidering."

"You've been—?" The slow, incredulous widening of Powers' eyes was ludicrous, a caricature of the yes-man's eternal travail as he sought to guess the next turning of his tethered fate.

"Begin at the point where I told you to find her," DuBois said. "Start there, and tell me everything. In detail."

"Yes. Well—" Once more, the pink tongue circled the

pursed, pale lips. As if to steady himself against seismic shock, Powers was gripping the arms of his chair, shifting his feet on the concrete surface of the deck, for better purchase. "Well, I—when you said you thought she was here, in Los Angeles, I decided to begin there. Here. I mean, I called MacCauley again. He's the one—the private detective—that I used first, to keep track of—of—" Helplessly, he shook his head.

"—of Ames' movements," DuBois said gently. "In Los Angeles."

"Y—yes." Gratefully, Powers bobbed his head, painfully swallowing. "I decided that since I'd already contacted him, he'd already have been—you know—briefed."

"Did you tell him Ames was dead?"

"I—ah—" Powers swallowed again. "No, I didn't. I—I decided I didn't want to tell him any more than was absolutely necessary."

DuBois made no response, gave no sign of either approval or disapproval. Instead, he lifted his right hand from the chair, signaling for Powers to continue. Then he touched one of the red buttons, angling the chair so that he could face the other man squarely.

"I just said that I knew they'd been up north, the two of them, but that now I thought they were back here—that she was back here, in the Los Angeles area. So we agreed that he'd assign someone to watch her apartment building."

"You told him he wasn't to interrogate anyone at Powers, Associates."

Quickly, Powers nodded. But, simultaneously, his eyes clouded. He'd made a mistake. Transparently, he'd made a mistake. A dangerous mistake, possibly. "What is it?" DuBois asked gently.

"Well, after I'd hired MacCauley, a man named

Bernhardt came to the office. Alan Bernhardt. He—he's a private investigator, and he was looking for Betty."

"You didn't tell me this, Justin. When I called you—told you to go ahead with it, with the plan for Betty—you should've told me about this man."

"Well, I—I thought about it, considered it. But it was so quick, that conversation you and I had. And we'd agreed—you told me earlier—that the less said the better, the less contact we had about this, you and I, the better. So I decided not to say anything to you."

"Tell me about him, what he said, what he did, this Bernhardt."

"Well, he—he told the receptionist—he implied—that he'd been retained by her mother, because of illness in the family. So when I heard that he was there, at the office—that he'd gotten that far—I decided I should see him, see what he had to say."

Gravely, DuBois nodded. "Yes, that was probably the right decision."

"There wasn't time to call you. And—and, even if there were time, I don't think I would've called. For the reasons we just discussed."

Once more, patiently, DuBois nodded.

"So I saw him, this Alan Bernhardt," Powers continued. "I asked him what he was after. And I found out that he hadn't been retained by her mother. Or, at least, I don't think he had. Because he—he talked about Nick Ames, about the fact that he was dead."

"The mother could still have retained him, though. Betty could have told her mother about Nick, and she was concerned for Betty's safety. Perhaps Bernhardt was lying about an illness for the sake of convenience."

Powers nodded. "Yes, that occurred to me."

"How'd you leave it, the two of you?"

"Well, I—I tried to hire him. I thought that as long as he'd found us, I may as well get him on our side."

"Did he accept the offer?"

"No, he didn't. But he left his card. And he told me where he was staying, in Santa Monica."

"But you don't know what his purpose was, what he's really trying to find out."

"Not really. He's very intelligent, I think. And he's probably devious, too. But I got the feeling that his purpose was to find her, find Betty. I didn't get the feeling he was concerned with Ames—with his death."

"Have you heard from him since?"

"No. Yesterday, I called his motel, but he'd checked out. And now I wonder whether he found her."

DuBois frowned. "I don't understand."

"Well, I'd already hired MacCauley, you see, before Bernhardt arrived. So I called MacCauley and told him that he might follow Bernhardt, put a man on him, in the hope that Bernhardt would lead them to Betty. And that could've been what happened. Because yesterday, MacCauley called, and said he'd located Betty in Borrego Springs, at the Ram's Head Motel. So it's possible, you see, that MacCauley put an electronic device on Bernhardt's car, and followed him to Borrego Springs."

"You didn't ask MacCauley whether, in fact, he did follow Bernhardt."

"No—" Apprehensively, Powers was shaking his head, anxiously watching DuBois, searching for signs of approval.

"Did MacCauley say whether Bernhardt is in Borrego Springs, too?"

"No, he didn't."

"You didn't ask."

"No, I didn't. I—" Powers hesitated, then admitted: "I didn't want to know any more than was necessary. I—I still don't."

DuBois let a moment of disapproving silence pass before he said, "So then you called your other friend. The one in Detroit. According to my instructions on the phone."

"Yes." As he spoke, Powers lowered his eyes. His voice was indistinct. In his lap, his pale fingers moved fretfully.

"Is your friend from Detroit in Borrego Springs now?"

"Please—" Powers raised his hands, as a supplicant might. "Please, don't call him that. Don't call him my friend."

"Sorry—" DuBois let another moment of silence pass. Then, speaking quietly, he said, "*Is* he there?"

"I think so. He should be, anyhow. He left four hours ago, from LAX. It's about a hundred fifty miles, from the airport to Borrego Springs."

"Will he contact you before he—" This time, it was DuBois who broke off, unable to pronounce the fateful words.

"N—no. At least, I don't think he will. We're going to meet Saturday, at LAX. I'll pay him off, pay him the other half, then."

"Does he have a phone number for you?"

"Just one. My private line, at home. It's under lock and key—the phone, and the answering machine, too."

"But you don't expect him to call."

"No, I don't. He implied that he wouldn't call, in fact."

"And you don't know how to contact him in Borrego Springs. You don't know where he's staying, of course."

"No, I don't. The only way I could contact him would be to—" Slowly, incredulously, Powers raised his eyes, finally meeting the other man's gaze. "I'd have to go there, and—" Once more, helplessly, he lapsed into silence. But his eyes remained fixed on DuBois' face, as if he were fascinated. Fatally fascinated.

"She's staying at the Ram's Head Motel, you said. Is that right?"

"Y—yes. As of yesterday, anyhow. Last night. W—why?"

"Because," DuBois answered, "I've decided to call her."

"But why? *Why?*"

"Several reasons. First, I've changed my mind. I don't want her killed. I don't think it's necessary."

"But you told me to—to arrange it, set it up. When I told you she'd been found, you told me to—"

"I'm well aware of that, Justin. But I've been considering the whole matter very carefully. And I think, if I can reach her by phone, I can make her see reason. After all, the purpose of the exercise isn't to kill her. The purpose of the exercise is to silence her. And I think I can do that. I think if I call her and tell her that there's someone who plans to kill her—someone in her immediate vicinity—then I think she'll understand that she has to act reasonably. I think she'll be frightened enough to understand. She's very upset now. That's perfectly understandable. She thinks she wants to make me pay for Nick Ames' death. But it's been my experience that, when a rational person realizes that death is imminent, a solid possiblity, he becomes more manageable. And Betty is essentially a rational person. I know her. Intimately."

"But she can ruin you. At least, that's what you told me. You said that—"

"She's always been able to ruin me. For years now, she's been able to ruin me. But she hasn't. And she won't, either. Not if she's handled properly."

"But she—she could ruin me, too. She knows about us, about our association. So she'd suspect that I'm the one who—" Helplessly, Powers began to shake his head.

"Justin—" Patiently, DuBois shook his head, then touched both the green buttons, moving the wheelchair a few inches closer to the other man. As if they were confidants—equals—he lowered his voice. "That was necessary. If we hadn't done that, silenced Nick Ames, I'm sure he would've made good on his threats. So you shouldn't feel badly about that. Not at all."

"It's not a question of feeling badly. It's a question of—of culpability."

"It'll work out, Justin. Believe me, it'll work out." Now he touched the buttons again, this time moving the chair back. It was a signal that the interview was about to end.

"We'll talk again, soon," DuBois said. "Keep monitoring your private line. If he should phone, call him off, tell him there's been a change of plans. Meanwhile, I'll call Betty, at the Ram's Head. When I've reached her, if that's possible, I'll call you, fill you in. We'll keep in touch."

"Wh—what about the money? The rest of the money, that I'll owe? On Saturday."

"You'll pay it, of course. A deal's a deal. Tell your man that the plans have changed, but that he'll be fully compensated."

"But why? Why change now? It—it seems risky for you to contact her. She could—"

"I've already told you, Justin. I think I can turn her around, make her see reason. And also—" He smiled: a faint, exhausted smile, the signal that, for today, he'd reached the end of his strength. "Also," he said, "I'm fond of Betty, genuinely fond. I don't want to see her harmed. Not unless it's absolutely necessary."

"But—" Suddenly Powers leapt to his feet, strode to the railing of the deck, turned to face the man in the wheelchair. "But this—" Vehemently, he shook his head, clenched his fists at his sides, took a single desperate step forward. "This is wrong. Don't you see how wrong it is—how dangerous? You—" His voice caught. He was blinking rapidly now; his mouth was impotently opening and closing, his knees were trembling, shamefully trembling. In all their years together, he'd never before defied DuBois, never before dared to question, to complain. "You say you'll call her, in Borrego Springs. You'll tell her someone's there, to—to kill her. But if you do that, scare her enough, she'll call the police, tell them about it. And if they believe her—if they catch him, because of what she tells them—then I could be involved. He could tell them where to find me, on Saturday, when we're supposed to meet. He could identify me. Th—they could arrest me. And besides that, there's no—" Suddenly his throat closed. His voice, he knew, would be cravenly unsteady as he said, "There's no way I can get hold of Fish—of *him*. No way I can stop him. Not unless I call every motel in town. And that wouldn't work, because he's undoubtedly using an alias. So th—that'd be another mistake. Because I'd be—" Once more, his throat closed, this time irrevocably, all hope gone. Thank God, he was standing close to the railing of the deck. Because suddenly he felt as if his legs were too weak to support him. And at his solar plexus, the center of himself, there was nothing left. Nothing but a terrible, shameful numbness.

As if he hadn't heard, DuBois sat motionless in the wheelchair, his eyes fixed on the ocean, and the deepening sunset. Aware that he'd lost control, aware that fear was tearing at his face as viciously as claws tore at carrion, Powers stood helpless, his legs braced wide, his right hand gripping the railing. Finally DuBois spoke: "This is the first time we've ever differed, Justin. This is a new dimension, an entirely new dimension."

"I—" Helplessly, he shook his head. His voice was hardly audible. "I realize that."

"How much will you pay him, on Saturday?"

"Twenty-five thousand."

"Do you have it? Now?"

"At home, yes. In the safe."

"Well, then," DuBois said, "I think you should go home, and get the money. Then I think you should get in your car and drive to Borrego Springs. It's almost six o'clock now. If you hurry, you can probably be there by eleven, maybe earlier. Find your man, pay him off, send him on his way. Then call me. At any time, call me."

Aware that, now, it was an incredulous, craven relief that he must try to conceal, Powers could only nod.

6

Aware that she'd risen to her feet, Bernhardt glanced up, saw her standing beside the pool, looking down into the water, obviously deciding whether she would go in. He'd seen her swimming earlier in the day. She was a good, strong, smooth swimmer, someone who probably loved the water, someone who'd probably had lessons. As she walked to the edge of the pool, their eyes met briefly, impersonally. Now she was standing poised, knees flexed, frowning slightly as she concentrated, took a deep breath—and committed herself to the dive. She entered the water cleanly, swam for a few yards underwater, then surfaced, changed to a crawl, began swimming to the far end where she turned, shook water from her eyes, began swimming back toward him. As he watched her, he wondered whether she suspected that he'd been keeping her under close surveillance wherever she went. Could she know that he'd watched her, stood guard over her? Last night, from the window of his cabin, he'd had a view of her front door. He'd been able to see the side of her cabin, too, the only side that had a window, except for one tiny frosted bathroom window, set high in the rear wall. She'd turned out her light about midnight. Sitting back from his own window, listening to his faithful Walkman, with his Ruger .38 on the floor beside his chair, he'd remained on watch until 3 A.M. before he'd finally surrendered to sleep. A car with only one passenger had arrived at the motel office about twelve-thirty, but the driver had been a white-haired man with a huge paunch and a debilitating limp, hardly the stereotype of a hit man.

Had it been a fool's errand, this trip that would cost several hundred dollars, this impulse that had begun with nothing more profound than yet another argument with Dancer? What would he have done, if someone had tried to kill her? He fired the gun once a year at the police range in Daly City, to qualify for the permit that allowed him to carry it. But he'd never drawn the gun in anger, much less fired it.

Yet when he did carry the gun, it comforted him— just as it had comforted him last night. The gun was a stainless steel .38 revolver with a four-inch barrel, one of the best revolvers in the world. Dancer had given it to him at the end of his first year with the firm, a symbolic gold watch for faithful service. But, as always, Dancer had attached a condition. If Bernhardt couldn't qualify at the police firing range with the pistol, he must agree to give it back. And—yes—he'd had to buy his own holster, ten dollars at a Mission Street pawnshop. It was a spring holster, the kind detectives used, the pawnshop clerk had told him.

After he'd bought the holster, exactly as if he'd been a kid with a new toy, he'd practiced his quick draws—and his combat crouch, and his snap firing. And, yes, he'd been aware of the pleasure it gave him, simply to hold the gun, to handle it—to fondle it, some would say. It was a deep, elemental pleasure—that much he'd discovered, to his own surprise. But what were the origins, the true origins, of that secret pleasure? He'd often thought about it, applied all the liberal-left theories he'd been brought up to believe: that a gun was the extension of his penis, a symbol of male dominance. But he'd never been very good at analyzing the symbols of his own libido. So he'd concluded that the gun represented power, more than sexual potency. If the male's sex drive was primary, which he believed, then the urge to protect the family inside the cave was certainly secondary. If the male instinctively fornicated, then he also instinctively fought. He fought with predators, for self-protection. And he fought with other males, for sexual dominance. So if the caveman's instinct was to pick up the fallen limb of a tree, his first club, then that same deep instinct accounted for the way the steel of a gun felt to the hand of the male—and the steel of a knife, too, another deep, elemental pleasure. And, without doubt, whatever they made the buttons from, that launched the missiles from their silos—that would feel the same, too.

At the far end of the pool, Betty Giles was getting out of the water. Bernhardt glanced at his watch. The time was six o'clock. If she did as she'd done yesterday, she would lie beside the pool for a half hour, drying out and reading. Then she'd go to her cabin, to change her clothes. At seven o'clock, give or take, she'd get in her car and drive to a restaurant, one of the two that were open in town. It would probably be dark, when she returned from dinner, almost completely dark. Understandably, she would be reluctant to let him into her cabin, after dark.

So it must be before she left for dinner, that he'd do what he'd come to do. Showered and scented, he would change into fresh clothes, with his gun concealed beneath his loose-fitting sports shirt. Then he would walk the fifty feet to the door of her cabin. He'd knock, and he'd smile—and he'd do what he came to do.

7

Almost before he finished knocking, he saw the curtains stir at the window beside the door. Good, she was being cautious. He stepped back from the door, took one of his newly printed business cards from his pocket, and smiled as the door came open on the chain. He'd rehearsed his opening lines, knew exactly what he wanted to say, and how he wanted to say it:

"I'm Alan Bernhardt, Miss Giles. I'm sorry to bother you, but we've got to talk. Here—" He extended the card. "This is my card. If you'd like to call your mother, to check me out, I'd happily pay for the call, put it on my credit card."

"My mother?" Her hand came through the space between the door and the frame; she took the card between thumb and forefinger. "You know my mother?"

"Yes, I do. We spent a long time together, talking about you."

"A private investigator—" Distrust was clear in her voice, plain in her small oval face behind the chain.

"Listen—" He stepped down off the small cement

door stoop, standing on the desert sand. "Listen, why don't we go and sit beside the pool? It won't take long, what I've got to say. But I feel dumb, standing here like this, talking through the door. I feel like a door-to-door salesman."

"Did my mother send you?"

"No, she didn't. But she'll be glad to learn that I'm here, I can guarantee that."

She didn't respond, but only looked at him appraisingly. How often had he suffered through this same suspicion-charged silence, standing on the wrong side of a stranger's door, trying to look harmless, and sincere, and reassuring—all while he labored to keep a fake smile in place.

"There's no one at the pool. Can we sit there for a few minutes, and talk?" He widened the smile. "I'll even buy you a Diet Coke. Or a Seven-Up. Your choice."

"All right. Just a minute. I've got to comb my hair."

"Fine." With his hands in his pockets, he moved away from her cabin to stand beside one of the head-high ocotillo cacti that defined this part of the low desert, and were protected by local statute. The motel owners had taken pains to protect the desert vegetation, outlining pathways with rocks, and the meandering driveway with fallen logs. A split rail fence, Abe Lincoln style, surrounded the entire tract. Rustic signs reminded tenants that the narrow driveway was one-way only, ending where it began, at the broad, graveled drive that opened on the county road. As nearly as Bernhardt could calculate, only a few of the twenty-odd cabins were occupied. Yesterday evening, he'd walked around the outside perimeter of the motel grounds, following the split rail fence as he familiarized himself with the sparsely populated neighborhood. Most of the nearby houses were upscale winter retreats built on

acre-plus lots. Most of the lots were unfenced and un-
defined, merging into the desert. Except for the full,
lush trees planted close to the homes, where water was
pumped up from the Borrego aquifer, the desert land-
scape was undisturbed: silent, vast, primeval.

He heard the night chain on her door rattle, saw the
door swing open. She was dressed in designer khaki
bush pants and a colorful Madras blouse. Both the
pants and the blouse were cut close enough to hint at
the fullness of a figure that her bathing suit had already
revealed. Her dark hair, cut medium short, was casually
combed. She carried a Mexican-style tooled leather bag
slung over one shoulder. Her sandals, too, were tooled
leather. As they turned together into the rock-bordered
footpath that led to the pool, he said, "Except for that
couple with the little girl, and a man that came last
night, I don't think there're any other people here but
us. At least, there're just four cars."

She made no reply, gave no indication that she'd
heard. She simply walked beside him, eyes front. The
set of her face, the way she walked, the way she carried
herself, all conveyed a kind of measured detachment, a
calculated aloofness. Or was it a shyness, an uncertainty of the spirit, her grim, silent secret?

Or was she, simply, afraid—and trying not to show
it?

At poolside, he gestured to the redwood lanai, and
the shade it offered. "How about here?"

She nodded. "Fine."

"I meant it about that soft drink—" He smiled, gestured across the driveway to the office, and the vending
machines beside it. "My treat."

"No, thanks. But you go ahead." She sat in a straight-
backed chair: a black metal frame covered with crisscrossed strips of white plastic.

"Not now. Later, maybe." He moved a companion

chair to face her, and for a moment they sat silently, looking at each other. In closeup, her features, like her body, were pleasingly formed, but slightly coarsened, denying her the kind of head-turning masculine attention that some women parlayed into a free trip through life.

"I guess," he said, "that I might as well start at the beginning, tell you why I'm here, the reason I've come."

Watching him carefully, she nodded—once. "Good."

"I came to Borrego Springs because, originally, I was hired to find you when you were staying in Santa Rosa—at the Starlight Motel."

Her reaction was instantaneous: a sharp, sudden shudder. Instinctively, she moved forward in her chair and shifted her feet, unconsciously poised for sudden flight.

"You—" She licked at her lips. "You were there? At the Starlight?"

He nodded. "I stayed right across from you and Nick. You were in room twelve."

"Nick—?" It was a half-choked whisper. Eyes wide, she glanced quickly to the right and left. It was another instinctive body movement, signifying her sudden shrinking from a terror remembered. "You knew Nick?"

"I didn't know him, any more than I knew you. As I said, I was hired to find you. And I did."

"Wh—who hired you?" As she spoke, she lowered her voice, moved forward in her chair. Responding, he moved his chair closer to hers, also confidentially lowering his voice:

"I worked for a large company at the time—Herbert Dancer, Limited. So all I know is what my boss told me to do—find you, and report to him, when I'd found you. He reported to his client. The next day, in the afternoon, I was taken off the case. I had an option. I could go back to San Francisco, or I could stay in Santa Rosa, since the room was already paid for. I decided to stay. And the next morning, I heard about Nick."

"It was DuBois," she said. "He hired you." She spoke softly, numbly, without inflection. Her eyes were blank. Her body was inert now, no longer poised for flight. Whatever she feared, she'd lost the will to resist, lost the strength to flee, even in her thoughts.

"Not me. Maybe he hired Dancer, I don't know. That's what I'm telling you. I was just the flunky." He paused, watched her face, watched her think about it—saw the rigidity of fear and shock slowly fade as her mind began functioning again, working with the pieces of the puzzle he represented.

He let the silence lengthen, watched her slowly sink back in her chair, watched her eyes sharpen and her mouth tighten as, plainly, she began to believe that he hadn't come to harm her.

"Who's DuBois?" he asked finally.

"He's a financier," she said. "And an art collector."

"Did you work for him?"

Clear-eyed now, pointedly refusing to answer the question, she said, "You still haven't told me why you're here."

"I think it's possible that Nick was killed by a professional killer. I'm not sure, but that's what I think—what the evidence suggests. And if that's true, then I was hired to set Nick up. I don't want that on my conscience."

"So you're trying to find the man who killed Nick." She spoke ironically, disbelievingly.

"No. That's for the police. I just want to find out what really happened in Santa Rosa. If the murder was a street killing, then I'm off the hook. But if it was planned, then I very well could've been involved. And if that's true, I want to know about it." He let a beat pass, watching her eyes narrow as she thought about it. Then he said, "That's why I wanted to find you."

"I don't understand your reasoning." She spoke coldly.

"There's nothing complicated about it. You could have the answers I need. Or, between us, we could have the answers. Your mother called me after you called her. She told me what you said, that you'd make them pay, for killing Nick. And you've just told me that you know who retained Dancer. So it's obvious that if you want to, you can tell me why Nick was killed. You could have the answer I'm looking for."

"What if you *are* involved? You could go to jail, couldn't you?"

"I won't know that until I know what happened— who hired who, and why."

"And you think I can tell you that."

"I think you can fill in some of the blanks."

"How do I know that you aren't doing what you did in Santa Rosa? How do I know there isn't someone on his way here to kill me?" She spoke evenly, calmly challenging him. Once she'd recovered from the shock of being discovered, she was thinking faster, gaining strength, beginning to ask the tough questions.

"Would we be talking like this, if I was setting you up? Being seen with you is the last thing I'd want. I'd make a phone call, and I'd split."

"Like you did in Santa Rosa." She spoke bitterly. Watching her, he approved. Slowly, surely, anger was displacing fear. Betty Giles was stronger than she thought—stronger than he'd thought, only minutes before.

Deliberately, he looked at his watch. "It's seven o'clock. What're you planning for dinner?"

"I'm not hungry. Not now." She hesitated, then ventured, "What about you?"

"Mostly," he answered, "I want to talk. I've got to get this settled. But I'm hungry, too. And—" He smiled at her, as warmly as he could, his big-brother impersonation. "And I always think better on a full stomach."

She remained motionless for a moment, measuring him with dark, solemn eyes. Then, plainly having made some significant decision, she rose to her feet. "I've got a kitchenette in my cabin—and some eggs. Would you like some? Then we can talk."

He rose to his feet and gestured for her to precede him down the path to her cabin. "Definitely, I'd like some eggs."

8

Racing the darkness, he'd been driving the Camaro steadily for two hours, windows rolled up, air-conditioning on, stopping only to make additions to the penciled map he'd drawn of the town, the first thing he'd done. Army officers, tac squad commanders, they all used maps, too. Because planning, that was the secret. You imagined everything that could happen, everything that could go wrong, accidentally or on purpose. Then you figured out an answer, a solution to the problem.

Accidentally on purpose . . .

It was something they'd said when they were kids, one of those catch phrases, one of the things kids say, words that meant nothing. And nothing times nothing was nothing, the story of his life, when he was young. Sometimes it seemed like a dream: all those years, one long nightmare, fading now—finally fading, finally leaving him in peace. But then, at odd times, odd places, the nightmare came back, as real as a hand at his throat, strangling him: the sights, the sounds, the smells, they all could come back, demons from out of nowhere.

Especially the smells.

Everything he did, then, everywhere he went, there was a smell to it, a smell for everything: garbage, piss, shit—sex—they all had smells. Sometimes it seemed like his life had its own smell, a smell he'd never forget.

Ahead was the circle, the center of Borrego Springs. He slowed the Camaro, flipped the turn signal lever, checked the mirror, everything squared off, everything righteous.

Why was it, right about now, making his plans, this close to doing it, why was it that scenes from the past popped and sputtered through his mind like electrical flashes gone wild, arcing in the dark, lighting up a place, a face, a fight, or a body, some bodies alive, some of them dead? Why couldn't he concentrate, make his mind do what it had to do? Because it was all he had, his mind. Whatever you thought, that's how you acted, how you were. He knew that now. Just about now: twenty-eight years old, going on twenty-nine. Just about now, he was figuring it out. Everything. Every little thing he needed to know. Finally.

Everything, and nothing.

Idling along, turning out of the circle and heading west, passing through the center of town now—by now familiar—he ticked them off: on the north side of the main street, Palm Canyon Drive, there was a restaurant, a hardware store, a variety store, a real estate office, a small, off-the-street shopping mall—and the sheriff's office, with a squad car parked in front.

Earlier, he'd seen a policeman standing beside this same car, talking to a man and a woman. He'd been a young man, the policeman, not more than thirty years old, short and stocky, wearing a khaki-and-green uniform and a wide-brimmed felt hat, hick Western. No question, it was a deputy sheriff he'd seen, probably one of two or three deputies. Plus the sheriff, certainly more than thirty years old.

Gently, he increased the pressure on the accelerator. He was passing a larger shopping mall on the left, very fancy, built to attract the people who came for the winter—the rich ones, with the big, expensive houses . . .

. . . the houses that, around the clock, the police would be watching, checking them out every round they made, especially now, before the season started, with most of the houses still empty.

While he'd been driving around, systematically checking out the town, he'd only seen one of the sheriff's cars, on patrol. They'd met each other east of town, between the town limits and the airport, on Palm Canyon Drive. The limit was forty-five, east of the central circle, so there'd only been a second that they'd been able to see each other. He'd decided to look at the sheriff, keeping his face expressionless, look him straight in the eye. And, yes, the sheriff had looked at him—a different sheriff from the one he'd seen earlier, or the one he'd just seen. Older, maybe the real sheriff, not a deputy.

His motel was ahead on the left, at the western edge of the town. Except for a gas station, on the right, the motel buildings were the last ones in town. It was here that the terrain began to rise, as the string-straight desert road began curving up into the foothills, only a few miles to the west. Looming above the foothills, the low mountains were close, less than ten miles away . . .

. . . ten miles to safety. Especially at night, in the mountains, with dozens of side roads to take, and at least two small foothill towns between the desert floor and the Los Angeles basin. And once in the basin, on a freeway, one car among thousands, traveling in darkness, he would be safe. He would drive to LAX, turn in the car, get a room at the airport Hilton, and wait until Saturday, when he'd get the rest of the money. He'd get a suite, and he'd rent another car, a Mercedes, or a BMW, this time, and he'd drive over to Rodeo Drive. He'd find a place that sold shirts for five hundred dollars, and slacks for three hundred. And he'd buy two of everything—all on "Fisher's" credit card.

Sometimes he thought of Fisher as a real person, a living, breathing person. It was important to do that, Venezzio had told him—important to get inside the person you create, the paper man, the front, the cutout, whatever. Because that man could be your only protection, the only thing between you and the gas chamber. And that's what he'd done: made up a real man, as real to him as a TV character. There was a real address, a small apartment way across town from his own apartment. Twice a month, at least, he got dressed in Fisher's clothes, and put Fisher's wallet in his pocket, with Fisher's driver's license, and Fisher's social security number, and Fisher's bank passbook—and, most important, Fisher's VISA card. And he stayed a night or two, in Fisher's apartment, telling people he'd been out of town, out of the country, whatever, on sales trips. Because Fisher was a salesman, a wholesale candy salesman, he'd decided. He'd even hired a kid, a good, dependable kid, to check the apartment, keep the hallway outside picked up. He'd been amazed, how easy it had been to create a man, a whole man, out of nothing. First he'd started a bank account—a cashier's check for eight thousand dollars. Then he'd gotten the apartment, and the driver's license, and the social security number. Every week, he churned the bank account, depositing, withdrawing, writing checks, thousands of dollars in and out. And after a year, he'd gotten what he needed: the VISA card, his passport to anything, anywhere.

Just ahead, he saw the last turnoff before the upgrade to the foothills began, a road that led north, toward a collection of expensive homes and condominiums surrounding a golf course with an artificial lake, everything lush green, with palm trees that waved in the strong desert wind, just like Palm Springs, where "shacks," someone had told him once, cost a "half million, give or take."

He could write a check, for a shack like that. He could walk into the real estate office, and smile, and sit down at someone's desk, some branch manager who made maybe twenty thousand a year, and he could write a check for a half million dollars.

He slowed at the intersection, checked traffic in both directions, then made a U-turn, back toward his motel, and the town center. He would make another pass down Borrego Springs Road, to the south. He would drive past the Ram's Head Motel, checking to see that her car was still there. Every twenty or thirty minutes, ever since he'd arrived, he'd driven past the motel, checking on her car. Once, about two hours ago, the car had been gone. For a moment, one instant, he'd panicked. No, not panicked. The word was "clutched," the new word. No car, no Betty Giles. No Betty Giles, no payoff at the airport—no twenty-five thousand dollars, to add to the twenty-five thousand already tucked in his suitcase. The money would be a casualty, another new word.

Once, years ago, he decided to learn one new word a day, for the rest of his life. And he'd done it, too—for a week or so.

The twenty or thirty minutes between drive-bys at the Ram's Head, they were his window of vulnerability, one more new word, from what a politician had said on the six o'clock news, just the other night. Because if she left the motel during that time, he'd lose her, probably never find her, because there were three ways out of town, so his chances of following her, finding her, were only one chance in three. But he didn't have a choice. He had to give her that window of vulnerability. Because otherwise, he'd have to stay parked on Borrego Springs Road, where he could see the motel driveway. And a black face in a black Camaro, parked on one road for hours, would stick out, way out. Even if no one checked on him, questioned him, the sheriff and the state police, they'd remember him. They'd slow down, take his license plate, run the number. And a rented car wouldn't do much to smooth out what they were thinking.

So, clutched, wound up tight, he'd done the only thing he could. He'd driven into town, looking for her car. And there it was, the blue Nissan, parked in front of the grocery store at the circle, one of only two grocery stores in town.

He was back at the circle—his tenth or fifteenth time around town. He turned down Borrego Springs Road, slowed opposite the Ram's Head—

—and saw her sitting beside the pool.

She was dressed in a colorful blouse and beige slacks, and she was talking to a man, both of them with their chairs pulled close, as friends would sit—or strangers, talking seriously. The man was about forty, tall, dark-haired, long nose, lean face.

Should he stop the car opposite the driveway, fixing the stranger's face in his mind? Should he risk it, risk her remembering him, the black man in the fancy black car? She hadn't seen him in Santa Rosa, he knew that, was positive of that. But the Santa Rosa police could've told her that a black man had done the job on her boyfriend. And if the stranger she was talking to should be a policeman, one from San Diego, only sixty miles away, or even from Los Angeles, then he'd be risking more than he'd gain, if he stopped.

So he kept the Camaro moving, kept driving south, toward the open desert. The dashboard clock read 6:50 P.M. Two more hours before it would be fully dark. There was time, then. Plenty of time to get ready.

9

"In some cultures," Bernhardt said, appreciatively pushing his plate away, "it would be considered polite to burp after an omelette like that—a long, loud burp."

She laughed: a full, rich chuckle, a ladylike belly laugh. Bernhardt nodded to himself. A belly laugh was propitious, a sign of confidence. And he'd need it badly, her confidence.

"Cooking eggs right is an art," he said. "My mother always said so. And now I see what she meant."

"It just takes lots of butter and high heat, at least initially. There's no mystery to it."

"For Horowitz, there's no mystery to piano playing, either."

This time, responding, she only smiled. The belly laugh had been an aberration, then, only fleetingly erasing the sadness, the wariness that still shadowed her dark, searching eyes. Yet, if she didn't trust him, didn't believe what he'd told her, beside the swimming pool, they wouldn't be here, in this tiny kitchenette, sitting at this platter-size Formica breakfast table.

"So you're just starting your own business, is that right?" She spoke conversationally.

He nodded. "Right. At age forty-three, I've decided I'm probably not very employable, not a very good team player, I guess."

"I saw you writing. All afternoon. You looked very serious about it."

"Do you ever go to little theaters, in San Francisco?"

Puzzled, she frowned. "Sometimes. Why?"

"The Howell Theater?"

She nodded. "A few times, yes. Are you—?"

"I direct at the Howell. And act, too, sometimes. And I write plays."

"So—" She moved her head in the direction of the pool. "You were writing a play."

"That's not something I always admit, at least not to strangers."

"Have any of your plays been produced?"

"One was produced off-Broadway, years ago. So far, that's it. So, to keep from starving, I moonlight."

"As a private investigator."

He nodded. "Right." He smiled across the table. "That's my shameful secret."

"I still don't know why you've come here—all this way, at your own expense." As she said it, he saw the suspicion return to her eyes, heard the caution in her voice.

"I've already told you—I want to find out whether I was used to set Nick up. And, frankly, I thought you might be in danger, too. I wanted to tell you that it could've been a professional, who killed Nick. Apparently you thought you were in danger, too. Otherwise, you wouldn't've run away from Santa Rosa."

He watched her eyes drop, saw her head lower—saw the sudden agony that bore down her, a palpable weight. She sat like some hopeless penitent in the confessional, all hope abandoned. "I shouldn't've done it," she muttered. "I shouldn't've run away. I—I'll always regret it."

He let a long moment of silence pass as he watched her. She was vulnerable now, burdened by a sad, nameless regret, by a deep, festering guilt. This could be his chance, his one chance to press, to finally open her up. This one moment, these next few words, they might be all he'd have.

"Who's DuBois?" he asked. "Why would he have done it—hired people to find Nick, then hired someone to kill him?"

Still sitting with her head bowed, hands lying inert in her lap, she spoke softly, with infinite regret:

"It was me, really. It was what I did—what I knew, that's how it started—how everything started."

Aware that he must prod her gently, cautiously, he said, "Why don't you start at the beginning? That's the easiest."

She sat silently for a last, long, lost moment. Then, as if she were exhausted by the effort it took to keep her thoughts secret, she began speaking in a low, lifeless monotone:

"I suppose it started about three years ago. I was working for Standard Oil, in San Francisco. I was an art major in college, and I got a job as a curator, with Standard. That was the job description, 'Fine Arts Curator.'" Briefly, she smiled: a wan, resigned twisting of her mouth. "It was a wonderful job, a better job than I ever thought I'd have. Because Standard encourages art, you see—all kinds of art. They have a two-million-dollar-a-year budget, just for art. They encourage the executives to hang paintings in their offices, and all their architectural specifications include statuary, or whatever. They encourage local artists, too—sponsor exhibitions, things like that. And I did it all. I arranged for the art to be rotated, and I did the acquisition, too. And after a while, when we had a piece for a certain length of time, I'd sell it, and buy something else. So I was a trader, too, just as if I'd been running my own gallery. It was wonderful, just wonderful—" She said it wistfully, regretfully.

"And then," she said, "I got a call from Justin Powers."

Hearing the name, Bernhardt realized that he'd suddenly tensed. But if she'd noticed, she gave no sign. Once she'd found the strength to tell her story, the release that confession could confer had become its own impetus. Having started the story, she must now finish it:

"It was a Thursday afternoon, I remember, that he called. He asked me if I ever got to Los Angeles. I told him that I'd only been in Los Angeles three times in my whole life. So then he told me that he had an opening on his staff that he'd like to discuss with me. It was the same kind of work I'd been doing, he said. Which meant, of course, that he knew something about me. But I didn't want to ask him about it, I remember. I mean, he called me at my office, and I didn't want to talk about another job, not then. So he asked me if I'd like to come to Los Angeles some weekend, all expenses paid. I agreed to it, right on the spot. Which isn't like me, not really. I've always been cautious, slow to make up my mind. But he asked me if I could come the weekend after next, which meant that I'd have time to check him out, check out Powers, Associates. Which I did, with D and B. And I was impressed. Amazed, and impressed. And flattered, too. And, besides, he laid on the whole package: Friday night and Saturday night in a suite at the Century Plaza, a rental car reserved for me—everything. He was even smart enough not to send a limo to the airport, because that would've been too much, too soon."

"He wanted something from you, then."

"He wanted something from someone like me. Not me, necessarily."

"But Powers, Associates isn't anything like Standard Oil. I mean, a two-million-dollar budget?" He let the skeptical question linger between them.

For the first time since she'd begun her story, she looked at him directly. "You know about them, then—about Powers, Associates."

"I talked to Powers in Los Angeles, just before I came down here."

Plainly curious, obviously tempted to question him further, she was nevertheless driven by some inner compulsion to continue: "I thought about that Standard Oil budget, too," she said, "when we talked on Saturday, in Powers' office. But then I decided that he must be thinking of a philanthropy, establishing an endowment, something like that."

"But that wasn't it."

"No," she answered, "that wasn't it." Eyes hardening now, mouth tighter, she spoke grimly.

"It was DuBois."

"Yes," she answered, "it was DuBois. You knew."

He shook his head. "No, I didn't know. You mentioned DuBois a few minutes ago. Is it the zillionaire? That DuBois?"

"One of the ten richest men in the world. Right. And Powers, Associates fronts for him, handles all his business dealings. Ostensibly, you see, Powers, Associates are investment bankers, venture capitalists, whatever. Actually, they're in the business of investing the DuBois billions."

"They're a front, in other words."

"Yes."

"And DuBois is an art collector."

"Yes," she answered, still grimly. "Yes, DuBois is an art collector. I found that out on Sunday, when Justin Powers and I went to see him. He's got one of the finest collections in the world, as you might expect. And Powers was fronting for him, as you say—screening people until he found someone he thought was right for the job of curator."

"And you got the job."

She nodded. "I got the job. Powers left us together, Mr. DuBois and me. We spent hours, looking at his collection. And it was wonderful, seeing it—wonderful talking with Mr. DuBois, about art. He's seventy-six years old, and he's had two strokes. He's an invalid, in a wheelchair. His mind is alert, though—incredibly alert. But all he cares about, the only thing that means anything to him, is his art."

"It seems strange, though, that he'd need a curator, just for a private collection."

"I thought so, too. I told him that I doubted whether I'd find enough to do. But he explained that he did a lot of buying and selling. It was part of his passion—buying and selling, manipulating the markets, and the dealers. It was all that was left to him, you see. All those energies—that genius for timing and bargaining—everything that made him one of the ten richest men in the world, it was all concentrated on art, on collecting. And obviously, he can't get around, except with great effort. So it seemed reasonable that he'd need someone to act for him, especially at auctions. That's what it's all about for the collectors—the auctions. And, even if he could get around, he wouldn't want to go to the auctions. They'd see him—recognize him—and prices would soar. So that part of it made sense, allayed my suspicions. And, besides, the money he offered me was more than I made at Standard—a lot more. And there were bonuses, too. If I found something good, a bargain, and we turned it over at a profit, I got twenty percent. But if it happened the other way—if we lost— he absorbed it. So it—" Sadly, she shook her head. "It sounded wonderful, a dream come true. And it *was* wonderful, too. It *was* a dream come true. At least for a while."

"So, what happened? What went wrong?"

"What happened," she said, "was that a month or two after I started working for him, I began to suspect that he'd lied to me. Or, at least, that he hadn't told me the truth. Not the whole truth."

Knowing that, now, nothing could keep her from finishing the story, Bernhardt decided to say nothing. He watched her as, visibly, she took the final decision, crossed her final bridge.

"There's a man named Edward Frazer," she said. "Ned Frazer. And it's a known fact that Frazer deals in contraband art."

"Contraband?"

She nodded. "Most of it comes from Mexico and Central America—Mayan statuary, primarily. Stuff that's smuggled out of the country illegally. Some of the pieces are actually national treasures. In Mexico, you see, if you bribe the right official, you can get anything."

"So DuBois has a collection of contraband Mexican art?"

She shook her head. "No, not Mexican art. DuBois only collects painters. As far as I know, he'd never talked to Ned Frazer, never dealt with him. But when Frazer arrived, DuBois was expecting him. Someone had apparently called DuBois, and told him that Frazer was coming. That's the first suspicion I had, that something was going on behind my back. Frazer and DuBois talked for almost two hours, privately. They talked on the deck that adjoins DuBois' study. Later I learned that when DuBois wants absolute privacy, he goes out on the deck. I'm not really sure why, maybe he thinks there's less chance of electronic eavesdropping, out there. Anyhow, when Frazer left, DuBois sent for me. He was excited. He—" Incredulously remembering, she shook her head. "He seemed to glow from within, that's the only way I can describe it. His eyes—they were on fire, it seemed. Obviously, it had something to do with Frazer, with his visit. And, of course, I was terribly curious. But I'd learned not to question him—about anything. And, besides, it was clear that he was going to tell me about it, about what happened, with Frazer. And he *did* tell me—eventually. He started out by saying that he had something very important for me to do, a very important acquisition. There'd be a bonus, he said, for doing it—a huge bonus. Which made it pretty obvious that he was talking about stolen art—a very valuable piece of stolen art." She broke off, let her eyes wander thoughtfully away. "I can still remember the thrill I felt, when I realized what was happening. I've often thought about that, about the thrill I felt. Part of it, certainly, was the thrill of actually coming into contact with a major work of art. Because that's what he was talking about, obviously—a major work of art. But I think there was also the thrill you feel when you do something illegal, something dangerous—that for bidden thrill a child feels when he steals a piece of candy from the candy store. I think it must be built in, that thrilling sense of sin—part of all of us, deep down."

"I think you're right," Bernhardt said, matching her speculative mood. "It's there, somewhere, in all of us."

"And, of course, there was the bonus," she admitted. "That's there, too, in all of us. It's called greed."

Ruefully, Bernhardt nodded. "I agree with that, too."

230

She sat silently for a moment, idly tracing a pattern on the tabletop with her forefinger. Plainly, she was recalling her meeting with DuBois, the meeting that must have taken place more than two years ago.

"As I look back," she said, "it was obvious that he was manipulating me—the way he's always manipulated people. It's incredible, really, how he does it. He's like a—a wizard, an ancient wizard, a sorcerer. He seems to be able to see deep inside people. He knows what they're thinking before they know themselves. I've seen him do it, time after time. He knows just which buttons to press, like a—a consummate musician. He doesn't bully people, either. That's not it. He doesn't use fear, either—at least not at first. He's actually very polite. Almost courtly, in fact. But, of course, there's always the stiletto, hidden in the sleeve." She paused, bitterly smiled. "Whenever I think of him, especially these last few days, I think of medieval imagery: wizards, Byzantine plots and counterplots—murders in dark castle corridors. And all of it's an extension of that wizen, corrupt little man in his electric wheelchair. He's a—a *presence*. An evil presence."

"So you took the deal," Bernhardt prompted. As he spoke, he looked at his watch. The time was eight-thirty; a moonless desert night had fallen. And somewhere in the night, a murderer could be waiting —watching—planning. Bernhardt had arrived late yesterday afternoon. Since then, he'd kept Betty Giles under constant surveillance—sometimes from across the swimming pool, sometimes at a distance, driving more than a mile behind her over the straight, flat, empty roads that led out from Borrego Springs into the desert. In all that time, he'd seen nothing suspicious—

—except the black man in the black Camaro.

Betty Giles' blue Nissan had been parked at a grocery store. He'd driven past the store and parked well beyond the entrance, so that he could see her car in the mirror when she emerged from the store, all according to accepted surveillance technique. She'd stayed in the store for more than a half hour—while he'd stayed in his car, baking in the afternoon sun.

About fifteen minutes into the stakeout, he'd seen the black Camaro approaching from the opposite direction, coming sedately toward him. As the Camaro drew even, he'd glanced at the driver—and then looked more sharply. Had it been the same black man he'd seen in Santa Rosa, following Betty Giles and Nick Ames as they left the Starlight Motel? He didn't know, could never be sure. If the witness at Santa Rosa hadn't said the murderer was black, he'd never have even speculated.

But he *had* seen a black man, following Betty Giles and Nick Ames.

And a witness *had* said the murderer was black.

And there *had* been a black man in a black Camaro, driving west on Palm Canyon Road yesterday evening.

"No . . ." She spoke slowly, pensively. "No, I didn't take the deal, not right then, not when we talked the first time. He's not as direct as that, it's not his style. He's a master of indirection, of timing. That first time, he just planted the barb, sowed the seed—" Impatiently, she gestured. "Whatever. Looking back, of course, I realize that he was far from calm. Because, behind that facade, he was possessed. Really possessed—a madman, almost, where art's concerned."

Impatient now, anxious to hear the end of her story, then excuse himself and reconnoiter the motel grounds, he nevertheless realized that he must not press her too closely. Instead, he must continue to methodically prompt her: "You did buy the painting, though. Didn't you?"

As she'd done before, she looked at him for a long,

resigned, deeply decisive moment before, trusting him, she finally nodded. "Yes, I bought it." Another moment of silence passed before she said, "It was Renoir's 'Three Sisters.' It had been stolen from the Louvre almost a year before Ned Frazer showed up."

"My God—" As memory of the news stories slowly crystalized, he shook his head in amazement. *"Renoir?"*

Once more, solemnly, she nodded.

"But it—" He realized that he was leaning across the small Formica table, gripping the table's edge with both hands. "But it's worth a fortune. And it's *stolen*."

She made no response. Instead, as if to punctuate the conversation, perhaps to demonstrate the release she felt, having revealed her secret, she rose, began clearing the table, putting the dirty dishes in the sink. "Coffee? I've got some instant. Decaffeinated instant, actually. I can't drink real coffee after four o'clock."

"Wait. *Wait*—" On his feet, facing her as they stood a few feet from each other, he raised his hand, as if to physically compel her to stand still, pay close attention. "Are you saying that this—this whole thing is about that—the 'Three Sisters'?"

"Partly that. And partly—"

"It's missing? Is that it?"

"No. It's hanging in DuBois' house right now—in a secret room, a room nobody's ever seen but him and me—at least, not after the first painting went up."

"You mean—?" He realized that he was gaping. Helplessly gaping.

"Basically," she said, "that's why he hired me. He didn't need a curator for the paintings he has all over his house. Everything I did was either make-work, or else I was essentially running errands for him. There wasn't anything I did for him that he couldn't have done for himself, or had his servants do—except take care of that room, that tiny gallery within a gallery.

He'd done it for a while, even from his wheelchair. He even cleaned the room, and serviced the humidifier. But he knew it was a lost cause, a rearguard action. Because, when he acquired a painting—a masterpiece—there wouldn't be anyone to take it to the room, no one to hang it. That's what was happening when he decided to buy 'Three Sisters,' you see. Before he could buy it, he had to tell me about the room. There wasn't any other way."

"There're other paintings in the room, then."

She nodded. "Five. There's a Goya, and a Van Gogh, and a Reubens, and a Braque—and a Rembrandt, too. A Rembrandt self-portrait, the one that was stolen from the Hermitage, six years ago."

"Jesus—" Once more, he shook his head. "It's incredible. It's absolutely unbelievable, that he'd put himself in that position, a man like that, with so much to lose. He's—Christ—he's receiving stolen goods. He's a common crook."

"No—" Infinitely weary, she smiled. "No, not a common crook. He's Daniel DuBois. And ordinary laws, meant for ordinary men, don't apply to people like him. You must know that."

"But the risk—"

"He's been taking risks all his life. Laws mean nothing to him. Stock market manipulations, currency violations, it's all part of the game, for him."

"That's white-collar crime—dummy companies, numbered bank accounts, money laundering. I can understand that. Whole countries do that. Panama and Colombia, for instance. But to actually—physically—take possession of a stolen painting, something worth millions, to put himself at that kind of risk—" Bernhardt spread his hands. "I can't understand it."

"It's a compulsion, like drugs. An addiction. That's the only way to understand it. He's possessed by the idea that no one—ever—will be able to see the 'Three Sisters' but him—at least, not during his lifetime. It's like he possesses a part of Renoir, you see. It's power—the ultimate power, the ultimate possession—better than oil wells, or a few castles. They're just steel and stone, after all. And he—"

"But it—it's sick."

"Sure, it's sick. But also understandable, at least to me. The first time I went into that room—the first time I saw those paintings—I was overwhelmed. Physically overwhelmed. There's a small bench, there, in the center of the room. And I had to sit down. I really did."

"You said no one will see the paintings as long as he's alive. What happens when he dies?"

"He'd written out instructions for me, and checks. We'd talked about it, too. For a year after his death, I was to have possession of his house, according to the terms of his will. During that time, I was to make arrangements for the paintings to be sold anonymously, back to the companies that insured them. From there, they'd go to museums."

"Are there other collections—other secret collections?"

"I'm sure there are. There's got to be. I don't know how many major art thefts have been committed over the past ten or twenty years. Let's say fifty. And out of that fifty, I'll bet that less than half were recovered, either by law enforcement or by ransom—insurance settlements, at fifty cents on the dollar. So that leaves twenty-five unaccounted for."

"It leaves twenty," Bernhardt said softly. "If we deduct DuBois' five."

Wearily, she smiled, gestured to the other room. "Do you want to sit in a softer chair?"

Shrugging, he followed her as he said, "There's something I want to do, something you can help me with. But first, tell me about Nick. How'd he fit into all this?"

She had gone into the other room, and was standing beside the queen-size bed. She was looking away from him, her back half turned. Bernhardt saw her shoulders sharply rise and fall as she sighed. Still looking away, she said, "We were together for a year, Nick and I. For whatever reasons, good or bad, we needed each other, depended on each other. I doubt that it would've lasted, though. I don't think we ever would've actually gotten married. Not unless one of us changed, anyhow—or both of us, maybe. But, anyhow—" She sighed again as he stood in the doorway of the kitchen, leaning against the frame, watching her from a distance. "Anyhow, we were together. We ate together, slept together, did things together. And when that happens—when one person lives with another person—they tell each other things. And—" Once more, she broke off. Her arms were folded now; she was standing with her leg touching the bed, as if she needed support. "And so I—I told Nick what I did, what work I did. I didn't tell him right out, not all at once. Because DuBois insisted on secrecy, absolute secrecy. Even before I knew about the 'Three Sisters,' about the locked room, he swore me to secrecy. But Nick kept asking me, over and over, about DuBois, about what kind of a man he was, how he made all that money. It got to be a fixation, I think, about DuBois, about his money. And the more I put him off, the more insistent he got. Once he even asked me to introduce him to DuBois. And I—" Slowly, she sank down on the edge of the bed. Despite his instinctive urge to reconnoiter, explore the darkness outside the cabin, Bernhardt nevertheless realized that she was saying something—confessing to something—that was important to her, and therefore perhaps important to him.

He left the doorway, went to the room's only easy chair, sat so that he could see her face. As he did it, she began speaking again: "I realized then, when he said he wanted to meet DuBois—I realized how far apart we were, really. Our tastes, our interests, everything—they were so different. Because, you see—" Helplessly, she gestured. "Because I couldn't imagine ever introducing them. It—it would've been ludicrous, the two of them, together. But then, of course, as soon as I realized that, I tried to deny it to myself. Maybe that's why I told Nick about the 'Three Sisters.' Subconsciously, anyhow, maybe that's why I did it. Maybe it was guilt—atonement, for what I was thinking about him. Or maybe it was just a slip of the tongue, that started it all. Or maybe, subconsciously, I wanted to confess to someone, to ease my conscience. Because, you see, I'd broken the law. I could've gone to jail, for what I did. When the 'Three Sisters' transaction was actually concluded—when I took possession—there were two men with me, to carry the money. And they both carried guns. One of them had one of those small machine guns, in an attaché case. It—it was like one of those dope transactions, from TV. Except that it was happening to me. *Me*." Hopelessly, helplessly, she shook her head. Sitting forlornly on the edge of the bed, shoulders slumped, hands limp, she was staring down at the floor, her eyes empty.

"So you told Nick the whole story."

She shrugged: an exhausted, defeated lifting of her slack shoulders. "I think, actually, that it started with a slip of the tongue—about the men with guns, in fact, something about them. Nick picked up on that—and guessed some of it, too. So once he knew part of it, there wasn't any point in not telling him the whole thing. And it was a relief, to tell him—tell somebody, anybody."

"Did you tell him about the secret room?"

Numbly, she nodded. "Yes. It was all a—a package deal, really. Once I'd told him about the 'Three Sisters,' the rest came out—spontaneously, it seemed. And, of course, Nick could guess a lot of it. He was very perceptive, really. A lot of people didn't realize that about him."

"So what happened next? Did he try to blackmail DuBois? Is that what happened?"

"Yes—" She nodded once, then nodded again, in another direction, as if she were including a third party in the conversation. Repeating: "Yes . . ."

"And then what happened?"

"Then they tried to kill him. It happened in a shopping mall, in Los Angeles—just a mile or two from my apartment. Incredibly, there were undercover policemen there, on a burglary stakeout. That's all that saved Nick. It was one of those terribly confused scenes, with everybody shooting. It was in the papers, in fact—except that Nick's name wasn't mentioned. But he had to stay overnight at the police station, because they thought he might've been a lookout, for the burglars."

"Did he tell them any different—tell them that he was a target?"

"No. He didn't tell them anything. He played the part of an innocent citizen who just happened to be in the wrong place at the wrong time. Which, of course, he was. And the man who tried to kill him was killed by the police, so that was the end of it. I was frantic, of course, wondering about him, where he'd gone, what happened. I thought he'd been in a traffic accident. They didn't let him make a phone call for hours—not until three o'clock in the morning."

"Had you known, then, that Nick was blackmailing DuBois?"

"No. I didn't know until he came home the next morning, from the police station. He woke me up, and told me to start packing. It—it was a terrible shock. I'll never forget it, those first few minutes, with him hanging over me, shaking me, telling me that they'd tried to kill him, that we had to leave, before they tried again—before they came there, to the apartment, after him. And I—I couldn't seem to understand it, understand what he was saying. I'd only been asleep for a few hours, and I—I felt like I'd been drugged, and he was trying to revive me, get me on my feet. It was unreal. Totally unreal, the whole thing. And all the time I was trying to understand it—why anyone would want to kill him. So then—God, I can still see him—he sat on the foot of the bed, and he told me the whole story. Everything. And then he said that I had a choice—that I could either stay, or I could go with him. I had to decide. Right then."

"Jesus—" Sympathetically, Bernhardt shook his head. "Talk about pressure."

"Yes."

For a moment Bernhardt made no response. Then, taking a calculated risk, he decided to say, "You shouldn't've gone. When you ran, you looked like an accomplice."

"I knew I'd lose him, though. If he left, I knew I'd never see him again. And I couldn't face that. Besides, I thought that, after a few days, I could talk sense into him. Because he was never sure, never absolutely sure, that DuBois sent the killer after him. It could actually have had something to do with the burglary gang—a coincidence, in other words."

"Did he believe that—believe it could've been a coincidence?"

"He—" She bit her lip. "He was starting to believe it, I think. In Santa Rosa, he was starting to believe it. And then they killed him. He got careless—got cabin fever, had to go out, have a few drinks. And they killed him."

"And then you ran."

"Yes . . ." She said it stoically, as if all guilt had been drained, leaving her empty of emotion.

"If you'd been in danger, though—if they'd wanted to kill you—they could've done it. Both times, in Los Angeles and Santa Rosa, they could've done it."

"Logically, you're right. But I wasn't thinking logically. I'm still not."

"What would happen," he asked, "if you were to call up DuBois, tell him that you want to make it up with him?"

Answering, she spoke in a dull, dogged monotone: "He had Nick killed. I can't forget that. I *won't* forget that." Her eyes were lusterless, cast down. The angle of her head, the set of her shoulders, both revealed a malaise that must surely numb the depths of her soul.

"Nick was threatening DuBois," Bernhardt said. "It figures that DuBois would react, do something. He couldn't very well call the police. And he's not the kind of man who's going to roll over and play dead. Besides, paying blackmail is usually a losing proposition. The blackmailer runs out of money, he makes another phone call. Nothing changes."

She made no response, either by word or gesture.

"So what now?" he asked. "What'll you do?"

She tried to smile—unsuccessfully. "Do you mean tomorrow? Or for the rest of my life?"

"Take your pick."

"No need. The answer's the same to both questions. I don't know. I haven't got the faintest idea."

"You've threatened DuBois. Is that right?"

"I said I'd make him pay, for having Nick murdered."

"How do you plan to do that? Are you going to tell the police? The papers?"

240

"I'm not really sure." She said it thoughtfully, speculatively. "I guess, originally, I wanted him to suffer. I wanted him to think about what he'd done—and worry, too, worry about what I'm going to do. He's someone that can't stand uncertainty. He's got to hear the other shoe drop. If it doesn't, he suffers."

"So, in fact, you might never actually tell the law what you're telling me."

"I—I don't know. I just don't know."

"If you *did* tell the police, you'd be taking a chance. Technically, you're an accessory to receiving stolen goods."

She made no reply, gave no sign that she'd heard.

Bernhardt glanced at his watch. The time was eight-thirty. He'd done what he'd come to do—what he'd come six hundred miles to do, what he'd probably spent four hundred dollars to do. He'd found Betty Giles. He'd made sure she knew she could be in danger. He'd consulted with her, advised her. And he'd offered her his protection.

No. Not really. He hadn't really offered her protection, or help. He'd been playing the part of the grand inquisitor, comfortably above the fray, the amiable moralist.

But he hadn't offered to help . . .

. . . and he hadn't told her about the black man in the black Camaro, proceeding so sedately down Palm Canyon Road.

At the thought, he rose to his feet. "Listen, I want to take a look around. And then—" Speculatively, he eyed her as she sat so forlornly on the bed. Earlier in the day, before he'd spoken to her, he'd thought of a strategy, a diversion that might determine whether, in fact, she was really in danger.

"You have a suitcase, don't you?" he asked.

"Yes. Certainly." As if the question surprised her, she raised questioning eyes. "Why?"

"I think there's a way that we can tell whether you're in any danger—any immediate danger."

As if she were indifferent to the possibility, she let a few seconds pass before she said, "How's that?"

"Before I answer the question," he said, "let me give you a little background." He paused, to organize his thoughts. "Now, there're two possibilities. Either there's someone here, watching you—or there's not. Right?"

She nodded. "Right."

"Okay. So the first thing we've got to discover is whether it's true—whether someone's here. Right here. Right now. Agreed?"

"I suppose so."

"Okay. Now, here's my idea—see what you think of it." To compel her attention, he let a beat pass, waiting until she raised her eyes to meet his. "Let's suppose," he said, "that there *is* someone. Let's say he's been in town for a whole day, watching you. Okay?" Encouraging her to join in the game of Let's Pretend, he smiled: a director now, trying to put the novice at her ease, trying to loosen her up, get her smiling, get her mind off herself, off the lines she might fluff, the mistakes she might make. Grimly repeating: "Okay, Betty?"

And, yes, the corners of her mouth had twitched. And, yes, a pale animation had kindled, far back in her dark, somber eyes.

Finally, she nodded. "Yes. Okay."

"All right, then. Now, if he'd been watching you today, he'd've seen you go into town, a little after noon. He might've seen me in town, too, seen us both at the store—you shopping, me parked outside. Of course, actually, I was following you, but he didn't know that.

"So then, he'd've seen us come back here—separately. He'd've seen us hanging around the pool, me writing, you reading, swimming, whatever. Then he'd've seen me making a move on you—introducing myself, smiling, trying to ingratiate myself to you, gain your confidence. The mating game, in other words."

Hesitantly, she nodded.

"He could be watching us right now. If he is, he's probably trying to decide about us, trying to decide what we're doing in here. Let's say he's a hit man, sent by DuBois to kill you." As he said it, he looked carefully at her face, calculating the effect of what he'd just said. There was no visible reaction, no sign of anxiety. Was it the numbness of loss, grief for a dead mate? Was it a death wish, an indifference to death? Or was it simple exhaustion, compounded by loneliness?

Probing, he said, "It's possible you know, that someone's out there. We'd be foolish not to consider the possibility. You must think it could happen. Otherwise, you wouldn't be here—running."

"I guess I was running when I left Santa Rosa. But I wasn't running when I came here. I was looking for—" Searching for the word, she hesitated. Then: "I was looking for peace. That's what I get from the desert. Peacefulness."

"But what happens next, after you leave here?"

"I'm not sure," she said. "San Francisco, maybe—Mother. She's all I've got, really. But wherever I go, I won't be running. That's over."

"What you should do is go back to Los Angeles. You should write a longhand account of what you just told me. You should date it, and get someone to witness it—me, for instance. You should put it in a safe deposit box, and you should give your mother one key. You should tell her to open the box in the event of your death. Copies of your statement should be addressed to the police in Santa Rosa, and the D.A. in Los Angeles—

plus a copy to me, maybe all of them in the box. Then you should tell DuBois what you did. And then you should get yourself a job in a museum, or whatever. You should get on with your life."

"You're probably right." Predictably, she spoke without conviction, without interest.

Compensating, he spoke briskly, with forceful animation: "In the meantime, though, I want to make sure that you're safe, at least for tonight. Tomorrow, if you want to, we can work on that written statement. Then we can leave. Or, at least, I plan to leave. But now, tonight, we've got to take out some insurance. Okay?"

"I—" She frowned. "I don't understand."

"I want to try and find out whether there's anyone out there. I figure it's maybe twenty-five percent that there *is* someone there. And I don't think four-to-one odds are good enough."

As he'd spoken, her eyes had sharpened, her mouth had tightened. But there was no fear visible in her face. Only a kind of resigned curiosity.

"Twenty-five percent?" she repeated.

"According to a witness, Nick was killed by a black man. Call that a fifty-fifty certainty. That's about what witnesses average, especially when they're describing a street crime that took place at night. However, when I was tailing you and Nick, I saw a black man following you in Santa Rosa. It could've been a coincidence, of course. But it changes that fifty-fifty probability, I think, makes it more like, say, seventy-five percent, that a black man killed Nick. Plus—" He hesitated, reluctant to alarm her. But her calm, stolid expression hadn't changed, hadn't faltered. "Plus, this afternoon, while you were shopping, I saw a black man driving a black Camaro. He wasn't following you, but in a situation like this, in a town this size, in the middle of the desert, he wouldn't have to stay on your tail. He wouldn't have to—"

"Was it the same man you saw in Santa Rosa?" Now, perceptibly, she'd grown anxious, apprehensive.

Ruefully, he smiled, shook his head. "I don't know. I hate to say it—because, literally, one of my best friends is black. But the truth is, in a surveillance situation, when you're talking about seeing someone passing in a car, I have trouble identifying a particular black man, distinguishing one from the other."

"'They all look alike.' Is that what you're saying?"

"I'm afraid that's what I'm saying."

As if to excuse his lapse, she nodded. Then: "How're you going to find out whether—" As her eyes shifted involuntarily to the door, she let it go unfinished. *Whether there's someone out there who might kill me*, was the sentence she was finishing in her thoughts.

"It's simple—" Involuntarily, he lowered his voice, leaned forward in his chair. "It'll just take a few minutes."

10

In his own cabin, Bernhardt walked to the window and carefully checked the overlap of the floor-to-ceiling draperies. Satisfied that no one could see inside the room, he took one of his two suitcases from the small closet. He lifted the suitcase to the bed, dug in his pocket for a key ring, and opened the suitcase. From under a miscellaneous collection of clothing he lifted out a bundle that had been wrapped in an oil-stained sweatshirt and secured with three strips of green cloth, each tied with a bow knot. He untied the knots, spread the sweatshirt on the bed, and took the shotgun in both hands. He'd bought the gun on impulse, for twenty-five dollars, at a garage sale. It was a double-barreled Browning, originally an expensive gun that had obviously been neglected over the years. He'd taken the gun to Jack Finney's mountain cabin. With some trepidation, at first using a large square of thick steel to shield his face, he'd test fired both barrels. Satisfied that the breech was tight, he and Jack had shot up a whole box of twelve-gauge shells, firing at tin cans weighed with rocks that one man threw into the air while the other man fired. Afterward, they'd calculated that their hits were less than twenty-five percent. And, yes, both their shoulders had turned black and blue the next day.

He'd taken the gun home, cleaned it, sprayed it with WD 40 and put it in his closet. The next day he'd bought a hacksaw. Feeling like a criminal, he'd disassembled the gun. Using a kitchen chair as an improvised sawhorse, holding down the barrels with his foot, he'd spent more than an hour sawing eighteen inches off the barrels. Then he'd sawed six inches off the stock, and two inches off the forestock. In two hours he'd fashioned an illegal weapon that, loaded with buckshot, could literally blow a man apart at close range. Broken down into its three parts, it could easily be carried in a grocery bag. Assembled, it could be concealed under a jacket, or even inside a pants leg. In two years, this was only the second time he'd ventured to take the gun outside his apartment.

Rummaging again, he found the plastic bag containing six rounds of twelve-gauge buckshot. He broke open the gun, slipped two shells into the chambers, and snapped the gun closed, carefully setting the safety, and testing it. As he slipped the four extra shells into his pocket, he glanced at his watch. The time was exactly nine o'clock. In five minutes, Betty would leave her cabin.

11

As he always did, Justin Powers had committed the route to memory: Interstate 5 to Oceanside, Route 78 across the mountains to S-3, which he would follow until it dead-ended at Borrego Springs. Years ago, when he'd been a student at Stanford, during the spring break, four fraternity brothers had made this trip. But at Borrego Springs they'd turned east, toward the Salton Sea, then on to Palm Springs, where they'd rented a motel room and proceeded to get drunk. Rick Foster, who'd been profiled in last Friday's edition of the *Wall Street Journal*, had proposed that they find two whores, and take turns. Bravely drinking, they'd all vowed to chip in, then screw their brains out. But when Rick had gotten sick and then passed out, the idea had died aborning.

Ahead, he saw the signs marking the junction of Route 78 and S-3, the two-lane highway that led out of the mountains and down to the desert floor. It had been fifteen minutes, at least, since he'd met a car; the dashboard clock read 10:15 P.M. As he'd calculated, he would arrive in Borrego Springs about eleven.

But to what purpose?

Following orders, always the good soldier, he'd done as DuBois had commanded: hurried home, changed into casual clothes, packed an overnight bag, and taken the twenty-five thousand dollars from his bedroom safe.

In less than an hour after leaving DuBois, he'd been on the freeway, driving south. At first he'd been eager to obey DuBois' order. If he could find Fisher, call him off, then that was an end to it. Even if the worst happened, and Betty made good on her threat to talk to the police, her target would be DuBois, not him. So it had seemed, at first, that he had everything to gain, making this trip. There would be no more murders, no further danger, if he could find Fisher.

But then, as the miles passed, the doubts began to surface—and then began to compound.

Arriving late at night, a stranger in a dark, strange town, how could he ever hope to find Fisher? He didn't know which motel Fisher had chosen, or what kind of a car he was driving. His only hope, therefore, was to actually see Fisher, a slim chance even in the daytime hours. And to make inquiries would connect them, he and the hired hit man. Inquiries would call attention to both of them, therefore endanger them.

As the junction came closer, he checked his mirrors, eased off on the accelerator, swung the big Mercedes into the left turn. This highway, S-3, was more difficult than Route 78: two narrow lanes clinging to the side of a small mountain, spiraling gently down. Calculating the curves ahead, sensitive to the sway of the car, he cautiously slowed to forty.

Time: 10:27.

Already, it could have happened.

Fisher could have arrived at Borrego in the late afternoon. He could have driven to the Ram's Head, where Betty Giles was staying. He would have familiarized himself with the town, with the roads in and out, possibly with the habits of the local police. Then, under cover of darkness, he could have killed her, then escaped into the mountains that, according to the map, surrounded the town on three sides.

At that moment, police could be puzzling over the body, searching for clues, interrogating witnesses.

Enter Justin Powers, the ultimate errand boy. Salary: a quarter of a million a year—plus bonuses, plus stock options, plus all the other perks: the club memberships, the travel cards, the corporate gifts. Year to year, he earned more than any of his friends.

Friends?

Did he have any, really?

Earned?

Was that the word, the legitimate word?

No, not earned. Rather, he collected his lackey's reward, his payment for services well and faithfully rendered, his five-figure tips.

Even when he made his own money in the market, separate from DuBois' money, he did it by buying whatever DuBois bought, selling whatever DuBois sold. Ten years ago, his dependency on DuBois sometimes secretly shamed him. Once, drunk, having just concluded an insider trading deal for DuBois, having dutifully offered the great man his craven gratitude for a ten-thousand-dollar tip, he'd considered blackmail. He'd been in bed with a party girl, a high-class hooker, an amenity provided by the third party in the three-cornered insider deal. Sylvia had been in Philadelphia visiting her parents, and the hooker had been hired for the whole night. After they'd done it—after he'd finally come, helped along by her knowing fingers and busy tongue—she'd gone to sleep beside him, gently snoring. Strangely, even though he was drunk, he hadn't been able to sleep. Instead, lying on his back, staring at the ceiling, listening to the hooker snore, he'd begun to fantasize. In the fantasy he began by selling his stocks and bonds, all of them. The proceeds, of course, would go to Switzerland, into his numbered account, leaving only a hundred thousand in Los Angeles, for Sylvia. Carrying another hundred thousand in cash and traveler's checks, he would fly to Brazil, secretly. He would allow a month to pass, perhaps two months. Then he would begin writing the letters to DuBois—extortion letters. Each letter would detail a crooked stock deal, or a currency violation, or a land swindle. And each letter would reap a golden harvest.

It was a fantasy that was to regularly recur over the next several years, whenever he'd had too much to drink. Until, finally, his doctor had provided the resolution. If he didn't quit drinking, his doctor said, his liver could fail. And when he'd done it, managed to finally quit drinking, the fantasies had faded, leaving him with the realization that he would never—ever—get the best of Daniel DuBois.

But Betty Giles had done it. Somehow, she'd done it—she and her boyfriend. A forty-thousand-dollar-a-year assistant and her ne'er-do-well boyfriend with the cowboy boots and the greasy hair had actually done it, actually shaken the throne.

But how?

How?

12

During the last two hours and twenty minutes the sheriff's car had driven past the Ram's Head twice—once before dark, when he'd been parked on a side road, and once after dark, when he'd been parked where he was parked now, about a hundred yards south of the motel, on Borrego Springs Road. The second time, pointedly, the deputy had slowed, looked him over, nodded politely, and continued on his way, patrolling.

On the next round, if he hadn't moved, the deputy would stop, check him out. Meaning that, if he hadn't already done it, the deputy would fix the face and the car firmly in his mind, along with whatever story he'd told.

Meaning that it was time to move, time to drive ahead, turn right, make a U-turn, park on another secondary road, facing Borrego Springs Road, close enough to let him see the motel driveway. He would stay there, in the car, for the next two hours. Then he would park the car on the road that ran behind the motel. He would park in the place he'd already picked. He'd picked the place when it was still light, in the late afternoon. It was near a dry wash, where trees grew twenty feet high, so the Camaro couldn't be seen unless the sheriff passed within a few yards of it. He would take everything with him—the Woodsman, and the .357 and the UZI, even the ice pick. On foot, he'd find a place to hide, a place that would let him see two sides of her cabin, the front door and the south side, with the window. And then he would wait.

He turned the ignition key, brought the powerful engine to life, switched on his headlights. Putting the gear selector in drive, he let the car move slowly forward, idling. The motel driveway was just ahead, with its blue neon sign and the lighted phone booth closeby. If anyone was watching, they would think he was driving at this speed so that he could check out the motel, see if there was a vacancy, without actually stopping. Now he could see the lanai—the illuminated swimming pool— the graveled track that led back among the trees and the cacti to her cabin. Low pathway lights illuminated the track, and her car. From this angle, briefly, he could see her cabin. He could—

Her cabin door was swinging open. She was standing in the lighted doorway.

Smoothly, he brought the Camaro to a stop. He must do it, must risk it, must stop here blocking the entrance, long enough to see what she would do next.

Because she carried two suitcases, one in each hand.

Now she was lowering the suitcases to the ground, turning, reaching inside the open doorway of the cabin as the lights inside the cabin went out.

He moved his right foot from the brake to the accelerator, pressed gently, sent the Camaro slowly forward—the tourist, still shopping, deciding to look over another motel before making his decision. Because it was important, very important, to keep playing the part, keep acting, keep thinking like someone else.

William Fisher, successful black real estate man—

—on vacation in his Camaro, celebrating a big deal he'd just made in Los Angeles, the biggest deal he'd ever made.

For William Fisher, black was beautiful, success was everywhere, all around him, living with him, breathing with him, *being* with him.

Behind him, out of sight, she was probably stowing her suitcases, getting in her car, settling herself behind the wheel. Checkout time was noon. So she was leaving money behind, starting out at night, at ten-thirty, driving off into the desert darkness.

Was it a problem?

Or a plus?

A big, fat plus?

Whichever direction she took out of town, she'd be driving on a two-lane highway. A dark, empty two-lane desert highway. If she went east, across the desert floor toward Palm Springs, she'd be driving alone on a straight, level road. He would follow her for a few miles, keeping well back. Then he'd roll the window down. He'd pick his spot and begin accelerating, as if he intended to pass her. He'd make sure the UZI was loaded, with a cartridge in the chamber, cocked, with the safety off. The gun would be lying beside him on the seat. He'd draw even with her, lift the UZI one-handed, give her a burst. If he could, he'd stop, back up to the crash site, get out of the Camaro, give her another burst, for insurance. Then he'd continue east. He'd leave his clothes and one suitcase—William Fisher's clothes and suitcase—in his motel room, unclaimed. He hated to do it, hated to lose his things, hated the idea of giving the police William Fisher, after all these years. But he didn't have a choice. For him, the next five minutes could mean everything.

If she drove south, or north, the same plan would work: follow her for a few miles, then move in. But if she went west, toward the nearby mountains, he'd have to do it quicker, just a few miles out of town, while the highway was still straight.

A quarter mile north of the Ram's Head sign, he switched off his headlights, pulled to the side of the road, put the Camaro in park. He unbuckled his safety belt, turned in his seat, lifted the saddle-leather suitcase from the backseat to the front seat, opened it, took out the UZI.

• • •

With the sawed-off rolled again in the sweatshirt, Bernhardt stood in the shadow of his cabin, holding the gun with both hands. To the casual observer, he could be carrying a bundle of anything: old clothing, perhaps, or something fragile, wrapped for protection—a computer component, or a surveyor's transit, or a camera.

If the police found him with a sawed-off shotgun, loaded, he could be arrested and charged with a felony, never mind that he had a permit to carry the revolver, holstered at his belt. So, to improve the odds, he should lock the shotgun in the trunk of his rental car, where the police couldn't look without probable cause.

But if he needed the gun, needed it in extremis, the time it took him to unlock the trunk could be a deadly eternity.

Still standing in the shadows, he heard the sound of a door opening. Fifty feet away, Betty was emerging from her cabin, carrying two suitcases. He watched her turn out the cabin lights, and close the door. She was walking to her Nissan, parked in its allotted parking space, the space outlined in whitewashed rocks. As they agreed, she was putting the suitcases in the car, in the trunk. Now she was slamming the lid of the trunk and walking to the driver's door. He stood motionless, watching as she got into the car, started it, switched on the headlights, began backing slowly out of the parking space. Once on the one-way driveway, she would pass among most of the other cabins before she arrived at the motel entrance. She would turn right on Borrego Springs Road, toward town. She would drive slowly, as if she were letting the Nissan's engine warm up before bringing it up to highway speed.

Once she'd cleared the motel entrance and her headlights were no longer visible through the screen of cacti and cottonwood that marked the northern property line of the Ram's Head, he would get in his own car. He would edge out of the motel grounds and follow her, leaving a mile, at least, between their cars. Reaching "the circle" she would turn east, toward the airport. Slowing his car, he would plan to leave the circle about the time she reached the airport, three miles to the east.

Still holding the shotgun with both hands, standing in deep shadow, he watched her as she drove around the meandering driveway, then drove past the pool to the motel's entrance. He saw her stoplights wink on, then off. Now, slowly, she was turning north, as they'd planned.

With his eyes on the entrance, now empty, he waited while he counted to a hundred. During that time, nothing passed on Borrego Springs Road except for the Nissan. He'd been breathing very shallowly, he realized, as he'd been counting, so that now it was necessary to take a deep, fateful breath before, moving quickly, he stepped to his car, unlocked the trunk, put the shotgun in, nestled in its sweatshirt wrapping against the spare tire. He slammed down the trunk lid, tested the catch, then moved to the driver's door. He opened the door, started the engine, and backed carefully out of his rock-bordered parking place.

• • •

Ahead, her blue car was entering the circle. In seconds, he would know: east, toward the open desert, north toward a mountain road that led up to a high plateau, or west, into the foothills and low mountains that separated the desert from the Los Angeles basin. He glanced in the mirror. Behind him, Borrego Springs Road was still deserted. Ahead, he saw the Nissan, turning out of the circle to the east. She was taking the two-lane highway that led past the airport and out across the desert toward the Salton Sea, and Indio, and finally north to Palm Springs. Of her three choices, this was the best for him, the easiest. It was good that he'd bought the maps and atlases, and taken the time to study them. Because planning—calm, careful planning—made the difference, all the difference. In a city, it was important to know every street, every alley, every doorway. In a city, two men carrying a mattress down a flight a stairs could make the difference, all the difference—life or death, in seconds. It had happened to him, in New York—two men and a mattress, blocking his escape from a third-floor walkup. Later, he'd laughed about it. Much later.

Slightly reducing his speed, he eased the Camaro into the right lane as he glanced again into the mirror. Now he saw headlights. In the last thirty seconds, someone had turned into Borrego Springs Road, and was following him toward town.

Following him?

Or just driving in the same direction?

Which?

Asking the question of himself, he felt his jaw tighten, the first sign of tension, of possible trouble. Because thoughts must be controlled, tightly controlled. Starting now, right now, thoughts must be controlled. So he must rethink it, switch it around, right now, before the rat's nibble of panic could begin. *Change it around, Willis, get it right:* No one was following him. Someone was behind him, yes. But not following him, not *really* following, not the law, not anyone who mattered. Two headlights in the mirror, that's all that had happened, all that had changed.

He was in the circle now, driving slowly. Already, the Nissan was almost a mile to the east: two taillights, pinpoints of red, alone in the blackness of the desert night. As he turned right, out of the circle, he glanced again in the mirror. Of course, the other car was following him into the circle. But the odds were only one in three that the other car would turn to the east.

Out of the circle, on Palm Canyon Road, he pressed the accelerator as he glanced at the speedometer. The town limit was still a mile ahead: maximum speed, thirty-five, until he reached the limits. She was more than a mile ahead of him, driving steadily. Beyond the airport, he would begin to close the distance between them.

But behind him, the headlights were still in his mirror.

There were three of them now: the Nissan, the Camaro, and the unknown car, all of them going east, about a mile apart.

There was a restaurant at the airport, one of the two restaurants that were open, not counting the French restaurant, north of town. The restaurant at the airport was called The Crosswinds, and so was the bar beside it, in the same building. Two hours ago, making his last tour before he'd settled down to watch the Ram's Head, he'd looked in through the window of the bar, and seen three people, two men and a woman. Townsfolk, obviously, not vacationers.

So the car behind him could be going to The Crosswinds. Or the car could be filled with teenagers, driving out in the desert to do a little drinking, a little screwing under the stars.

Or it could be the sheriff, on patrol.

Or a house painter, visiting a friend.

Or a Mexican family, going to—

Ahead, the Nissan's left turn indicator was flashing. She was slowing, beginning a turn across the highway and into the parking lot of The Crosswinds.

● ● ●

When he'd seen the driver of the parked car switch on his lights and begin following the Nissan, Bernhardt had instinctively lifted his foot from the accelerator, dropped back.

Was the car between him and Betty a Camaro? In the darkness, at this distance, he couldn't be sure. And to draw closer could risk everything.

Risk the plan . . .

Risk their lives.

257

• • •

She slowed, checked the mirrors, signaled for a left turn into the small parking lot that served both the airport and the restaurant.

Soon—in minutes—they would know.

• • •

Seeing her turn into the parking lot, Bernhardt was conscious of a small, secret surge of primal excitement, an elemental rush. The first time he'd felt it, this primitive quickening, he'd been shaken. Had he spent a lifetime in conscious pursuit of the aesthetic while, in his unconscious, the beast within was straining at its chains?

The first time he'd felt it, this exhilaration, he'd recognized the sensation for what it was: the simple pleasure of the chase, whether or not the prey was brought to ground. Only later did he realize that the beast craved more than mere titillation.

The town's last intersection lay just ahead, a four-way stop midway between the circle and the airport. Beyond the intersection, on the right, were the school grounds: three buildings surrounded by playing fields, with a parking lot large enough to accommodate a half-dozen school buses. He stopped for the intersection. Then, under way again, he quickly switched off his lights, turned into the school's parking lot, stopped the car close beside a line of cedar trees that would conceal his car from anyone coming from the east. Leaving the engine running, he inched the car forward to the edge of the treeline's protecting shadow. A car was approaching from the east, from his right, coming fast. Was it Betty, so soon? They'd agreed that she should remain at The Crosswinds for two minutes, lights out, before she drove back into town. He watched the headlights, saw the car begin to sharply slow for the four-way stop, only fifty yards to his left as he faced the road. The car was a large, dark sedan, not the Nissan. And now headlights were coming from his left, from town. It was a pickup truck that only slowed for the intersection, quickly accelerating now, eastbound. From inside the truck, through open windows, came the blare of rock music.

• • •

Drawing abreast of The Crosswinds, he slowed to twenty-five, as slow as he dared. His peripheral vision was good, something he'd used to his advantage, one reason he was the best, the most expensive. So he could pretend to look at the road ahead while he watched the Nissan as it pulled to a stop in the restaurant's parking lot, headlights switched off. The parking lot was dimly lit, but he could see her sitting behind the steering wheel. Was she combing her hair, collecting her purse before she went inside? If he was parked beside her now, in the empty space beside her, to her left, he could simply slip over to the passenger seat, lower the window, raise the Woodsman with its silencer, do the job, pop pop pop. But the seconds were passing—and the Woodsman was still in the suitcase, no clip in the handle, nothing. So, the prisoner of his own plan, he must continue driving straight ahead, at least for a mile or two, still driving slowly. Then he would make a U-turn, drive to The Crosswinds, make sure her car was empty, make sure she was inside the bar. He'd park the Camaro in the parking lot beside the restaurant, where three or four cars were already parked. He would park—and he would plan, make another plan, one more plan—one last plan.

As he drove, he kept his eyes on the outside mirror until the restaurant building cut off his view of the parking lot. Then, quickly, he shifted his attention to the rearview mirror. The mirror was black. Whoever had been following him had turned off, probably at the four-way stop near the city limits.

• • •

She looked both ways, backed out of the parking space, turned onto the highway as she switched on her headlights. In both directions, ahead and behind, the highway was deserted.

Ostensibly deserted. Not actually deserted.

Because, back at the four-way stop, Alan Bernhardt was waiting, lights out, hidden.

And in the other direction, somewhere to the east, lights out, the murderer could be waiting, too—waiting for her next move.

Bernhardt hadn't told her his whole plan, his strategy, not really. But his reasoning was transparently simple. First, he wanted to determine whether, in fact, the anonymous murderer had found her, tracked her down. If that had happened, then Bernhardt might try to help her.

If it hadn't happened—if she was safe—then she would do as he'd told her. She would write it all out, tell her mother what she'd done, put the envelope in her safe deposit box, sealed and dated, to be opened in the event of her death.

They could get through this night together, she and Alan Bernhardt—the actor who eschewed the dramatic, the quiet, thoughtful man, so gentle, so self-effacing, and yet so resolute, so solid, so determined. Somehow, they would get through. Then, tomorrow, she would begin the process of reassembling the shattered fragments of her life. The days, the weeks, the years, would pass, all the empty years, the years of longing, of loneliness. She knew this present ache would subside. She knew that eventually Nick's image would fade from her thoughts. But she also knew that as his image faded, she would be diminished.

• • •

Quickly, Bernhardt switched off the engine, took the keys from the ignition, swung open the door. Careful to keep his eyes on the highway, he unlocked the trunk, took out the sweatshirt-wrapped shotgun. He closed the lid of the trunk, slipped behind the wheel, closed the driver's door. As he was bending across the seat to put the bundle on the floor, he heard the sound of an approaching car, saw the intermittent flash of headlights through the screen of cedar trees, coming from the east. The car was slowing for the intersection as it cleared the line of trees, came into full view on the road before him.

It was the blue Nissan.

He thrust a key into the ignition switch, twisted, brought his engine to life. Gently, he touched the accelerator, revving the engine to guard against loading up, flooding.

As the Nissan accelerated out of the stop, Bernhardt began slowly counting. At the count of one hundred, if the Camaro hadn't appeared, he would switch on his headlights, venture out onto the highway, drive to the circle, finally to the motel, following Betty Giles at a distance. Then he would knock on Betty's door and invite himself in for a drink.

• • •

There were two possibilities. Only two. Either she'd done it on purpose, planned it—or else she hadn't planned it, hadn't done it on purpose.

She'd put her suitcases in the car, two suitcases. Meaning that she was leaving town. Why?

Why?

Was she scared, and running? Or was she just moving on, leaving this town for another town? Earlier in the day, he'd seen her in the phone booth. Could she have been warned?

She'd driven to the airport, parked, waited until he'd come to a stop beside the highway, more than a mile east, out in the desert, out of sight behind a low rise.

Then she'd started the car, gone back the way she'd come. Why?

Why?

Had she simply changed her mind—decided to leave, then decided not to leave, decided to go back to the motel, wait until morning? Was it as simple as that?

Ahead, the Nissan's taillights were winking as she slowed for the four-way stop. Only a half-mile separated their cars. The mile-long stretch of road from the four-way west to the circle was deserted. The UZI was on the seat beside him, cocked, with the safety off, a cartridge in the chamber, ready. One burst—two seconds—and it would be over. Everything.

As if the thought had turned to action, his foot was pressing harder on the accelerator. The engine surged, the car leaped forward—

—just as, from the circle, a headlight beam was curving, steadying, coming directly toward him, a mile ahead. Meaning that he couldn't do it, not now, not with a car coming toward him on a two-lane road.

Still automatically, his engine came back to idle; the Camaro was slowing for the four-way stop. Once more, one more time, his body had taken over from his mind, made the right decision. It was like an override, everything automatic: a machine, making the decisions. Or an animal, going on instinct.

"You've got reflexes like a cat," Venezzio had said once. *"Just like a big cat. A tiger."* He could still remember the pride he'd felt, hearing Venezzio say it.

• • •

Even before the Camaro actually appeared, Bernhardt's heart had begun to race as the headlights had shown up, a half mile behind the Nissan. And now, incredibly, the Camaro was less than a hundred feet ahead of his car, the manifestation of a fear that had miraculously materialized, the thought that had become reality, a clear and present danger. It was as if Bernhardt had designed a fictional computer image and pressed the computer's button and watched as the car and the driver had come to life in the empty screen, a perfect match. Surreal green letters might appear on a black screen: *This is your killer's car. This is your killer, the black man behind the wheel. Soon, he will attack.*

Because in minutes—moments—as soon as Betty turned the Nissan into the city center circle and then turned out of the circle toward the south, returning to the motel, the killer would suspect that he'd been tricked, that he was under suspicion.

And Bernhardt's car, also turning into the Ram's Head driveway, would confirm it.

The Camaro was accelerating now; in another few seconds it would disappear, cut off by an angle of the school building on Bernhardt's left.

So, on cue, a reluctant actor trapped by his own script, he must now enter the action, begin playing his part.

He took his foot from the brake pedal and placed it gently on the accelerator. As the car began moving slowly forward, he put his left hand on the switch that controlled the headlights. His hand was trembling.

• • •

Ahead, the Nissan was turning into the Ram's Head entrance. Behind him, headlights were curving out of the circle, following him.

Was it the sheriff's car, behind him?

Could they have gotten to Carter, whoever he was, and arrested him for the Santa Rosa murder? Could Carter have turned him, to get a deal?

Had the Los Angeles police called the sheriff? Could the sheriff have contacted the woman, told her to put her suitcases in the Nissan, drive out to the airport, suck him in, then drive back to the motel, still with him following, exposing him?

If it had happened, if Carter had turned him, then there would be more than one car, more than just one car. There would be five cars filled with police: deputy sheriffs and state police. They'd be hiding in the motel grounds, cowboys and Indians, the fucking wild west.

He glanced at the speedometer. Yes, he was driving at a steady thirty-five, exactly the speed limit here. On his left, the motel entrance was coming up fast, too fast. He lifted his foot from the accelerator, let compression slow him down, no brake lights showing. Minute-to-minute, second-to-second, the angles were changing as the motel office came into his line of vision, and the lanai, and the floodlit pool, no one swimming—and the Nissan parked in its regular parking place, lights out, the Nissan and only one other car, a guest's car, nothing changed.

Now the Camaro had carried him beyond the entrance, cutting off his line of sight. At the next intersection, he would turn left, then left again, bringing him behind the motel grounds. If they were hidden among the motel cabins, with their M16s and their riot guns and their vests, he'd see their cars. In the desert, so empty, they couldn't hide their cars. Not in the few minutes it had taken him to drive out to the airport and then return to the Ram's Head, they couldn't hide their cars.

• • •

Should he follow the Camaro out into the desert? The Camaro was faster than his car, much faster. He would—

Ahead, at the first intersection beyond the motel entrance, the Camaro was turning left. Immediately its headlights disappeared behind the motel's buildings, flickered intermittently between low-growing trees and high-growing cacti—then disappeared again.

If the black man turned left again, behind the motel, parked, got out of the car, stepped over the low split rail fence that surrounded the motel grounds, crept through the desert flora to her cabin, he could break down Betty Giles' door, kill her, and escape, all within minutes—one minute, two minutes.

Quickly, Bernhardt turned the wheel sharply left, braked to a stop in the motel's driveway, beside the small neon sign. He swung open the driver's door and walked to the phone booth: five long, urgent strides. As he walked, he kept his gaze on the head-high oleanders that divided the motel grounds from the road. Growing only a few feet from the phone booth, cutting off his view of the cabins, the oleanders would offer a killer perfect cover. But he must take the chance, must use the phone, his only hope now. Because the telephone system inside the cabins was inoperative, still being repaired.

Inside the lighted booth, a helpless target for anyone concealed nearby, desperately scanning the darkness, he lifted the receiver, listened for a dial tone, touch-toned 911. The dial tone ceased when he touched the "9," began again when he touched the "1." The line began ringing: three rings, four—five rings. From the south, headlights were coming fast; a large sedan hurtled past, toward town. And from the north, other lights were approaching, two pairs of headlights. They were—

"—help you?" It was a woman's voice: a sleepy-sounding voice.

"Yes. I—this is an emergency. I want the sheriff's office. My name is Alan Bernhardt. I'm a private investigator, from San Francisco. And I've—"

"—are you calling from, please?"

"I'm calling from Borrego Springs, at the Ram's Head Motel, from a phone booth there. And I've got to—"

"—moment, please."

He heard the hollow-sounding clicks as she made the connection and another voice came on the line. It was a recorded voice, speaking in metallic officialese:

"You've reached the San Diego County Sheriff's office, at Borrego Springs, California. We're out on patrol right now, but we'll be checking for messages every fifteen to thirty minutes. So please tell us the nature of your report, or problem, and leave your address and phone number when you hear the tone. Also, leave your name. Speak slowly and distinctly, and take your time. If any further assistance is required you can call the California Highway Patrol, located at Indio, California. Their number is—"

Indio—forty or fifty miles to the north. Bernhardt waited for the message to conclude, and the beep to sound. Then: "Yes, this is Alan Bernhardt speaking. I'm a licensed private investigator from San Francisco. I'm registered at the Ram's Head Motel, and I've got reason—good reason—to believe that one of the guests here, Betty Giles, in cabin number seven, could be in danger. The phones at the motel aren't working, so please come to cabin number seven, at the Ram's Head. We'll be there, the two of us, waiting for you. And hurry. Please hurry."

He replaced the phone on its hook, and returned to the car. The driver's door was still open, and the engine was still running.

And on the floor, on the passenger's side, was the oil-stained sweatshirt, bundled around the shotgun.

• • •

She set the night chain, took the empty suitcases to the closet, put one suitcase on the floor, one on the shelf.

Bernhardt hadn't told her what would happen now, after they returned. He'd told her, in detail, what to do, where, when: drive to The Crosswinds, park, switch off the lights, wait two minutes. Switch on the lights, start the car, drive back to town, back to the motel. Take the suitcases inside, lock the door. Wait.

Obediently, she'd done as he'd asked, not questioning him. But she knew, of course, the purpose of the plan. She knew he suspected someone was following her. But, strangely, she hadn't asked him for details. And, strangely, the possibility that a killer was out there hadn't really troubled her.

In everyone's life there were moments when death lost its sting, and the void beckoned. When she was younger, a teenager, she'd often wished she'd never been born. But during those years anything, it seemed, could plunge her into deepest despair: a bad grade in school, a trivial argument with her mother—a giggling group of girls in the high-school hallway, avoiding her eyes as she approached. And the wish not to have been born, she'd once read, was only one step removed from—

A knock sounded: two raps in quick succession. Quickly, she strode to the door.

"Yes?"

"It's Alan, Betty. Let me in."

As she slid the night chain from its slot and turned the knob, she was aware that the sound of his voice was evocative, suddenly something special. Only a few hours had passed since he'd introduced himself, given her his card, showed her his license. But in those few hours, incredibly, he'd placed himself between her and—

—and what?

Death?

Before he came inside he looked carefully behind

him, then to the right and left. Then, quickly, he entered the cabin. He was carrying a bundle, which he put on the bed and began to unwrap as she relocked the door and slid the night chain into place. When she turned to face him, he was holding a gun in his hands: a short, obscene-looking gun, with two short barrels. His smile was rueful, gently apologetic. His eyes, too, were soft and gentle: the poet, playing at this warrior's game, uncertain of his role—and sensitive, certainly, to the sudden fear he must see in her face.

"I'm not sure," he said, "but I think we could have a problem."

As if she were a patient who'd just received a doctor's death sentence diagnosis, she felt her knees weaken, felt her solar plexus contract, felt her center go suddenly hollow. There were only two chairs in the room: an easy chair and a straight-backed chair. She reached for the straight-back, and moved to sit in it.

"No—wait." He put the gun on the bed and gestured for her to sit in the easy chair. "Sit there. I want to use this."

Obeying, she watched him jam the chair under the door's knob, then watched him check the draperies, tightly drawn across both the room's windows, one of them a picture window beside the door, the other a small, high window above the bed. Now he strode into the bathroom. The tiny, head-high frosted glass window above the toilet was too small for a man to climb through. Leaving the window open a few inches, he half closed the bathroom door and sat on the edge of the bed to face her, verifying that it would be impossible to shoot through the bathroom window and the half-opened door and hit either of them.

"Did you see him?" she asked. "The black man—did you see him?"

"I saw *a* black man," he said, emphasizing the single

article. "He was driving a black Camaro—the same car I saw earlier today. It was probably the same man I saw earlier, too. But I don't know whether it was the same man I saw in Santa Rosa." Apologetically, he spread his hands. "I just don't. The car was different. But that doesn't mean anything."

"He did follow me out to the airport, though. Just like you planned for him to do."

"Yes, he followed you. Both ways. Out to The Crosswinds and back."

"And now—" Irresistibly, her eyes were drawn toward the picture window. "Now he's out there, somewhere."

Bernhardt sighed, shook his head. "I don't know, Betty. I just don't know. I called the sheriff's office, and left a message. I told them to come by here, as soon as possible. I told them it's an emergency."

"The phones—" She looked at the useless telephone, beside the bed. "If only we had a phone."

"All we could do is call the sheriff, or the state police. But I imagine that, since this is the sheriff's jurisdiction, he'd have to check it out first, before the state police would get involved. That's the way the police operate—by jurisdictions."

"But if it's an emergency . . ."

"It's not an emergency until something happens, or unless we have proof—either proof, or pull. And I don't really have either."

"But you're a private investigator."

He grimaced. "As far as most policemen are concerned, a private investigator is nothing but a pain in the ass."

She tried to smile—but failed.

• • •

He set the UZI's safety, then held the gun with his left hand while he rested his right hand on the top rail of the split rail fence. The fence was waist high, just high enough to make him put one foot on the first rail before he could safely, silently, climb over the fence. Cautiously, he placed his right foot on the bottom rail, testing its strength. He would—

From his right came the sharp, sudden sound of something scurrying through the underbrush—an animal, instantly gone. Earlier, he'd seen jackrabbits: two of them, bounding through the sagebrush. The rabbits were the first wild animals he'd ever seen. Twenty-eight years old, and he'd never seen a jackrabbit. Rats, yes. Thousands of rats. But no rabbits.

Again, he set his hand, set his foot, found his balance—and stepped over the fence, one giant step, and he was back on the ground, crouching low. Her cabin was straight ahead, on a direct line with the swimming pool. From her side window came a shaft of pale yellow light. A second cabin, to his left, was dark, with no car in its parking spot. Another cabin, to his right, was also dark. Beside the cabin to his right, a car was parked: a Reliant, driven by the man she'd been with earlier, the tall, dark-haired man she'd taken into her cabin—

—and into her bed, now?

Where had he been, the dark-haired man, while Betty Giles was sucking him in, faking him out? Could he have been in the car behind, the headlights he'd seen in his mirror? He should have found out. If possible, he should have found out. He should have parked the Camaro as soon as he'd turned off Borrego Springs Road and driven behind the motel grounds. He should have waited for the car that was following him to pass—or not pass. He could have—

Another rustling in the underbrush, this time closer: a soft, sinister rustling.

A snake? A rattlesnake, five feet long, in front of him, inches from his foot? If he stepped on it, and was bitten, he could be dead in an hour. And snakes came out at night. He'd heard the motel manager warning a woman not to walk in the desert at night. There weren't as many rattlesnakes in the desert as there were in other places, places with more water, the manager had said. But the rattlers here were bigger, deadlier—diamond backs, the worst rattlers of all.

The thought had stopped him, straightened him from his stalker's crouch, left him helpless, wet with sudden, shameful sweat. In daylight, he would be safe. In daylight, he could see a snake, walk around it. But now, in the dark, he was—

Headlights were swinging off Borrego Springs Road, into the motel's entrance. A car stopped in front of the motel office. As the headlights died and the door swung open, he saw light bars on the car's roof.

The police!

Quickly he stepped behind a head-high desert bush as the policeman strode through a pool of light to the door of the motel office. As he watched, Dodge touched the .357 holstered at his belt on the left side, touched the Woodsman with its silencer that hung beneath his left armpit, suspended in its own special holster. An ice pick in its leather scabbard was at his belt, on his right side, and beside it a Buck knife, razor sharp. Everything was carried next to his skin, concealed by his loose-fitting shirt.

Everything but the UZI, too big to hide. If a policeman saw him with the UZI, it was shoot or be shot—kill or be killed.

The policeman was stepping back from the door of the office as a man came out—the hotel manager. As they talked, the two men turned together, facing Betty Giles' cabin. The manager raised his arm, pointing. The policeman nodded briskly, turned, and strode toward the cabin. He walked confidently, with long strides, looking straight ahead: a spit-and-polish cop, doing his duty.

Dodge waited for the policeman to disappear behind the angle of the woman's cabin before he moved away from the shelter of the bush and advanced toward the cabin. He was only a few feet from the rear of the cabin when he heard the knocking: three loud, hard knuckle-raps, a cop's knock. Close beside the cabin now, standing in its shadow beside a small, frosted, head-high window, a bathroom window, he forced himself to scan the terrain slowly and systematically, left to right. The tall man's cabin, dark, was first on his left. Another cabin, farther back, was also dark. A third cabin, to his right, was lighted. Between the second and third cabins, farther back, he saw a storage shed and a dumpster, both of them behind a screen of low-growing trees. Through the trees and the cacti, he counted three other lighted cabins. The only illumination for the grounds came from dim, ground-level lights that outlined the paths and the curving driveway, everything natural, the close-to-nature gimmick. In the silence, nothing stirred. The only sounds were the voices from inside the cabin: two men's voices, and the woman's voice. The small sliding bathroom window was open a few inches. A screen covered the window. Behind the window, faint light glowed.

After one final long, searching look around, he turned his back on the motel grounds. One slow, cautious inch at a time, he brought his right eye into line with the frosted window.

13

Years ago, in the first acting class he'd ever taken, the teacher had urged her students to practice expressions in front of the mirror. Pain, pleasure, rage, love, hate, envy—Bernhardt had dutifully practiced them all. Because facial expressions, after all, were an important part of his stock in trade. Therefore, out of habit, he kept a running inventory of his own expressions.

So that now, listening to this petty, officious, stuck-up asshole of a less-than-thirty-year-old sheriff's deputy, he could vividly imagine his own expression: a mixture of exasperation and frustration and anger and—yes—probably desperation, fueled by fear.

"What I'm really getting at, sir," the deputy was saying, "is that we don't have the personnel. I mean, we've got a population of less than two thousand people, here—five, six thousand, during the season. So there's the sheriff and the deputies, and that's it, 'round the clock. And right now there's just me, on duty. Now—" The deputy took a half step forward, then resumed his stiff, regimental stance, arms rigid at his sides, chin lifted, chest arched. "Now. I'll certainly check. I'll certainly make it a point to check here at the Ram's Head, check the grounds. And I'll tell my relief, too, tell him to drive through here. He comes on at one A.M. I'll fill him in, and tell him to come by on his very first round." Now the fresh, scrubbed-looking face broke into a fatuous smile, a smile that was calculated to reassure the timid. "But—" Projecting a regret that was

273

obviously fake, he shook his beautifully barbered head. "But I just can't get someone assigned here all night, sir. That would mean authorizing special time. And the truth is, I just don't have that authority."

"And you won't call the sheriff."

Again, the other man regretfully shook his head. "Sorry, sir. If we were talking about—you know—some real, live problem, or a highway accident, something like that, it'd be a different situation. But we're talking about suspicion, here. You—ah—" He hesitated, then said, "You said you're an investigator, sir. So you should be able to understand what I'm talking about. I mean, we've got guidelines, here. Strict guidelines. Just like you do in San Francisco, I'm sure."

Bernhardt drew a long, deep breath as he looked at Betty Giles. She sat on the edge of the bed, shoulders slumped, eyes downcast. Dejected. Scared, and dejected.

"What you should understand, Deputy Foster," Bernhardt said, "is that as soon as you leave, I'm going to write up a complete account of our conversation, everything that was said. So—" Grimly, he paused, compelling the younger man's reluctant, long-suffering attention. "So if I were you, and anything should happen here tonight, I'd advise you to find that report, and flush it down the toilet. Otherwise, sure as hell, your ass will be in a sling. Do I make myself clear?"

The cherubic mouth tightened, but the parade-ground stance held. The other man's Adam's apple bobbed once, though, before the chin lifted an officious half inch, and the brown eyes raised to focus on Bernhardt's forehead.

"Yes, sir," came the answer.

"Good—" Bitterly, Bernhardt gestured to the door. "Well, Deputy Foster, you'd better be getting back in your car. There's no telling what could be happening, out there."

"Now, sir, there's no call to—"

"I do have one more bit of advice for you, though," Bernhardt said. He let a heavily ladened beat pass. Then: "If I were you, and I saw a black man of about thirty, driving a black Camaro with a California license plate, I'd use extreme caution. Because he'll be armed and dangerous. Will you try to remember that, Deputy Foster?"

Once more, the Adam's apple bobbed. But, a disappointment, the reply came quietly, steadily, with studied indifference to Bernhardt's anger. "Yes, sir, I will."

• • •

With the only illumination coming from the small ground-level lights set along the driveway, it was dark enough to let him walk between the cabins without fear of being noticed, being remembered. To someone watching, he'd just be a shadowy figure moving among the low-growing trees and the tall, clustered cacti they called ocotillo. They'd think he was a motel guest, out for a walk, keeping off the driveway because he liked everything natural. Or he could be taking a short cut between the motel office, where he'd gotten ice, and his cabin, where he had someone waiting for him—someone ready to take off her clothes after one more drink, a woman he'd found in a bar, a white woman, stepping out on her husband, some rich movie company executive.

"Imagination," Venezzio had always said, "that's what makes the difference. You imagine what the other people think they're seeing, not what it feels like they're seeing."

Because most people beat themselves, that's what Venezzio was saying. A cop stops you for speeding, you think it's the big one, the end of the line—come out shooting, get killed. It's not the police that beat you, it's yourself, your own imagination. If you feel like everyone's looking at you, suspicious, that's how you act. And that's how they got caught, the other ones—everyone but him.

So, walking easily, play-acting, he stepped out from behind a cactus, crossed the graveled driveway, and walked in front of her car to the rear of her cabin, into the shadow of a small tree that grew twenty feet behind her cabin. He checked his watch: ten minutes after eleven. Forty minutes ago, the sheriff left, drove away in his squad car.

Meaning that, soon, he'd probably be back, checking. That much he'd heard: that the deputy would come back.

Listening at the open crack of the small screened bathroom window, standing on tiptoe so he could just see into the dark bathroom with its half-open door, he'd heard them talking: the woman, a few words only, and the deputy, talking tight-ass, and the tall, dark-haired man, coming on strong. He'd only been able to pick up a few words, one word out of five, maybe. He could've heard more, if he'd been able to move around to the south side of the cabin, press his ear to the window glass in the living room. But he couldn't risk it, even for a minute, in plain view from the office, and even from the highway, beyond the driveway.

They'd called the sheriff, that much was clear, even one word in five. And the deputy wasn't buying their story, that was clear, too. Whatever they wanted, whatever they were selling, the deputy wasn't buying. And five minutes later, the deputy was gone. He hadn't even walked around the cabin, checked it out. He'd just gotten back in the car, and driven through the grounds on the one-way driveway, then driven off toward town.

And the man and the woman had been pissed. Badly pissed. And scared, too. Badly scared.

He'd been ready, if the deputy had come checking. He'd been ready with a plan, thinking ahead. He would have fallen back—like soldiers did, in battle, fallen back to a prepared position: his car, hidden behind the small stand of trees that grew in a dry gulch, about two hundred feet in back of the split rail fence. He would have gotten in the car, gotten behind the wheel, with the UZI in his lap and the Woodsman on the seat beside him, both guns loaded and cocked, safeties off, the silencer on the Woodsman, screwed down tight. He'd heard enough through the bathroom window to know that there'd be no backup for the deputy. So it would've been one on one, him and the deputy. He would've pretended to slump over behind the steering wheel, maybe drunk, maybe dead. Both windows would've been open, ready. And when the deputy came alongside, he'd get a face full of high-speed .22 hollow points: three, four of them—and one more, through the temple.

Then, quickly, he would've reloaded the Woodsman, and put it back in its holster. He would've taken the UZI, and gone back to the cabin. Maybe he would've thrown a trash can through the floor-to-ceiling living-room window and gone in behind it, using the UZI. He'd done that before, wild west, shooting up everything: a union vice president and his wife and daughter, all of them watching TV, fat and happy. He'd used one clip to put the three of them down, then used another clip to make sure they stayed down. Five, ten seconds, that's all it had taken.

Or maybe he would've tried the front door, tried to kick it in, always a risk. Because if he had a gun in there, the dark-haired man, and the night chain held for even one kick, then it was a shootout, kill or be killed.

And if the room was dark, with him in the doorway, outlined, the odds could be too long. One lucky shot, and that was the end.

From where he stood, he could see the east side of the cabin, the bathroom side, with the one tiny window. He could see the south side, too, with the chest-high window. But he couldn't see the front of the cabin, the side that faced the office and the pool, the side with the picture window, and the door. And it was through them, through the window or the door, that he had to go in. Either the picture window, behind the trash can—or the door, kicked in.

And every minute, the odds changed. Plus and minus, kill or be killed, the odds changed.

If he did it now, right now, with the room still light, everyone was a target, a disadvantage. But the sooner he did it, the less chance that the sheriff would find the Camaro, hidden behind the trees.

If he waited—one hour, two hours, even three hours—and if they went to sleep inside, both of them in bed, then his chances improved. Five seconds through the window, while they were waking up, and five seconds with the UZI, rat-a-tat-tat, and he was out of there, making for the Camaro, the empty clip in his pocket, a full clip in the gun, ready. Thirty seconds to the Camaro, and another three, four minutes out of town, driving carefully, conservatively. Fifty thousand richer, another satisfied customer.

But between now and then, once or twice, maybe more, the sheriff would come by, checking. It was guaranteed, that he'd come by. And if the Camaro was discovered, everything changed. Without a car, carrying three guns, on foot, he might as well be an animal with no place to hide, running off across the desert.

14

"Will that be one night, Mr. Carter?" As he asked the question, the clerk turned the registration card for him to sign, and handed him a ballpoint pen.

He nodded. "Yes. I'll be moving on in the morning." He took the pen, looked down at the card. Incredibly, until now, this very moment, it hadn't occurred to him that he should've been ready with a complete alias: a fictional first name to go with "Carter," and a fictitious address, too, and a fictitious occupation, a business phone, and all the rest of it. And the license number, too—he hadn't decided about that, either. If he wrote down the right number, and if anything went wrong, then they could check out the number in the police computers. But if he wrote down a wrong number, and the clerk checked, looked at the Mercedes, parked outside, then the clerk's suspicions would be aroused.

But now he must write down a first name: James— yes, James Carter. Two "Js": Justin and James, easy to remember.

He wrote slowly, while he tried to think of an address. The clerk was watching him—suspiciously? He finished the name, decided on a fictitious apartment on Wilshire: 2942 Wilshire, #1205.

And now the license number. From where he stood, at the counter, he could see the Mercedes parked, in a bright cone of light, with the license plate clearly visible. It had been planned that way, without doubt. The layout had been planned so that the clerk could unobtrusively check the license plate. So, writing from memory, he entered the license number, the right number. And beside "employer" he entered "self." Now he handed over the pen, along with two twenty-dollar bills and one ten. As he watched the clerk fill out a cash receipt, Powers asked, "How many motels are there in Borrego Springs?"

"Three," the clerk answered. "At least, there's three in town, here—this one, the Ram's Head, and The Arches, just down the road—" He pointed. "Then there's the Del Soro, southeast of town, about five miles. But the Del Soro is as much a resort as a motel, really. You know—tennis courts, a dress code for dinner, that sort of thing." He finished the receipt and pushed it across the counter, along with a few dollars in change and a room key. "That's unit nineteen, three doors down on the right."

Accepting the receipt and the key, he decided to pick up the bag he'd hastily packed and take one step toward the office door before he turned back to the counter, as if he'd just remembered a minor point.

"There's a man named Fisher. He works for me. He's black—a black man. We're supposed to meet here. In Borrego Springs. He's got something for me, some business papers. Is he, ah, registered here, by any chance?"

As if the question puzzled him, the clerk frowned. Then: "Does he drive a black Camaro? Is that the one?"

"I—ah—I don't know what he's driving, to be honest with you."

Should he explain—expand?

Or would it be a mistake, a serious mistake? Always, under pressure, people talked too much, revealed too much.

"The reason I asked," the clerk was saying, "I happened to see a black man this afternoon, driving a black Camaro. But he's not registered here."

"Oh. Well—" He waved a casual hand. "I'll try the others, the other two motels in town, here. The—what—the Ram's Head? Is that it?"

The clerk nodded. "Right. And The Arches. The Ram's Head is south of the town center. That circle, that's the center. And The Arches're west, about a quarter mile." He pointed.

"Oh, Good. Thanks. Thanks very much." He smiled, waved with his free hand, and left the office.

Thoughtfully, the clerk watched the customer as he walked to the top-of-the-line Mercedes. He waited until the customer had reparked the Mercedes and disappeared inside unit nineteen before he consulted his Rolex and punched out a number on the telephone console. Still eyeing the big Mercedes, he tapped his finger on the counter until the recorded message was finished and the beep sounded before he said, "Yes, Sheriff. This is Jerry Tricomi, at Granger's. It's eleven-thirty. And I just wanted to say—wanted to leave a message—and say that there's a man just checked in here who's maybe asking about the same man that Charlie Foster—Deputy Foster—was asking about, a black man driving the black Camaro. Charlie came by about a half hour ago, I guess it was, asking about this black man. So I thought maybe I'd better—you know—touch base. The man's name that just checked in here is Carter. James Carter, and he's in unit nineteen. He's driving a Mercedes 380SL, I think it is. Anyhow, it's a Mercedes coupe, silver." He glanced at the registration card. "License number CVC 916 J."

15

"I want to turn out the lights," Bernhardt said. "I think it'll be safer. Why don't you close your eyes, try to sleep?" Sitting in the room's only armchair, he spoke softly, cautiously. The armchair was placed facing the door and the picture window, closely draped. The shotgun and the revolver lay on a side table, drawn close to the chair. The straight-back chair was still jammed beneath the knob of the door. Sitting at an angle that allowed him to face the front door, Bernhardt's back was half turned to the woman, lying full length on the queen-size bed, pillows stacked behind her head.

"You can turn out the light," she said, "but I won't sleep."

He rose, flipped the light switch beside the door, returned to the armchair, sank into it with a sigh. At the same time, she switched off the bedside lamp.

"That gun," she said. "The shotgun. Did you make it?"

"Yes."

"It looks—deadly. Obscenely deadly."

"It *is* deadly. At ten or twenty feet, there's nothing deadlier than a shotgun, especially if it's loaded with buckshot. The shot pattern's maybe a foot across at that range, so you can hardly miss. That's not true of a pistol or a rifle."

"But a pistol or rifle has a longer range."

In the darkness, he nodded. "Right."

"Have you—" She hesitated. "Have you ever shot anyone?"

"God, no. I'm a lover, not a fighter. This is only the fourth or fifth time I've ever carried a revolver. And only the second time I've ever had the shotgun out of the house." He hesitated, then decided to say, "That's because sawed-off shotguns are illegal. It's a felony, just to own one."

She made no response, and as the silence lengthened Bernhardt became aware of small sounds: a subdued whir of the room cooler, coming from the kitchen, a car passing on Borrego Springs Road, a radio playing soft rock—and the faint, faraway sound of an animal's cry.

Finally, in the darkness, she spoke: "I haven't thanked you for this—for what you're doing."

To himself, Bernhardt smiled. "You sound very formal, very proper."

"And I haven't asked you why you're doing it, either. I mean, you could've warned me, then got in your car and left."

"To be honest," he answered, "I'm not really sure myself. Maybe it's got something to do with the dominant male."

"But you're not like that, not macho."

"Not to the naked eye. But the last hour or so, I'm beginning to develop the theory that the veneer of civilization isn't all that thick. Men've been conditioned to stand guard at the entrance to the cave, protecting their women."

"That's the point, though. I'm not your woman."

"You're *a* woman, though. Nature designed you to bear the children. Men have a different purpose, designwise."

"We aren't going to have an argument about sexism, are we?"

"Maybe we are. Some of my best friends are feminists, but sometimes we argue. Because I maintain that men are basically—*structurally*—more aggressive than women. I'm not saying that's good. I'm saying it's a fact. A demonstrable fact. Men and women are different. Basically different. Inherently different. But the women—some women—say it's all a matter of socialization, of conditioning. Which is bullshit, in my opinion. Walk past a schoolyard, sometime. The little boys are beating on each other. Not the girls, though. They're playing jump rope, or whatever."

Once more she chose not to answer. This time, Bernhardt decided not to break the silence. Whatever might happen, whatever was coming, it would be safer to wait for it in silence, listening to the night sounds.

"God, it's hot." As if she'd tuned in on his thoughts, she spoke sotto voce. "I can't understand why they don't air-condition these cabins, instead of just using a cooler."

"Ordinarily, we'd have that open—" He pointed to the picture window. "For cross ventilation."

"Is the bathroom window open?"

"Yes, but it only opens about a foot."

Another silence. Then, in a small, cowed voice, she said, "Do you really think it's possible that someone's out there?"

"I don't know. But if someone *is* out there, and Deputy Foster finds him, I wouldn't give much for the deputy's chances."

"I know—" She let another moment of silence pass. Then: "God, if only the phone worked."

"You feel unconnected, without a phone." As he said it, he was aware that their conversation had become slightly disembodied in the darkness, recalling other conversations in other rooms: dormitory rooms, exchanging undergraduate confidences under cover of darkness—pillow talks in long-forgotten bedrooms, with long-forgotten bed partners.

"It sounds like—" Reluctant to put the thoughts into words, her voice died. Then, hesitantly: "It sounds like you—like you're expecting something to happen."

"All I know," he answered, "is that a black man killed Nick. And, sure as hell, a black man followed you, tonight. So we'd be just plain stupid, if we didn't assume that he's out there. Especially since you did, after all, threaten DuBois. Which, obviously, wasn't the wisest thing to do, under the circumstances. Especially since you knew—or should've known, anyhow—that Nick was killed for doing exactly that same thing."

"It wasn't blackmail, though. I didn't ask for money."

"You wanted to make DuBois pay—wanted a piece of his hide, for God's sake. If I were DuBois, I'd worry more about you than about Nick. He could've been bought off. You can't."

"That's all in the past now, though. It—it evaporated, that anger of mine. Just—just now, just tonight, it's gone."

"Good. Being mad doesn't get you anything but trouble. We all know that."

"'Don't get mad, get even . . .'" Her voice was hushed, reflective, almost intimate.

"Except that you don't get even with people like DuBois. Ever."

"I know . . ."

Another silence settled down, this one longer, drowsier. Bernhardt picked up the revolver, went to the picture window, drew back the curtain a few inches. The time was just after midnight, and the swimming pool lights had been turned off. The motel office, too, was dark. As he watched, headlight beams appeared on Borrego Springs Road, brightening as they entered the frame of the motel entrance before they abruptly disappeared. How many minutes would elapse, Bernhardt wondered, before another car passed?

He let the curtain fall back, stepped into the tiny kitchenette. The compact cooler occupied the lower half of the kitchenette's small window, leaving a space too small for a man to come through. He checked the closure of the gingham curtains above the cooler, then pushed open the bathroom door. The small frosted window above the toilet was half open, but the angle of the wall made it impossible for anyone to shoot through the window into the living room.

Leaving the bathroom door half open, for ventilation, Bernhardt returned to the living room, sank down in the chair, put the revolver on the table. In the dim light that filtered through the draperies, it was impossible to see whether or not Betty's eyes were closed.

Then she stirred, spoke softly: "Do you think it would've been better to pack up and leave—take our chances on the road?"

"I don't know," he answered. "He's got a Camaro. And these roads are deserted, at night. I was wondering about asking the sheriff for an escort out of town to the west. It's only a few miles, to the foothills. But it's pretty obvious that wouldn't've worked, not with Deputy Foster, anyhow—the goddam jerk."

"You said you were going to write a report about his behavior. Are you?"

"Probably not. All I'm thinking about now is getting through the next five or six hours, until it's daylight. Then we can get packed. It'll take you an hour or so to write your statement about DuBois. After you've done that, we can leave, go back toward Los Angeles. We'll go convoy style, you in front, me following. I'll talk to the sheriff in the morning, ask him for an escort for the first ten miles out of town. If he refuses, I'll demand that he make a written report to verify my request.

That's one thing I've discovered about cops. If there's something on file—a piece of paper, on someone's desk—your chances are better of getting action. But even if we don't get his attention, we're still a hell of a lot safer in the daytime than we are at night. Especially if there're two of us."

"If the killer's out there somewhere, watching, he'll've seen Deputy Foster come. That's bound to help. And Foster will drive past, too."

Decisively, Bernhardt nodded. "Right." Then, surreptitiously, he stifled a yawn. After another drowsy, darkness-shrouded silence she asked, "Are you married, Alan?"

"No. I was married, years ago. She died."

"Oh—I'm sorry." She said it the way most people meant to say it: quietly, respectfully. But most people failed. Pamela had said it like that, too: with deep, true compassion. He let a beat pass, then asked, "What about you?"

"No—" A small, pensive sigh. "No, I never married. I'm afraid that Nick was as close as I've come. And that really wasn't very close. I thought it was—I thought it was as close as you get. But I was wrong. I can see that now. It hasn't even been a week. But already I can see that it never would've worked, with the two of us."

"I—I'm sorry."

"Me, too—sorry for myself, for being too dumb to see it sooner."

"It's not a question of intelligence. That's got nothing to do with it."

"What *does* it have to do with?"

"Need, I suppose. And loneliness, too. If you're lonely—if you need someone—then you can't really afford to look too closely, sometimes."

"Do you need someone?"

"Everyone needs someone," he answered quietly.

"You included?"

"Me included. Definitely, me included. Listen—" He stifled a yawn. "Listen, why don't you go to sleep? I'll stay awake. Then you can keep watch, tell me if you hear anything, wake me up. Okay?"

"Yes—" She yawned, too. "Yes—okay."

• • •

Twenty-five minutes ago, their lights had gone out. Fifteen minutes ago, the sheriff's car had come back, driven among the cabins on the one-way driveway, engine idling. Hidden behind a tree no taller than himself, he'd seen the police car pass within a few feet of him. It had been a test, a test he'd set for himself, to prove his nerve, his courage—like deliberately cutting into his own flesh, to prove he could do it, stand the pain. He'd done it once. He'd been drunk, sure. But he'd done it— taken a knife and cut himself, the only one at the table who'd dared. The scar was still there, on the inside of his forearm—still there, like a badge.

If the sheriff had seen him, he would've been ready: same plan, really, but different, slightly, a little different. Because instead of using the Woodsman, for the noise, he'd've used the UZI, get the job done, never mind the noise. Then, with the shit already in the fan, he'd throw a trash can through the window, go in behind it, with the UZI.

But the sheriff hadn't even glanced in his direction, hadn't taken more than two minutes, to drive around the grounds. So he didn't have to risk it, risk breaking in, risk making himself a target, if the tall man had a gun.

And then, suddenly, it had come to him, how he could do it, how he could get them out of the cabin, where they'd be the targets, not him. He'd heard how someone did it once, did exactly what he had to do. All it took was a knife, and a little hose. He'd already seen a hose, lying between two cabins—a garden hose. And he already had a knife, his Buck knife, that he always carried on a job. And the rest of it, everything else, he could find that in a trash can, almost any trash can.

• • •

Switching off the air-conditioning, Powers touched another switch, lowered a window on the driver's side. The desert air was pure and sweet, an ecological revelation, after the chronic Los Angeles smog. And, yes, the stars were closer, brighter, more mysterious. Ahead, a sliver of moon had risen over the far desert horizon.

Was it a killing moon?

Could she already be dead, lying on a blood-soaked bed at the Ram's Head Motel? Could Fisher already be far away, safe from pursuit, making preparations to meet him at LAX, collect the rest of his murderer's pay?

He'd passed the Ram's Head, driving into town from the south, more than an hour ago. It had been a shock, seeing the sign. Until then, that very instant, it had all been an abstraction: a report from MacCauley, a call to an anonymous number in Detroit, an envelope handed over at the airport—one of thousands of transactions he'd made during the year, buying low, selling high, bargaining for the best possible terms.

But when he'd seen it, that blue neon sign materializing out of the deep desert darkness, the sudden shock had been shattering. This wasn't an abstraction. This was murder, bought and paid for.

Involuntarily, seeing the sign, his foot had come off the accelerator. Almost of its own volition, the Mercedes had slowed. Because, in minutes, it could have been over. He could have found her, told her that she was no longer in danger, that DuBois had decided to give her back her life. Then he could have warned her that she wasn't safe until he found the man he'd hired to murder her.

But then, searing his consciousness, the truth had struck like a blow: If he warned her, saved himself from involvement in another murder, he admitted to her that he had ordered Nick Ames' murder. He would put himself at her mercy.

So he must find Fisher, before Fisher found Betty Giles.

A black man in a black Camaro, the motel manager had said . . .

• • •

Setting the safety catch, he carefully laid the UZI on a large flat rock. But he must make sure, absolutely sure, that he remembered, about the safety catch. When it came down to seconds, kill or be killed, he couldn't take time to snap off the safety. It had happened to him once. Only once.

Coming out of a crouch, he took the Buck knife from its case at his belt. As he opened the blade, he scanned the two nearest cabins, both of them dark. If someone was inside, looking out into the night through their big front windows, they could see him. But all they'd see, from twenty-five feet away, in the dark, was a figure who'd just bent over, put something on the ground, then straightened, taken something from under his shirt. And now they'd see him bend down again, make a motion with his two hands that could mean anything—while, quickly, two slashes of the knife got him a three-foot length of garden hose.

He replaced the knife in its snap-over sheath, picked up the UZI—still with the safety on, he must remember—and began the careful, dangerous walk back between two more cabins. One of the cabins still showed a dim light, and a blue-white TV glow. Ahead was the screen of close-planted trees that concealed the dumpster he'd seen earlier, before it got dark. This time, he must lay the UZI directly on the coarse, sandy soil, lay the length of hose beside it. Now, after another quick look at the nearby cabins, he leaned over the side of the dumpster. An instant's flash of bitter memory was as strong as the garbage smell: stinking hallways, stinking alleys—stinking lives, his own and all the others.

On top of the trash, he found the perfect one: a half-gallon wine bottle. And rags, too—everything, right there. He straightened, thrust the rag in a trouser pocket. Carrying the bottle and the hose in his left hand, the UZI in his right hand, he moved cautiously to the rear of the motel grounds, to the split rail fence, just high enough and rickety enough to be a problem. This time, though, carrying everything, balancing like an acrobat, he giant-stepped over the fence, another flash of childhood memory: baby steps, giant steps, hide and seek, you're it, you're screwed. All of them, screwed before they even started. Everyone but him.

Another two hundred feet took him to the Camaro, doors unlocked, windows down. He put the UZI inside, on the driver's seat—still safetied, remember, still on safety, loser lose everything, if he forgot. Moving to the rear of the car, he took off the gas cap, put it on the car—remember, the roof of the car. *Remember*. And the bottle was on the ground beneath the gas tank. And the hose—yes, it fitted—thrust down inside the tank. And now, suck—*suck*—as he lifted the bottle, ready as, yes, the gas was coming, gagging him. Hose into the bottle, back on the ground. Gurgling, gurgling—gas overflowing now. He freed the hose from the tank, reached for the rags, still in his pocket.

Should the rag be soaked in the gas, before he—?

The cap. He'd forgotten the gas cap, on the roof of the car. He twisted the gas cap down tight, tested it. This was the time when everything counted, when he couldn't forget anything. This was the time when—

A match.

He'd done it all, a fucking miracle. Found a hose, a bottle, everything. Made the cocktail—whatever they called it, named for a Russian, some kind of Russian.

All useless. Nothing, without a match.

A match . . .

At a store, in town? No, not now, not after midnight.

In a house, someone's house? Break into someone's house, risk everything, just for a fucking—

A bar.

It had to be a bar. Two bars in town, one at the circle, one at the airport. It was no better than fifty-fifty, out of season, that they'd be open after midnight. But he had to do it. Either do it, get a match, or forget about it, about everything but crashing in, glass breaking in the middle of the night, the middle of nowhere, taking a chance, maybe that one last chance, one chance too many.

• • •

"Yeah," the bartender said, "there was a black guy in here, left maybe fifteen minutes ago." He nodded, poured Powers a brandy, took the five-dollar bill to the register to make change. "Nice fella, very nice spoken, too, very polite. Said he just wanted to use the bathroom, and get a book of matches. Smiled about it, very good-humored. And then I noticed he left two dollars on the bar. How about that?"

• • •

He placed the bottle on the ground close beside the house, placed the UZI beside the bottle. Then, as he'd done before, once before, an hour ago, maybe longer, he moved inch by inch to the right, until he could see into the bathroom through the small, high, screened bathroom window. The window was open about six inches. It was an aluminum window, and slid side to side. But the screen was nylon, not aluminum. It was a break, that the screen was nylon. Possibly his biggest break of all. Because if he could cut away the screen, and slide back the window another six inches, he could do it, throw the gas bomb inside—throw it hard, so it would break. Or, no, just lob it in, a grenade, so it would break on the tile floor of the bathroom, not go as far as the carpet of the other room, maybe not break.

Instantly, the gas would explode. Inside, they'd panic. With the UZI—safety off, remember, safety off— he'd go around to the front, wait for them—do them when they came out, screaming. Two bursts—one clip—and they'd go down. Clip out, new clip in. Remember to release the slide, release the fucker, make sure there was a bullet in the chamber. Then another short burst, the insurance burst, to her head. Then back over the split rail fence, back to the Camaro—fifty thousand richer. Start the car, drive, disappear in the night, sixty-five miles to Palm Springs, across the open desert, gone.

• • •

The monster was turning, coming back, leering down on him, a fire-breathing, four-wheeled monster, shattering the high, wide, raging sky with a doomsday roar. And he was helpless, trapped, held fast by—

"*Alan.*"

Opening his eyes, he saw her face close to his, saw her eyes, fearfully wide in the half light. It was Betty, whispering his name. Betty Giles, the target. Terrified.

"Wh—"

"*Shhh.*" With her hand on his arm, to quiet him, she moved her head to the left, in the direction of the bathroom door. "Listen—"

And as he sat up straight in the chair, he heard it: a faint, alien sound. Was it an animal, gnawing?

A man, coming for them?

As he rose to his feet and picked up the sawed-off,

his heart began to hammer, his knees went weak. Gripping the shotgun, his hands trembled violently.

The safety . . .

He must take off the safety, right thumb pushing the catch forward.

Twenty-five dollars, he'd paid for the shotgun. Not enough, not nearly enough. Not now, not enough. Suddenly not now.

"Get back," he whispered, gesturing with his head for her to move aside, away from the bathroom door. Then, with legs that were leaden, with the roar of blood pounding in his ears, throat gone dry, he was moving forward—one step, two steps—and one last step, bringing him squarely facing the bathroom door. Taking his left hand from the sawed-off's forestock, fingers cravenly trembling, he slowly, gently, pushed the door fully open.

In the rectangle of the bathroom window, slid to the side, fully open, he saw something changing the quality of the outside darkness. Not a hand, or a head, or a solid shape, but a film without substance, a thickening, then a thinning—

—the screen.

It was the screen, moving, folding back, disappearing.

• • •

With his right shoulder pressed against the cabin wall, with the gasoline-filled bottle on the ground beside the UZI, both of them in front of him, he crouched, swept the nearby darkness one last time with quick, probing eyes. Then he looked up at the window, two feet above his head, its nylon screen folded back.

A lob—a hook shot, really, from his crouched position beneath the window—a left-handed hook shot, followed by a right-handed grab for the UZI. And then the sprint around the side of the cabin, UZI cocked, safety off, finger on the trigger, ready. Followed by the ten, twenty-second wait, listening to their screams from inside, trapped in the flames—trapped until they tore open the front door, desperate to escape the fire.

As he held his breath, listening, he took the matches from a hip pocket, opened the folder. Had someone spoken, inside the cabin? Had something stirred? He allowed himself five more seconds, the last five seconds, listening. Then, winner take all, he struck the match, hesitated one last, final moment, then touched the tiny flame to the gas-soaked rag, the wick. Instantly, orange flame blossomed; bits of burning rag flared, fell away from the bottle. He dropped the matches, used both hands to grip the bottle below the flaming wick. He straightened from his crouch to stand close beside the window. Pain seared one hand, both hands.

Quick. It had to be quick.

• • •

He was out there. The black man, come to kill them. He was out there, just outside the window. Was this the time to run, tear open the front door, try for safety, scream for help? Frozen at his center, Bernhardt could only raise the shotgun, trained on the window's foot-square opening. At five feet, six feet from the window, the buckshot would—

Beneath the window a glow began, followed instantly by a tiny flame in the dark rectangle of the window. The shotgun bucked; the blast was palpable, a flash of gouted orange in the darkness, deafening him—

—as fire filled the window frame, an explosion of flame, blinding him, the black of night flaring daytime-bright, acrid, deadly dangerous.

• • •

He braced himself, used both hands to lift the bottle level with the window—

—heard the shotgun blast, saw flame explode, felt the

heat searing nostrils and throat, saw the darkness fuse with the fire, first into a blinding-bright whiteness, then into the last long, sudden darkness . . .

. . . as his voice, screaming, filled everything: the last sound so quickly fading: all the pain, finally gone. Too late.

16

As Powers switched off the bedside lamp he heard the siren: a high, thin wail, rising and falling in the night. He'd heard this same sound in small towns before: the siren on the firehouse, summoning the local volunteer firemen.

Or it could be the police: the Borrego Springs sheriff, or the state police, racing to answer the homicide call. Betty Giles, dead. Murdered at the Ram's Head Motel.

In the darkness he sat up in bed, listening. If it was the police, the sound of the siren would soon fade as the car left the center of town, outward bound.

But even if it *was* the police, it wasn't necessarily murder. It could be an accident, on the highway. Or a robbery. Anything.

But it wasn't the police, because the sound was stationary, still rising and falling, a monotony of undulating shrillness. And now, closeby, he heard excited voices, heard car doors slamming. The motel manager, doubtless, was a volunteer fireman, and was answering the call.

He got out of bed, went to the window, drew back

the drape. Yes, an engine was revving nearby, a car was moving, spurting gravel from its rear wheels.

Grimacing at the sound of the siren, he switched on the lights and strode to the bureau, and the bottle of Cutty Sark. Was there still ice in the ice bucket? Yes, enough for one drink, one generous drink. He filled the plastic glass with ice, poured in the Cutty Sark. The TV was beside the brown plastic tray that held the bottle, the glass, and the ice bucket. Giving the ice in his drink time to melt, he looked at the local TV log, on top of the set. An old John Wayne movie had just come on: *Flying Tigers*, made during the war. He switched on the TV, turned the channel selector, saw John Wayne in the cockpit of a vintage fighter plane, maneuvering to elude a villainous Japanese, a propaganda turn.

As he picked up the highball, the sound of the siren suddenly died. Enough firemen had responded; the truck was ready to roll. He carried the glass to one of the room's two easy chairs, sank down, propped his bare feet on the edge of the bed, and sipped the scotch as he watched the whirling, roaring, smoke-spiraling dogfight.

The TV's digital clock read 12:45 A.M. He'd left a call for six-thirty. He would dress, get in his car, make the rounds of the town's motels, all four of them. In the darkness, he could have driven within a block of the black Camaro, and never seen it. But tomorrow, in daylight, he would find him, find Fisher, pay the killer off. Then he'd pack his bag and return to Los Angeles, all danger passed, all problems resolved.

He yawned, settled himself, sipped the Cutty Sark, then set the glass aside. Surprisingly, perhaps, considering the situation, he could feel his eyes growing heavy . . .

• • •

Something had startled him, brought him suddenly awake, eyes wide, heart thudding. His attention was groggily focused on the TV screen: John Wayne, chin-to-chin with another man, both of them angry, voices raised, fists clenched.

But the sound came from the door: a knocking, three quick, firm knuckle-raps.

"Yes?" As he spoke he rose, went to the TV, switched it off, looked at the digital clock: 1:30 A.M.

"Mr. Carter?" It was a man's voice, medium loud.

Still groggy, he began to shake his head. Then memory returned, a rush of random images: the envelope filled with money, exchanging hands at the airport—the narrow, winding road, coming down out of the mountains, straightening on the desert floor—the motel clerk's transparent suspicion as he answered questions about the black man.

Mr. Carter was really himself. Justin Powers. Both were the same. Here, now, both were the same.

"Mr. Carter?" More insistently, now.

As he turned uncertainly toward the door, he was aware that he wore only shorts, because of the desert heat.

"Yes. Who is it?"

"It's Deputy Foster, Mr. Carter. Could I talk to you for a few minutes? Ask you some questions?"

"But it—it's late."

"I know that, sir. But there's been an accident. We need some help, sir."

He was standing close to the door now, close enough to touch the knob. But he couldn't do it, couldn't open the door. Not now. Not wearing shorts, and nothing else.

"Just a minute." He took his slacks from a chair, slipped into them, put on the sports shirt he'd worn earlier, finger-combed his hair. He'd forgotten to pack slippers, and as he stepped to the door he was conscious of his bare feet.

Standing close to the door, he squared his shoulders, lifted his chin, drew a deep, uncertain breath.

James Carter. He must remember it, remember the name. *His* name. His identity, now. And ludicrously, also the name of a president. How had it happened that, for anonymity, he'd chosen Jimmy Carter's name? How could he have been so incredibly stupid?

He slipped off the night chain, twisted the doorknob, stepped back as he swung the door open.

Deputy Foster was a young, muscular, fresh-faced man who spoke in a high, clear, self-important voice: "This won't take but a minute, sir—" As he said it, the deputy sheriff moved purposefully forward into the room, leaving Powers to close the door behind him: an inferior, waiting on his betters.

Standing in the center of the room between the bed and the bureau, the deputy turned to face him squarely. For a moment Foster said nothing, standing with his legs slightly spread, both thumbs hooked into his tooled leather equipment belt. His wide-brimmed beige felt hat, Powers noticed, was impeccably creased and sat precisely square on Foster's large head. The flesh of Foster's face and neck glowed with good health.

"Do you have any identification, Mr. Carter?"

Identification . . .

Yes, of course he had identification: a wallet stuffed with money and credit cards . . .

. . . everything in the name of Justin Powers, of Beverly Hills, California.

"Well—well, yes, certainly. Of course, I've got identification."

"I wonder—could I just take a look at your driver's license, please?" As he spoke, Foster glanced pointedly at the bureau top, at the wallet and the keys and the small change and the pocket knife, a random scattering, somehow so intimately revealing.

"Well, I—" His gaze, too, was fixed on the wallet. Helplessly fixed. Hopelessly fixed. "I suppose so. But why?"

"Your car—is that your car, outside? The Mercedes? License CVC 916 J. Is that yours?"

"Well, yes. Certainly. It's—"

His car. Registered to Justin Powers. Not to James Carter. But to Justin Powers. Beverly Hills, California.

If he were there, in Beverly Hills, he would call his lawyer, demand to see his lawyer. He'd make this banal, boyish policeman miserable, make him crawl.

But not here. Not in this motel room, rented in the name of James Carter.

Not with his identification made out to Justin Powers, lying on the bureau. Not with the car's license, also registered to Justin Powers.

"Yes," he heard himself answering, "yes, that's my car. But—" Betraying him, his throat closed.

But was it really a betrayal? Or was it his body, his mind, involuntarily protecting him? Because he mustn't do this—couldn't do this—couldn't put Justin Powers here, in this tiny town, with Betty Giles and her killer.

But he couldn't lie, either. Because the police computer could catch him. In seconds, the computer could catch him, expose him, prove that the Mercedes was his.

But, God, he had to say something. He couldn't simply stand here, feeling his eyes betraying him.

In his own ears, his voice sounded weak: a low, hoarse croak: "But my real name is Powers. Justin Powers. I'm—ah—traveling incognito. Because of—"

Because of what?

Business?

A woman?

Money or sex, which was it? Which would protect him, impress this spit-and-polish policeman most?

"Because of business—" He waved his right hand in a quick, ragged gesture. "We're working on a deal—a real estate deal. My firm is Powers, Associates. In Los Angeles. That's my head office, in Los Angeles. And we're putting together a deal, a big real estate deal. You can check. You can—" Once more, he gestured raggedly, this time toward the wallet. "I've got business cards. Everything, all kinds of identification."

"Ah—" Now the deputy was nodding. Was it a sign of encouragement? Or cat-and-mouse complacency? "Ah—that checks, then. Jerry Tricomi—the manager, here—he says that you're in Borrego Springs on business, that you're self-employed."

He nodded. "Yes. Th—that's right."

"And you're in real estate." As he spoke, Foster smiled—a false, fatuous smile, transparently calculating.

"Well, actually, it's really investments, that I'm in. Venture capital."

The truth. The precious truth—until now, that moment, he'd never known how wonderful it was, to tell the truth.

"Jerry says you came here looking for someone who works for you." A pause. And as the silence lengthened, Deputy Foster's smile was fading. Gone. Cat-and-mouse gone.

How fleeting it had been, the unimagined luxury of simply telling the truth.

"Is that true, Mr. Car—Mr. Powers?"

He was nodding. Cautiously, watchfully nodding. In business, in the boardroom, he'd learned to watch their eyes, read their eyes. And in Deputy Foster's boyish,

China blue eyes, he saw the kind of smugness that could clearly mean trouble.

But he couldn't retract the nod. The single quick, ill-considered, self-incriminating bob of the head was forever gone, eternally beyond recall.

"A black man, Jerry said. About thirty, driving a black Camaro. Is that the man?"

"I—I don't know what kind of a car he's driving."

Another silence lengthened as Deputy Foster's innocent blue eyes remained fixed on him. Then, softly: "His name was Fisher. Is that right, sir? William Fisher?"

Was?

Was?

"Y—yes—" He felt a surge of sudden relief. Because he could be spared. He could be—

"*Is* that right—the right name?"

"Y—yes. That's—" Once more, his throat closed. But words were without meaning now. Everything, he knew, was revealed in their faces—his face, and Deputy Foster's face. "That's him. William Fisher. Yes."

As soon as he said it, he saw the other man's demeanor change. As if he were no longer capable of concealing his pleasure, Deputy Foster let a long, self-satisfied beat pass while he restored himself, regained his previous petty, officious poise. Then, incongruously, he looked down at Powers' bare feet. When he finally spoke, his manner was elaborately formal—chillingly formal: "If you wouldn't mind, sir, I wish you'd get some shoes on, comb your hair, whatever, and then come with me. There's—ah—something you can help me with."

An accident, Foster had said earlier. Then he'd used the past tense, referring to Fisher. Perhaps, after all, there was hope. Perhaps, now, a bit of role-playing was called for, to remind this fresh-faced bumpkin deputy of his real status, of their relative importance.

"I think," Powers said, "that you'd better tell me what this is all about, Deputy Foster."

Instantly, the China blue eyes narrowed, the parade-ground stance stiffened.

Could it have been a mistake, challenging this underling? If Foster felt forced to call in his superiors, the strategy could backfire—badly. So, softening his manner, trying for a more colloquial tone, Powers asked quietly, "What's happened, anyhow?"

"There was an accident, sir," came the prompt response. "A bad accident. And William Fisher is dead."

"How—" He cleared his throat, licked his lips. "How'd it happen?"

"There was a—" Cautiously, Foster paused. Then: "There was a fire, sir."

A fire . . .

"Well, if he's dead, then I don't understand what you need from me. I mean—" He spread his hands. "I mean, what's the urgency? What's the point of my—" Unsure how to finish it, he frowned, spread his hands, tried not to reveal the numbness of relief that struck him squarely in his center, as sudden as a blow.

"Identification, I guess," Foster replied. And now, plainly feigning an indifference he didn't feel, he spread his big-knuckled hands and smiled. "I don't know, to be completely honest with you. All I know is, the sheriff sent me here, to ask you to come on over, help us out."

"Well, then—" With a false smile in place, Powers decided to elaborately, amiably shrug as he stepped to the bureau, pocketed his wallet, his keys, his change, his knife. "Well, then, I guess I'd better comply." Quickly, he slipped on the boat shoes he'd decided to wear, ran a comb through his hair, and gestured for the deputy to precede him through the door, out into the desert night, cooler now, a welcome balm. The sheriff's car was parked in the driveway, blocking the Mercedes.

"Why don't you go ahead," he said, speaking casually. "I'll follow you."

"No, sir—" Diffidently, Foster swung open the patrol car's passenger door. "No, sir. I think it'd be better if you came with me." Boyishly cheerful now, he smiled. Genially explaining: "Bosses' orders."

FRIDAY
September 21st

1

Bernhardt glanced through the archway and into Pamela's tiny kitchen, where a clock hung on the wall over the Cuisinart. He'd been talking for almost an hour, telling her everything, every detail. He'd once seen Ruth Gordon interviewed on PBS, a celebration of her eightieth birthday. She'd been asked for her thoughts on marriage. In her gravelly voice, she'd said that the real meaning of marriage was that you "had someone to tell it to." Driving from his apartment to Pam's, he'd remembered the line. Because, during the drive up from Los Angeles, the closer he got to San Francisco, the more clearly he realized that, yes, he wanted to tell it to Pamela, the whole story. And when he'd called her, heard the instant lilt of pleasurable recognition in her voice, when she'd invited him to dinner that same night, pasta and salad, he could bring the wine, he'd experienced a quick, breathless excitement that had left him, literally, laughing out loud, a teenager again.

"My God—" Sitting across the table, eyes wide, she incredulously shook her head. "It's amazing, an amazing story. It's like a—a movie, a damn good movie. Where's Powers now? In jail?"

"I doubt it. But I doubt that he's sleeping very well."

"Did you and the woman—Betty Giles—confront him at the scene, with the"—mischievously, she smiled—

307

"with the barbecued corpse, and everything, right there?"

He nodded. "That's right. At least, she told the sheriff what she suspected, that Powers hired Fisher, or whatever his name is. And the fact that several people, including the motel manager, will testify that Powers said he was looking for a black man who worked for him, that pretty much ties up the package."

"And what about Daniel DuBois? Did she implicate him?"

Bernhardt shook his head, at the same time refilling her glass, then refilling his own. "No, she didn't. Maybe she will, down the line. But she didn't do it then, not in the first hour or two."

"She wrote out the statement, though, and gave her mother a key to the safe deposit box."

He nodded. "Yesterday." For a moment they sat silently, their eyes meeting, sharing the moment. Bernhardt shook his head. "It's amazing, when you think about it. A second, two seconds, and your whole life changes. Forever." As he spoke, their eyes still held. If he'd been writing the scene in a play—or, more like it, in a B movie—the protagonist might continue to hold her eyes as he said, *"The way my whole life changed when I met you."*

Did she feel it, feel this sudden, special closeness? If she were writing the scene, what lines would she give herself?

Finally, softly, she said, "And Powers arriving on the scene like that, it's amazing. I wonder why he did it, put himself in jeopardy like that?"

"I don't know. Once he saw the body, he just quit talking. All he'd say was that he wanted to call his lawyer."

"Did he spend the night in jail?"

Bernhardt nodded. "Yes. And maybe the next night, too. They took him to San Diego."

Another companionable silence settled between them as they sipped their wine and looked into each other's eyes. As the moment lengthened, he saw her expression change. As if she'd experienced sudden pain, her eyes darkened, her mouth tightened. "It must've been horrible for you. I mean, seeing him burning, running until he dropped, it must've made you—" Helplessly, she broke off.

"It made me sick to my stomach," he answered quietly. "Very, very sick to my stomach. But then, later, it was okay. I mean, if I'd actually shot him, killed him, I probably would've felt worse, a lot worse. Because they say there's a moment, one split second, before you pull the trigger to kill someone at close range, that you hesitate. Because you know—you realize, suddenly— what it means, killing someone, killing that particular person. But this was different, you see. Because all I saw was something inside the window frame—a half-gallon bottle with the wick burning, a Molotov cocktail. He was going to burn us out, then kill us, with his machine pistol, that's pretty obvious, now. But I didn't know any of that, obviously, when I shot. It was a re-flex. The simplest, most elemental reflex. I saw something move, and I fired. And that was it. I hit the bottle and it broke, and the next second, the next split second, he was a human torch."

"You must be a good shot."

"Not really. I had a shotgun—a sawed-off shotgun. From six or seven feet, it has pattern of about a foot, maybe more. So I could hardly have missed. But, still—" He dropped his eyes, drained his glass of wine. "Still, I'll have nightmares for a while. And Betty will, too." As he spoke, he was remembering the sheriff—Alvin

Gates, a fat, fortyish, slow-talking man with small, shrewd eyes. While Bernhardt had told his story, Gates had stared thoughtfully at the sawed-off, lying on the bed. Neither man had mentioned the gun, an unspoken bargain between them, noblesse oblige. And now the sawed-off was impounded, in Gates' charge. With luck, Bernhardt would never see it again.

Another short silence passed before, decisively, she rose to her feet, picked up their empty plates. "Time for dessert," she announced, taking the plates into the kitchen, where she put them in the sink, and turned on the tap. Bernhardt picked up two serving dishes, and followed her. As he put the serving dishes on the counter beside the sink, she remained motionless, staring down into the sink. He stood silently for a moment, looking at her profile, half turned away. Then, hardly aware that he'd intended to do it, he lifted his hand to touch the curve of her neck, just below the ear. He felt her start at the touch, then felt her raise her shoulder, incline her head toward his touch, move almost imperceptibly closer. Now, still turned away, she put her hand on the tap, shut off the frothing stream of steaming water. For a moment they remained motionless, deciding. Then he moved his hands to her shoulders, gently turned her to face him. Neither moving closer nor moving away from him, she gravely raised her eyes to his.

"I'm sorry for your nightmares," she said. "Truly sorry."

"Thank you."

"I'm also sorry for that crack about the barbecued corpse. Sometimes I—I say those things. I see pictures in my mind, and the words come out."

"I know. It's okay." He spoke softly, intimately. Then, still with his hands on her shoulders, he drew her slowly toward him until, yes, her breasts were touching his chest. At the touch, he felt her body quicken—as his body, too, was quickening, tightening.

"I thought about you when I was gone," he said. "I thought about you a lot."

"I know you did. I thought about you, too, Alan. A lot."

"I'd like us to—" He broke off as she lowered her head to rest her forehead on his chest. "I'd like us to be lovers," he whispered.

"I know . . ."

He moved his hands down from her shoulders to the small of her back, still drawing her closer. He felt her reluctance to make this final commitment of the body, yet also sensed her reluctance to move away from him. With his lips against her forehead, he whispered, "You need time. I understand that."

"Yes . . ." Against his chest, he felt her nodding. "A little time. Just a little."

"It's okay, Pam. Believe me, it's okay. I can wait."

He felt her stir, felt a quickening—this time a whimsical quickening. With her face buried now in the hollow of his shoulder, still with her body close to his—close enough, for now—he heard her chuckle.

"How long can you wait?" she asked.

"Almost as long as you can," he answered quickly, "but no longer."

BESTSELLING BOOKS FROM TOR

THE BEST IN SUSPENSE

☐ 50105-5 CITADEL RUN by Paul Bishop $4.95
  50106-3   Canada $5.95

☐ 54106-5 BLOOD OF EAGLES by Dean Ing $3.95
  54107-3   Canada $4.95

☐ 51066-6 PESTIS 18 by Sharon Webb $4.50
  51067-4   Canada $5.50

☐ 50616-2 THE SERAPHIM CODE by Robert A. Liston $3.95
  50617-0   Canada $4.95

☐ 51041-0 WILD NIGHT by L. J. Washburn $3.95
  51042-9   Canada $4.95

☐ 50413-5 WITHOUT HONOR by David Hagberg $4.95
  50414-3   Canada $5.95

☐ 50825-4 NO EXIT FROM BROOKLYN by Robert J. Randisi $3.95
  50826-2   Canada $4.95

☐ 50165-9 SPREE by Max Allan Collins $3.95
  50166-7   Canada $4.95

Buy them at your local bookstore or use this handy coupon:
Clip and mail this page with your order.

Publishers Book and Audio Mailing Service
P.O. Box 120159, Staten Island, NY 10312-0004

Please send me the book(s) I have checked above. I am enclosing $_____
(please add $1.25 for the first book, and $.25 for each additional book to
cover postage and handling. Send check or money order only — no CODs.)

Name _____

Address _____

City _____ State/Zip _____

Please allow six weeks for delivery. Prices subject to change without notice.

THE BEST IN PSYCHOLOGICAL SUSPENSE